HIDDEN REALM

THE LIVING ORACLE
BOOK ONE

MELISSA McSHANE

Night Harbor Publishing

CHAPTER 1

A light breeze fluttered my shirt and died away, not dimming the screams and shouts coming from all around me. I tilted my head back, squinting at the top of the castle, where a stocky figure stood silhouetted against the cloudless summer sky. "No!" I shouted. "It can't be you!"

"It is me!" the warrior shouted. "The terror of the kingdom! Fear me and my mighty wrath!"

I strode toward the castle across the soft lawn and onto a carpet of wood chips that shifted underfoot. "You'll never take me alive!"

The mighty warrior scowled. "I am the most powerful! Watch this!"

I gasped and darted forward as Duncan threw himself over the parapet and grabbed the rope dangling from it. Like a monkey, my son descended hand over hand until he reached the ground. I came to a halt about three feet away. Giving Duncan room to express himself without getting hurt or killed was a full-time job.

"You're right, that was impressive," I said, not letting panic reach my voice. "Now—"

"I challenge you to a duel!" another small voice shouted. Sophia came running around the corner of the castle-shaped play structure. She was armed with two long sticks she waved at Duncan. "Fear me and my mighty wrath!"

"I don't think so," Judy said from behind me. "No stick fighting, not after what happened last week." She disarmed her daughter and tossed the sticks in the direction of our picnic blanket. "You can take yourselves and your mighty wrath to the slide. Maybe you could take turns being the fastest."

"I'm the fastest," Sophia promptly said.

"No, *I'm* the fastest," Duncan replied. "Watch this!" He ran off, spreading his arms wide like a tiny blond airplane. Sophia was on his heels in the next instant, her dark hair trailing her like a comet's tail.

Judy and I returned to sit on the blanket. Viv, who lay sprawled on her back chewing her plastic straw, removed it from her mouth and said, "They're either going to kill each other or end up married."

"Fortunately, that day is far in the future," Judy said. She idly started collecting wrappers and uneaten sandwich crusts and putting them in the hamper. This was the last weekly picnic my best friends and I had before school started, and it was bittersweet to think of how our children were growing older.

"They nearly killed each other last week," Viv pointed out. "Reenacting the final battle from that video game they're so crazy about. *Legend of Kerrigor* or whatever."

"*Legend of Kerigon*, and I blame Jeremiah—and by extension you— for giving it to them," I said. "I'm getting tired of hearing 'fear my mighty wrath' whenever it's time for a bath. Duncan doesn't need any help being obstinate."

"Duncan is six. Obstinate is part of the age," Viv said. "I remember being just like him back then."

"You're still obstinate," Judy smirked. "You're just old enough to call it 'strong-willed.'"

"They aren't all obstinate." I pointed at the swings, where Alastair pumped his legs back and forth as he sailed peacefully higher and higher. "I swore I'd never compare my children to each other, but sometimes that is really hard. Though Alastair gives me different worries."

"It's got to be easier while school is out," Viv said. "Less temptation for him to...you know."

"I do." I sighed and pinched the bridge of my nose, though my head didn't hurt. Yet. "He wants to help. There's nothing wrong with that. But he's an oracle, and that has to be a secret."

"Would you still say that if magic was practiced openly?" Judy asked, a trifle more heatedly than I expected. "Wouldn't his gift—your gift, all the children's gifts—benefit the world if you didn't have to conceal it?"

I bit back the hasty words her near-antagonism prompted in me. "I want them to have a normal childhood, as far as that's possible. That can't happen if everyone knows they have prophetic powers. They'd be swarmed—have all the wrong kinds of attention—it's not what I want for them."

Judy frowned, but as she began to speak, little Jenny stirred and sat up from where she'd been napping in the shade. Her blonde hair was mussed on one side, and there was a crease across her plump cheek from a fold in the blanket. "Mommy," she said. Her eyes, brown-blue like her brothers' and mine, flashed silver so quickly I almost missed it. Then she let out a scream that drew the attention of everyone within twenty feet of us.

I scooted over and gathered her up in my arms. "Shh, shh, don't cry, sweetheart," I said, my heart aching with a familiar pain. "It can't hurt you. They're just pictures. Don't be afraid."

Jenny buried her face in my shoulder and shook with the intensity of her sobs. "Don't like it," she gasped when the crying wound down. "There was a strange lady, and she hit her little boy, and he was so scared—"

I couldn't tell her everything was all right. She was only three, but she was smart enough to recognize the lie. "Be still, and let me look," I said. I turned my attention inward, letting my awareness of the rest of the world fall away.

Ten years ago, I had been the custodian of Abernathy's Bookstore, which was secretly the world's only oracle, and after defeating alien invaders who had tried to destroy our reality, it and I had become one entity. Now I was the oracle, able to prophesy the immediate future, and after ten years of practice, I felt confident in my ability to manage the oracular gift. But nothing had prepared me for having a child who was possessed of the same gift and was terrified of it. I couldn't stop her having visions. All I could do was share them.

Originally, I had needed words to commune with my power, but that time was past. Sometimes I still silently verbalized my query, but often I simply let the knowledge of what I wanted sink deep within me. The answer emerged in images and feelings and sometimes just the same bone-deep knowledge, as if the truth lived within me and surfaced for the asking.

My query about what had frightened Jenny returned several fleeting images—a gray house faced with red bricks, a woman standing over a cringing child, a cuckoo clock striking three o'clock—and a sense of fear I guessed was the child's. Nothing that gave me any indication of the house's location or who the woman was.

Frustrated and angry, I tried again, focusing not on the house but on the clock. The more seemingly random the image, the more likely it was to be key to the prophecy. This time, I saw a street sign and then a road map. I drew in a deep breath and cuddled Jenny more closely. "It will be all right, I promise," I said, hoping it was a promise I could keep.

One-handed, I retrieved my phone from my bag and called Lucia, custodian of the magical nexus called the Gunther Node and head of magical law enforcement in the Pacific Northwest. Gone were the days when she screened my calls; now she picked up within two or three rings. "Yes?"

"Are there any Wardens living near Arrowdale Court in Salem?" I asked. The Wardens, guardians of the secrets of magic in our world, could do something about Jenny's vision.

"I don't know every Warden in the Pacific Northwest, Davies," Lucia said, but without her usual brusqueness. "I can find out."

"There's a woman who's been beating her child. I don't know why it matters—I mean, obviously it matters that we protect children, but I don't know if there's more to it than that—"

"That's enough. I'll take it from here." Lucia paused. "It was Jenny's prophecy again, wasn't it?"

"She'll grow into it," I said, not very sincerely to my ears. "Thanks."

Lucia hung up. I lowered my phone and said, "Lucia will find the little boy, all right? You did a good thing, sweetie."

Jenny shook her head. She was still trembling. "Can I have a cookie?"

"Of course." I found an Oreo in the mostly empty package and handed it over. "Go ask Alastair to push you on the swings."

When Jenny was out of earshot, Viv said, "It's not getting better, is it."

"We don't know what to do," I said, swallowing tears. "The boys never experienced these terrors. And neither of them saw the horrible things Jenny does. I thought the oracular gift...I don't know if 'understand' is the right word, but it always seems conscious of human limitations. I never have a spontaneous prophecy when it would endanger me, like while I'm driving. And the boys always received visions that were innocuous when they were Jenny's age. I don't understand this at all."

"She's still so young," Judy said. "Isn't it likely she'll outgrow it? Or —not outgrow, precisely, but the human brain develops over time, and she'll gradually gain more understanding and ability to cope."

"We hope," Viv said. "Even if that's true—" She glanced at me and shut her mouth.

"I know." I brushed dark cookie crumbs off my fingers. "If these visions continue to hurt her, who knows what kind of damage that might do before she does outgrow them?"

We all fell silent. I wished desperately for a change of subject, but it seemed all of us felt the burden of the conversation. I looked past the swings and the play fort to the street, and then beyond the street to the shops lining it on its far side. Men and women strolled past, dressed for the unexpectedly hot day in shorts or lightweight dresses. Traffic was light at this hour, and aside from one dark green panel van with no logo on the side, no one was parked on the street.

Judy closed the hamper. "I should get going. I have to stop in at the store before going home."

"Uh-huh," I said absently. Two men and a woman had emerged from the van. Though they wore sturdy boots, the kind with steel-capped toes, they were otherwise dressed casually in shorts and T-shirts, not in coveralls the way I'd expected. I wasn't sure why I'd assumed the van belonged to some construction or maintenance company, given the lack of logo, but their appearance surprised me. "I wonder what they're doing."

"What who are doing?" Viv asked. She sat up and ran her fingers through her short chartreuse bob, straightening her hair.

"Those people. They're not workers, and—" The three had walked into the street, and I gasped as a car drove straight at them. Instead of slamming on the brakes, the driver slowed to a stop and then carefully maneuvered around them. I didn't see rude gestures or any other indication that the driver was angry or upset.

"What are you talking about, Helena?" Judy asked.

I glanced at Judy and Viv, who were looking in the direction of the van. "Those—" I turned to watch the three, who were now kneeling in the street with no concern for passing traffic. Another car drove up, slowed, and its turn signal came on as it waited for an oncoming car to drive past before moving into the opposite lane and driving around the trio.

"You don't see it," I said.

"I see a maintenance truck blocking off that lane," Viv said. "Good thing it's so quiet now, because that would be a real nightmare come rush hour."

"It's an illusion," I said.

I stood and brushed off my rear end, though I hadn't been sitting on the grass. My inborn ability to perceive the truth beneath illusion never indicated when something was under an illusion, and I depended on other people to know what I ought to be seeing or hearing. "There's a van, and three people kneeling in the street. I don't recognize any of them. Viv?"

"Hang on," Viv said. She dug around in her capacious pink bag printed all over with images of Tinker Bell and eventually emerged with a flat box twice the size of a typical glasses case. Inside was a pair of pale blue glass lenses, flat round circles connected to each other loosely by a twist of gold wire. Viv settled the lenses over her eyes, with the wire across the bridge of her nose, and steadied them with one hand. A deep blue haze bled across each lens like an ink spill and then vanished.

"Huh," Viv said. "I don't know them either. And that's not a Gunther Node van, obviously."

"What are they doing?" Judy asked.

"No idea," Viv said. "They're just kneeling there—no, now the woman is standing."

I watched the woman walk to the rear of the van and open the doors to climb inside. In a moment, she was back, hefting a jackhammer with a bright orange case. The two men made room for her, and she settled the tool firmly right where they'd been sitting. I winced as the jackhammer noise split the air, louder than the traffic, louder than the shouts of children playing nearby.

"I can't hear it," Viv said. "These things are only good for piercing optic illusions." But she kept watching the tableau. "This is so damn weird even I can't believe it's happening."

"Lucia?" Judy said. She had her back turned and was watching the children at play, but her brow was furrowed the way it got when she was intent on a phone conversation. "Do you have anyone digging up the road across from Riverside Park? No? Well, there's somebody—no, I can't see them, they've set up an illusion—Helena says—how many, Helena?"

I held up three fingers.

"Three people, and from the look on Helena's face they're making an unholy racket." Judy fell silent, but the intent look didn't leave her face. "All right. No—well, of course. Goodbye." She lowered her phone. "Lucia doesn't know anything about it, and she's sending someone."

"So she wants us to sit here and wait?" Viv asked. She put away the lenses and stretched. "What if we had things to do?"

"I have to go soon, but you have nothing to do until you get a new case, or whatever you call it," Judy said.

"Jeremiah calls them bountyheads, but he watches too much *Cowboy Bebop*," Viv said airily. "That private investigator firm has offered us a permanent job, but I think we'd rather stay independent. Get our own licenses. Even so, I'm not sure I want to wait on Lucia's schedule."

"You're right," I said. The jackhammer had stopped, and the three people were gathered around the hole it had made. "Watch the kids."

"Helena!" Judy exclaimed. I ignored her and strode toward the van.

A tiny part of me insisted this was madness. I had no idea who these people were, no idea what they were up to, and they might not be friendly. But the rest of me was caught up in the rushing, swooping sensation of the oracle guiding me.

I reached the sidewalk, checked both ways, and crossed the street, hoping my children wouldn't see me jaywalking. I'd only just convinced Duncan that street lights and stop signs mattered. But the street was empty except for the van, and I reached the hole in the ground without having to dodge traffic.

The three people didn't look up as I approached. I had the strange sensation of being the one under an illusion, invisible to everyone but myself. I wasn't exactly being stealthy, but all three of them were staring into the hole as if it was a vista on some wonderful hidden treasure. Even when I came to a halt beside the skinnier of the two men, they didn't look up. I paused for a moment, feeling awkward, and then cleared my throat. "What are you doing?"

That got a reaction. All three of them jerked upright, and the plump man rose fully to his feet. They stared at me like I was a cop and they'd been caught trespassing. "You can see us?" the plump man said.

"I swear the illusion is holding," the woman said, rising more slowly.

"It is," I agreed, "but I'm Helena Campbell."

None of them looked enlightened. In fact, the skinny man looked more puzzled than before. "Who?"

That sent up all sorts of warning bells. No one who was part of our magical world would fail to know my name. That wasn't arrogance, it was pure fact. "You're not—" I began, then caught myself. That was something I'd learned both from my husband Malcolm and from Judy's favorite spy thrillers: never let on to an enemy how ignorant you are. And if they didn't know me, they might be enemies. "I'm guessing you don't have permission to dig here. Do you want to tell me what you're after, or should I call the authorities?"

Their amusement at this statement made me worry I'd said the wrong thing. I kept a straight face and refused to let them see my uncertainty. "The authorities," the plump man said. "You don't know anything, do you?"

"She saw through the illusion," the woman said.

The plump man waved in a dismissive gesture. "That means nothing."

"You're not sure about that," I said, making a guess. Sure enough, he looked a lot less certain. "In fact, you're asking yourself who might be interested in learning what you're doing."

The skinny man cursed. "Adepts," he said. "Kill her now."

"There's only one of her. She's no threat," the plump man said, but he reached behind him and brought out a small but lethal-looking pistol. "Back away, lady, and don't make me use this."

With the oracle's warning still surrounding me, I felt no fear. "You won't shoot," I said, acknowledging what my prophecy told me as well as challenging him. "Get in your van—"

"Step back," the plump man repeated, gesturing with the gun. Then he looked past me, and his eyes widened. The gun moved to point at something behind me. I turned and saw Viv, holding the blue lenses to her face, running as fast as her long legs would take her toward us.

I swung back around to see the plump man's finger move to rest on the trigger. Without a second thought, I kicked his knee and ducked away from the gun. My foot in its sandal couldn't do much damage, but he grunted in pain and his arm sagged. In the next moment, I was beside him, grabbing his wrist and sinking my nails deep into his flesh. He cried out and dropped the gun.

It all happened so quickly his partners had only just begun to move. The woman backed up and reached for her own pistol. The skinny man fell to his knees beside the hole and reached into it. I kicked the fallen gun away and pushed past the plump man to shove the woman off balance, or at least I hoped I would manage that. Fighting competently still wasn't one of my skills.

The woman took a step backward under my assault, but stayed upright. She grabbed my wrists and shoved me to the ground. I found myself eye to eye with the skinny man, who froze in his scrabbling at the hole. Then Viv was there, dropping the lenses inside her shirt and body-checking the plump man. It was his turn to hit the ground.

Viv moved smoothly past her fallen victim to challenge the woman. Unlike me, Viv knew what she was doing after eight years of kickboxing training. She and the woman circled each other, looking for an opening.

That was all I noticed before movement caught my eye, and I saw the skinny man pull something out of the hole in the asphalt. I grabbed his wrist, and for a moment we stared at each other like a couple of stunned deer facing the same oncoming car. I recovered first and reflexively slammed his wrist against the edge of the hole. He dropped whatever the thing was and wrenched out of my grip.

"Go, now!" the plump man shouted. I looked up. Viv was on the ground, and so was the woman, but the plump man hauled her up and dragged her to the van. I snatched at the skinny man's legs, but managed only to brush the sole of his work boot before he was out of my reach. He threw himself into the driver's seat and gunned the engine. Viv grabbed me and dragged me out of the van's path as it sped away, bumping once over the new pothole but not stopping.

I sat on the sidewalk, panting, beside Viv, who wasn't nearly so out of breath. I really needed to get more regular exercise, though attacking strangers wasn't in my daily routine. "Thanks."

"You have got to stop running into danger," Viv said. The illusion was gone, because traffic had resumed its normal course, though there still weren't many cars. All of them swerved wide of the hole in the street, sending up honks whenever their paths took them into oncoming traffic.

I crept forward from the sidewalk and looked into the hole. Whatever the skinny man had found there, he'd dropped it again, and it was visible only as a vague, oblong shape. I dug my phone out and turned on the flashlight, and aimed the beam into the hole. "Wow," I said, forgetting that my head was inches from oncoming traffic.

The object was a stone about half the size of my head, with rounded edges and a smooth texture. But what had astonished me was the glass embedded in it. Emerald and ruby and sapphire fragments caught the light and gleamed with deep, liquid hues. It looked like the concrete stepping stones the kids had made for our friends the Kellers last Christmas, only this was clearly granite and not concrete and I couldn't imagine how the glass had gotten there.

I put away my phone and reached into the hole, and got another surprise: the stone weighed practically nothing, certainly not as much as granite and probably not even as much as the glass pieces all together. I showed it to Viv, who'd crouched beside me. Viv whistled in appreciation.

"That's something," she said. "What is it?"

"I have no idea," I said. "You're a glass magus—is the glass magical or something?" Any magus, a Warden who could wield magic, could tell if an object was imbued with magic, but of the six types of magi, the glass magi specialized in seeing what was hidden.

Viv dug in her shirt for her lenses. "I don't get it," she said after a minute of observing the stone in silence. "I can't tell if it's magical or not. It's not a warded stone, that's for sure, but it's also not definitively non-magical."

I stood, cradling the stone in the crook of my arm, and waved to Judy, who was poised in the terrible still pose that told me she was going to erupt if we didn't return immediately to tell her what was going on. "Those people weren't Wardens," I said, "unless there are Wardens who've lived in caves for the past ten years and don't know the Long War is over. But they could definitely do magic."

Viv led the way across the street. "We should turn everything over to Lucia and let her figure it out. If those were rogue magi, it's her job to track them down. Unless the oracle has a different idea?"

I saw Jenny swinging and laughing as her brother pushed her, saw Duncan and Sophia holding the high ground of the fort against a couple of other children, and my desire to dig into the mystery diminished. "Lucia will tear me a new one if I don't let her handle this. The oracle isn't a policeman. But..." I brushed my fingers over the smooth glass shapes. "But I think this is the start of something serious."

CHAPTER 2

Lucia's office hadn't changed in all the years I'd known her: battered melamine desk, an office chair much nicer than the desk, metal bookcases piled high with binders and boxes of paperwork. The newest addition from a few years ago was a magazine rack on the desk's corner, filled not with magazines but with tablets in varying shades of gray and black. I didn't know what was on each tablet, but Lucia never got confused.

The stone rested in the center of her desk, the colored glass gleaming in the white lights illuminating the room. Compared to the angular, modern furnishings, it looked like a prop from a fantasy movie.

"Huh," Lucia said. She prodded the strange stone with her forefinger. "This looks like one of those tchotchkes people buy at seaside tourist traps to put in their gardens."

"A stepping stone, yes," I said, not mentioning the similar ones my children had made. "But one made by a master sculptor. Don't you think it looks... I don't know, deliberate? Like it wasn't just thrown together."

"And it's got magic bound up in it somehow," Viv said.

"Yes, you said." Lucia's voice sounded distant, like she was thinking about something else. "Tell me more about the people who dug it up."

"Just what I said. They didn't know who I was. And they—oh, I'd almost forgotten this—they said something about adepts. Like I might be an adept, whatever that is."

"Not Wardens."

"Definitely not," Viv said. "What does that mean?"

"A pain in the ass for me," Lucia said sourly. "People who can work magic who aren't Wardens like us...that suggests rogue magi."

"Maybe the last remnants of the Mercy?" I said. The rogue magi group called the Mercy had been in league with the alien invaders, and the invaders' defeat had weakened but not entirely destroyed them.

Lucia shook her head. "We eliminated them for good six years ago, I'm confident of that. I'd say some splinter group that wants to stay secret from other magi, but even a splinter group would recognize your name, Davies." Lucia called everyone by their last name and called me by my maiden name, possibly because keeping track of more than one Campbell annoyed her.

Lucia pushed her chair back from her desk and stood. "Leave it to me. You take your brood home and don't worry about it."

"But—" I closed my mouth on a protest. There really wasn't anything I could do short of prophesying, and I'd tried that already and gotten no visions or impressions. That generally meant either that something was none of my business, or that it didn't affect me or anyone close to me. "All right. Will you tell me what you learn?"

"If it matters to you, sure," Lucia said with a familiar sardonic smile. "You need to stop carrying the weight of the world, Davies. There are magi for that. Not that I think you're capable of *not* trying to help regardless."

The three of us left Lucia's small office and followed the long hallway back to the Gunther Node's central hub. The scent of gardenias, so familiar, came to my nose briefly. Why gardenias in this cold, concrete warren that escaped being called a bunker because it was enormous, I had occasionally wondered. No one ever mentioned it, and I never asked because I felt superstitiously that my drawing attention to it might make it disappear. Or maybe I was the only one who smelled it, and everyone would look at me funny if I said anything.

The central hub was a gray concrete dome some three stories tall that should have echoed with all the traffic that went through it. Why it didn't was another of those mysteries, like the gardenias, only this one I didn't care enough to pursue. Colored lines painted on the floor in a spaghetti tangle led from the hub's center to each of seven doors the size of warehouse gates, also rimmed in color. At the moment, few people strode through the hub, though "few" still meant dozens. I'd seen the hub at its busiest, so this qualified as practically nothing by comparison.

I opened the first door inside the green-rimmed opening and said, "All right, time to go!" Then, "Oops—sorry for the interruption!"

I hadn't known the Gunther Node had a day care until Alastair was almost a year old. Natural light, not artificial—that was another thing I hadn't known, that magic could produce actual sunlight, not an illusion —lit the cheery room painted with birds and trees and animals that would never coexist peacefully in Nature. The day care smelled pleasantly of fresh-baked cookies rather than gardenias and was unexpectedly quiet. I'd interrupted story time.

Frank Hale glanced up from the picture book he held. "Almost done, Ms. Campbell," he said.

But Jenny popped up from where she'd been sitting, shouting, "Lucia! Lucia!" and ran for us, flinging her arms around Lucia's legs. Lucia bent and swept her up, holding her upside down so she giggled.

"You need to let Mr. Frank read, peanut," she mock-scolded Jenny, and set her down on her feet.

The other children, gaping, turned back to the book with its pen and watercolor art of monsters being led by a boy in a white wolf suit. Even Alastair was listening, though he sat at the back of the group so he could pretend disinterest. Alastair could read before he was three, and he'd often been the one reading aloud to the other kids in kindergarten, but he still loved being read to.

I listened to the comforting, familiar last pages of *Where the Wild Things Are* without impatience. This was one of those days where I had nothing to do except start dinner in a few hours, and I enjoyed the peace. When Frank closed the book and said, "All right, Campbells, we'll see you again sometime, yes?" I straightened from where I'd leaned against the wall and waited for Alastair and Duncan to join us.

Julie Northrup, one of the other day care workers, wandered over with a toddler in her arms. The sleepy child had her head against Julie's shoulder. "It's good to see the kids," she said quietly. "You know they're welcome any time."

"I'm grateful," I said. "It's been a real blessing." Not all my days were this peaceful, between handling requests to the oracle and business related to my corporation. The oracle still charged for its services, but it wasn't as if I needed the money personally, so I'd incorporated my "consulting business," paid myself a nominal salary, and organized a charitable giving program to handle the rest of the funds.

Alastair came to my side. "I'm ready."

"Duncan," I called, not loudly as I was conscious of the sleeping child Julie held.

Duncan kept driving a Tonka truck across the carpet and ignored me.

Sighing inwardly, I said, "Duncan, don't forget we're going to watch a movie this afternoon."

That brought him to his feet and hurrying toward me. I cringed inwardly at Julie's regard. She would never criticize, and maybe she didn't even think a criticism, but I felt guilty nonetheless. These days it seemed I resorted to bribing Duncan a lot faster than I used to, even if it wasn't technically bribery. His disobedience reminded me painfully that I really had no idea how to raise children.

We said goodbye, peeled Jenny off Lucia's leg, and headed back to the hub, where Viv found a black-clad tech to work the teleportation circle that sent us outside. The heat of the day felt worse after the cool air-conditioned comfort of the Gunther Node, and I opened the doors of the Tahoe and fanned the air inside into motion while the kids ran in circles around the car. How they still had so much energy in this heat baffled me.

Viv paused with the front door of her car open, clearly as reluctant to step into the oven as I was. "Girls' night tomorrow?"

"As always," I replied. "It's Judy's turn to choose, so I figure she'll text us."

Viv nodded and climbed in to start her car. She'd driven her Econoline van into the ground, not willing to admit it was past its best-by date, until Jeremiah had taken her to a used car lot a few years back and she'd fallen in love with this battered Lexus GX that looked like it had been through the wars. No one would ever believe it was a luxury automobile. She'd immediately named it Clarence.

"Don't worry about it," she told me.

"Worry about what?"

"The stone. Those weird people. Whatever's coming, we'll have plenty of warning. I feel it." She shut the door, waved, and drove off down the short incline to the road.

I watched her go until she vanished out of sight around the bend. Ever since becoming a glass magus, Viv had become prone to premonitions. They weren't as clear as oracular visions, and not as precise as the precognitive visions our friend Victor Crowson had, but they were always accurate, even if sometimes their accuracy wasn't obvious until the event was over. That one hadn't been particularly helpful, not in the sense of telling me what more to expect, but it was reassuring.

I came to myself and herded the kids into the car. "Seatbelts," I reminded Duncan and Alastair, then checked to make sure they'd fastened them properly. Surprisingly, Duncan never fought me on the need to stay strapped in, possibly because Alastair didn't. Alastair was better at getting Duncan to do things than I was. Older brother, possibly cooler brother—whatever the reason, Duncan looked up to him, and I had to resist the urge to put the burden of Duncan's obedience on Alastair. That wasn't fair to anyone.

I put the Tahoe in gear and trundled down the road. We'd bought it when Jenny was born and the Accord couldn't fit us all anymore. Malcolm was the car nut, not me, so I'd let him choose, but I'd balked at the size of the enormous SUV. "It would be like driving a tank," I'd complained, but Malcolm had pointed out the conveniences of a full-size SUV for a working mother like myself, and I'd agreed to test it. Just to see. And I'd been surprised at how much I'd liked it. Even so, I called it my land yacht, with myself as skipper.

The journey from the Gunther Node to our house was about half an hour long, but at this time of day, traffic wasn't heavy, so I sailed along the freeway half-listening to the conversation Alastair and Duncan were having. Alastair was telling Duncan the plot of some book, but he kept looping back to insert important parts he'd forgotten in his excitement. It was reassuringly normal in my genius son, that he wasn't perfect. Sometimes he was a little too much like a small adult, between his intelligence and the oracular gift.

Jenny didn't speak, but I heard her tapping the sides of her booster seat in rhythm with the quiet music playing in the background and knew she hadn't fallen back asleep. Too much sleep during the day made her cranky and unable to sleep at bedtime. I relaxed, and realized I'd been tenser than I'd thought. Now that I could go over that encounter in memory, I was shocked at how casually I'd ignored the guns. I'd been certain they weren't a threat, and I had no reason to doubt my insight, but the possibility of being wrong still chilled me.

I made myself contemplate dinner, something light and cool, until we reached home. The kids, released from their seatbelts, raced inside, and I followed more slowly. We'd lived here for more than ten years, it was familiar, but familiarity had bred contentment in me rather than contempt, and I always entered the house with a sense of relief. Here, I could shut out the world when the demands of the oracle became too much.

I kicked off my sandals and put them in their cubby, shouting, "Alastair! Duncan! *Shoes!*"

Running feet sounded in the hall outside the mud room. "Movie?" Duncan asked.

"Get cleaned up first. I'll make popcorn." Again, the sense of calm filled me at the thought of such a normal interaction. I really had the best life imaginable.

The feeling of peace persisted through the movie, a cartoon chosen by Duncan. Judy had expressed astonishment that my children were willing to sit through an entire seventy-five minute movie without losing interest, something Sophia apparently never did. That, I had no explanation for, but it was something else for which I was grateful. Afterward, they spread out through the house to play while I started dinner. The idle thought that this was too good to be real struck me as I was chopping vegetables to go in the salad. I told myself that was fool-ishness and went back to singing along with the *Annie* soundtrack.

But the thought wouldn't go away. It didn't feel like a worry or anxi-ety, and it wasn't the oracle; it was just the sense that I was fortunate, and I shouldn't take that for granted. I wasn't sure I was in danger of that, but memories of serving as the oracular bookstore Abernathy's custodian, of all the things I'd endured in that position, started coming to mind. It would be easy to tell myself I deserved peace after everything I'd experienced, after giving my own life for the sake of defeating the monstrous invaders that wanted to destroy our world, but that was never true. In fact, wasn't the reward for success traditionally supposed to be yet another job?

With that, I heard the back door open, and footsteps along the short hallway heralded Malcolm's appearance. I left the knife on the counter and met him halfway, kissing him more fervently than I usually did. "I'm glad you're home."

"So am I," Malcolm said, taking me in his arms and returning my kiss. "Did something happen?"

"No—well, yes, but nothing awful. You just saved me from dwelling on memories." I took his hand and led him back to the kitchen. "I'm so glad I have you and the kids."

"Now I'm worried." Malcolm took a sliver of red bell pepper off the cutting board and ate it. "You're sure you're all right?"

I ate a slice of bell pepper myself. "Don't you ever feel like we're *too* fortunate? I mean, we have the ideal life, financial security, jobs we love, three wonderful children—maybe it's too good to be true."

"If I believed there was some force in the universe intent on balancing the scales, I might worry. But remember everything we endured to get to this point, Helena."

I sighed. "That occurred to me, too. Just because it's been years since the last time my life was in danger doesn't mean it didn't happen. I don't know. It was just an odd thought." I swept the chopped vegetables into a bowl atop a bed of lettuce and tossed the mixture with the salad tongs. "But let me tell you what did happen today. It was so strange."

Malcolm loosened his tie and freed the top button of his shirt. "Not dangerous?"

I considered his probable reaction to learning about the guns. "Not seriously dangerous." Before he could dig deeper into that statement, I told him about the three people and the stone they'd unearthed and tried to take.

Malcolm's frown deepened the longer I spoke. When I finished, he said, "Non-Wardens, but magi?"

"I guess. What else could it be if they were capable of making illusions? But none of it makes sense. And I haven't had any prophecies regarding it."

"You're right, though, that any Warden would recognize your name." Malcolm took off his suit coat and folded it over his arm. "So, what haven't you told me?"

"Um...one of them pointed a gun at me. But I knew he wouldn't shoot! So, technically, I wasn't in danger."

To his credit, Malcolm's sudden tension didn't erupt into chastisement. He simply shook his head and said, "I realize your prophecies are always correct, particularly the ones that rise out of circumstance, but that doesn't stop me worrying about your safety."

"It worried me, too, in hindsight. But I trust the oracle, especially now the oracle is me." I set the salad bowl on the counter and made a grab for the tongs as they threatened to overbalance and fall. "Go get changed, and then if you'd bring the kids, dinner is ready."

I gathered a handful of forks from the drawer and then paused as the swooping, gliding sensation of a spontaneous prophecy overtook me. For a moment, I saw a narrow, two-lane road, lined on both sides with pines that cast their needles over the paved surface. A gap appeared between the trees on the left, clear of undergrowth, with deeply rutted tracks that said many cars had passed there over the years. In the vision, I took that left turn and bounced through a passage so narrow pine branches brushed the car on either side. Then the vision faded.

I realized I'd dropped the forks and swiftly bent to gather them up and toss them into the sink. As I removed more silverware from the drawer, I contemplated what I'd seen. No indication of when it would happen, at least not beyond "daytime" and "summer," but in my heart I felt it would be soon. Combined with that sense was a feeling of satisfaction, the kind of rightness I felt when I'd done something good.

I hadn't gotten that feeling from a vision in a long time, not because my visions were evil, but because they were usually impersonal. I was grateful for that, because I didn't think I could endure being emotionally affected by every vision, even the ones about pleasant things. That might be what hurt Jenny so much. If so, I hoped she outgrew it fast.

With the table set, I listened to the distant noises of children playing upstairs. My earlier sense of peace had evaporated, replaced by a need to take action. I remembered what I had said about the strange stone—that it meant the beginning of something serious. At the time, I'd meant it was a mystery the Wardens would need to unravel. Now I wondered if it meant something else. Something personal. Maybe I wasn't wrong to consider how fortunate my life was, if something was coming that would disrupt it. In any case, I was sure the oracle would be at the heart of it.

CHAPTER 3

I stood at the loft window and gazed out over Portland at sunset.
From where I was, most of Portland's downtown was to my right,
putting those buildings in silhouette against the sky. Clouds
tinted the most outrageous shades of orange and peach and pink caught
the last light of the sun like they were auditioning for a burlesque show.
Between myself and downtown, the Willamette snaked past, with the
Morrison Bridge straddling it. If I squinted, I could make out the red-
brick building that housed the Board, no longer the Board of Neutralities that had governed the Wardens and the magic-producing nodes, but
still a powerful force in the magical world.

"I'm hungry," Viv murmured.

"Shut up. Judy needs us to be patient." I turned around and leaned
against the window with my arms crossed over my chest, not because I
was impatient but because that was a comfortable pose. The loft was
brightly lit despite the sunlight, and its white walls and ceiling made it
seem even brighter. The floor, on the other hand, was nearly black and
varnished to a point where my shoes slipped if I stepped incautiously. I
glanced down at my wavery, dim reflection. I looked like someone in
need of a cheeseburger. Maybe I was hungrier than I thought.

Judy walked toward us, not having any trouble with the floor despite her four-inch stack-heeled sandals. "I am really sorry," she said in a low voice. "We're almost done here. I'll buy dinner to make it up to you."

"It really is all right," Viv said.

"No, but Katrin is...this is her first Fashion Week, and I don't want her freaking out and doing something stupid like pulling her collection the night before it's shown." Judy rolled her eyes. "She has nothing to worry about. It's not like this is Milan."

"It's still a big deal for a young designer, though," I said, looking past Judy at the clothing on racks and the models being fussed over by a short, round young woman wearing overalls over nothing but a pink bra. The clothing was as brightly hued as the clouds and in the same colors; orange and day-glo pink were apparently trendy, as were wide legs, lots of what I would call costume jewelry that Judy and Viv would no doubt say was vintage, and shirts with large, irregular triangles cut out of them. I couldn't see myself wearing any of it, but I still found the look appealing.

"A very big deal," Judy said. "I want to feature her clothing in the store, but it will sell better if her show goes well. Which means she has to *have* a show." She walked back to the woman in overalls, who had just torn the sleeves off the nearest model's dress and looked ready to burst into tears.

"Dramatic," Viv said in a low voice. "I guess it could be worse. She's not a diva. Katrin, I mean."

"She's not?" I controlled my surprised outburst. "What would a diva look like?"

"Oh...treat the models like mannequins, change her product line a dozen times before release, insist that it's all crap and she's a disaster..." Viv shrugged. "It's amazing how different designers' personalities are."

"How long were you a fashion model, again?"

"Three—no, four months." Viv examined the turquoise finish of her nails. "I think Judy's ready. Let's go."

I nodded, and the room moved with me. "Stop," I said. In the next moment, I felt a rush as if I'd been caught up in an eagle's talons and lifted into the sky. The loft fell away, and I saw a table in a forest, not a wooden picnic table but an ornately carved oak dining table complete with eight chairs. Scattered across its shining surface were playing cards —no, these were too large for playing cards, and their backs, for they all lay face down, had a bright pattern of a purply sky scattered with stars. Tarot cards.

I watched as a wind lifted two of the cards and flipped them over. I didn't know enough about tarot to recognize the cards, but one of them had a wheel at the center and a winged animal at each corner, all of them surrounded by clouds. The other showed three women dancing in a circle, holding fat goblets over their heads. Then the wind blew harder, hard enough that I felt it, and all the cards went sailing away over the tops of the pine trees, and the vision faded.

I blinked several times to clear my sight. Prophecies left my eyes feeling itchy, as if I'd had them open for too long, which was probably true. I lost all awareness of my real body when I had a spontaneous prophecy. Dimly, I heard Viv saying, "...a minute, she's coming around."

I focused on the figure in front of me, who turned out to be Judy. She looked mildly concerned, but when she said, "I hope Katrin didn't see that," I realized she hadn't suddenly become worried for me. After ten years of spontaneous prophecies, my best friends were accustomed to my occasional bouts of stillness in the middle of some other activity.

"Another one I don't understand," I said. "I—are we ready to leave?"

"We are, unless you need to tell us what you saw," Judy said.

I shook my head. "It can wait until we get food. Nothing urgent."

Judy drove to Giuseppe's, our favorite Italian restaurant. "I was planning on trying that new restaurant on Burnside," she said, almost apologetically, "but Katrin has exhausted me and I want something comforting and familiar, like meatballs the size of a baby's fist."

"I'll never complain about Giuseppe's," I said. "And the other place will still be there next time."

"Unless it's so trendy it closes in three weeks, and we'll be grateful we missed it," Viv said.

Giuseppe's had been around for at least two decades, but the recent remodel had freshened its appearance so it looked, not brand new, but youthful again. The owner had kept the rich, dark interior that had always given it a warm and comfortably intimate air, but the tables were bigger now, the booths wider, and the lighting was brighter. I liked the changes, something Viv and Judy had teased me about, given how reluctant I was to embrace change. I figured if something was working, why "improve" it? That didn't make me stodgy, it made me...well, "conservative" was probably the wrong word, but I liked it better than "intractable."

Leonard greeted us cheerfully—we did go there often, so it was natural we knew all the hospitality staff by name—and showed us to our favorite booth. If I was conservative, half of the reason was that everyone around me conspired to make me so. We ordered without benefit of the menu, a server named Elise brought us water, and Viv excused herself to use the restroom. When she returned, she said, "So, what did you see?"

"Oh," I said. "Actually, you could help. It was a tarot deck, spread out face down on a picnic table in the middle of a forest. The vision showed me two of the cards." I described the cards, coming up with more details than I'd registered at the time.

Viv listened intently, her eyebrows furrowed. "The Wheel of Fortune," she said, "and the Three of Cups."

"What do they mean? Not something bad, right?"

"I don't think so. The Wheel of Fortune means change, which can be good or bad—usually that depends on the question or the other cards you draw. But the Three of Cups doesn't refine that meaning much. It represents friendships, positive relationships. I suppose both together implies a change in a relationship, for good or bad. I'm not really an expert tarot reader."

"So...maybe making new emotional connections?" I asked.

"Or losing existing ones, if it's a negative meaning," Judy said.

"I hate that interpretation," I said. "Three women on the card, and there are three of us." I shook my head. "No. It's a prophecy, not a tarot reading. If it's symbolic, that doesn't have to mean tarot symbolism. It makes more sense to say change is coming, and the three of us are involved. Because it's not like we've never been at the heart of a Warden crisis."

"I don't think it's predicting something will happen to us," Viv said, "but if change is coming, that change could involve making connections with someone new. I wouldn't disregard that possibility."

"Is that a premonition?"

"No, just a guess."

Conversation paused as Elise reappeared with our food. When she was gone, we ate for a while in silence. I forked up fettucine Alfredo, twirling the fat noodles around my fork, and contemplated my vision. "And it was in the forest," I said when my mouth was empty.

"What was?" Judy said. "Oh, you mean the vision. How many is that now?"

"Four. All the spontaneous prophecies I've received in the last twenty-four hours have had something to do with a forest. Two of them were of the same road through a forest." I twirled my fork in the pasta again, but didn't take a bite. "This has never happened before, a sequence of related visions instead of one vision that makes sense by itself."

"But they're not in order," Viv said. "How are you supposed to know what to do if it's just a bunch of images?"

"It's more than that, though. There's always a feeling of anticipation, like I'm moving toward understanding. It's like I'm accumulating puzzle pieces, only I think they'll assemble themselves once I have enough of them, and the picture will make sense." I took a drink of my beer—Harry Keller's best efforts hadn't been able to turn me into an appreciator of wine—and set the glass down with deliberation to the right of my plate.

"Well, don't do anything stupid," Viv said. Her eyes widened. "I don't know where that came from. You're not stupid."

"That sounded like a premonition," Judy said.

"It was." Viv took a long drink of wine and wiped her mouth. "Damn. I wish those were less obscure."

"That one suggests danger," I said. "That's specific enough for me."

———

I WOKE EARLY the next morning and decided to make pancakes for breakfast, even though it was Malcolm's turn. I padded barefoot around my spacious kitchen, humming as I pulled flour and salt and baking powder out of the cupboards. My mother always made her pancakes from scratch, and I liked the flavor better than a mix.

I heard small feet pounding down the stairs, and soon Duncan came into view, his blond hair sticking up in tufts all over his head. "Pancakes!"

"Yes, and can you bring me the eggs?"

Duncan carefully set the cardboard carton on the counter by the mixing bowl. I glanced at him in time to see his eyes flash silver. Swiftly I put out a hand to steady the egg carton, but despite his sudden stillness, his hand didn't relax. After a few seconds, he blinked and stepped back.

"What did you see?" I asked, trying for a casual tone.

Duncan wouldn't look at me. "I don't know," he said. "It was too fast."

I didn't need the ability to detect lies to know Duncan hadn't been honest. I hesitated only a moment before saying, "Duncan. You know you shouldn't conceal a prophecy. Suppose it could help someone?"

"It can't. It wasn't important," Duncan said stubbornly, and ran out of the room.

I put both hands on the counter for support and bowed my head, carefully not voicing the words in my head. Again, I couldn't resist comparing. Alastair had taken to being an oracle as naturally as breathing. If anything, Malcolm and I had had to teach him not to prophesy when that would draw attention to himself. I sometimes let him do some of the official requests for prophecies people sent, under my supervision.

But Duncan, stubborn beyond belief, seemed to feel the oracle was a bossy adult, something he reflexively fought against. In the last year, he'd started claiming not to understand the prophecies he received when he didn't pretend he hadn't received them at all. Malcolm and I had come close to arguing about what to do. Malcolm thought Duncan would outgrow what he called our son's "oppositional phase." I countered with the plain fact that the children's prophecies, while not usually about anything vital, had nevertheless helped many people, and maybe they had a duty to act on what they saw. To which Malcolm had said, "They have a whole lifetime to use their power to help others. Duncan's only going to resent the oracle more if we force the issue."

That last statement had influenced me more than the rest. Duncan shouldn't resent something that was so deeply a part of him; that would be like hating himself. So I spoke gently, hoping Duncan would respond to that. It wasn't working so far, at least in terms of getting him to open up, but at least he and I were no longer at odds all the time.

I cracked eggs one-handed into the bowl—I'd learned that from the movie *Sabrina*, the one with Bogie and Hepburn—and stirred until the yolks were pale yellow. Three young oracles, each with their own problems. At one time, I'd wondered if I should have more children, to bring as many oracles as I could into the world. Now I contemplated each of my children and wondered if I was doing right by them. It was one thing for me to be an oracle, with my years of experience both with Abernathy's and with the magical world in general. The children had come into the world with the gift and no preparation. All they had was me, flailing around and doing my best to strike a balance between giving them a normal childhood and preparing them for a unique destiny.

Jenny toddled in and clung to my legs, but didn't cry, so I guessed she just wanted morning cuddles. "Daddy's in the shower," she said. "I want pancakes."

"Just a few minutes." The griddle was almost hot enough. "Where's Alastair?"

"In bed."

"Why don't you go tell him about breakfast. Duncan?" I called Duncan's name again, and eventually he came into the kitchen, slouching the way he did when he felt guilty about his behavior and didn't want to admit it. I pretended nothing was wrong. "Duncan, please set the table."

"Okay." That was the best I was going to get from him. I reminded myself he was six and finished making the pancake batter. Malcolm was right; Duncan would figure things out eventually.

After breakfast, I left Malcolm and the children to clean up and shut myself into my office for the morning's business. Today I hurried through my personal email before booting up the second computer, the one dedicated to the oracle's communication. Fifteen requests. That was fewer than average. Now that requests were exclusively made via email, I'd originally expected to have a lot more of them. But as soon as word got around that prophecies were, if anything, more expensive than Abernathy's auguries, the initial rush had faded.

I'd also originally resisted making people pay for prophecies. What had been commonplace for Abernathy's felt strange when it was me doing the prophesying, like charging people for the privilege of talking to me. But I remembered how Abernathy's had operated, how it priced its auguries in a way that ensured their recipients didn't take them for granted, and I'd realized I needed to do the same unless I wanted to be overwhelmed with requests.

Now I opened the first message and read:

My son is struggling to find a job. He doesn't have a college degree, but he's bright and I think if he found the right job he could make a career out of it. How can I help him?

The swooping, falling sensation of a prophecy swept me up immediately. I let out a deep breath and began typing a response. *Your son has quit every job he's ever had after less than two months. It doesn't matter now what job he takes so long as he stays with it for a year. If he does that, he will discover his career.* I knew more than this: that the job the son chose would not, in fact, be his future career, but part of my understanding of a prophecy included how much I should tell the asker.

I attached the payment link to my reply, not worrying that I'd given the person information without demanding money up front; if they took advantage of the oracle and didn't pay, they'd never receive another prophecy. My instincts told me five thousand dollars was reasonable and within this person's means. The fact that the money would almost all end up as grants for deserving organizations soothed any remaining qualms I had. That, and I never charged for spontaneous prophecies. That would be awful, giving someone a prophecy they hadn't asked for and then hitting them up for payment.

None of the requests were difficult, and I sailed through all fifteen in less than an hour. I shut the oracle's computer down and stretched. The room moved with me, and I closed my eyes and let the new prophecy rise up within me. The forest again, only this time I was moving backward on the road through the pines and firs. I emerged from the trees and saw I was on a road running through a city, not a large one based on how few buildings there were. It had the look of a road stop somewhere along I-5, except I saw no freeway—

and with that, the vision faded, and I was looking at the blank monitor again. I drew in a deep breath and blew it out, slowly. I was increasingly certain the visions were building toward revealing a location, complete with directions. What lay at the end of that road, I had no idea, but I felt eager to learn.

I checked the clock. Malcolm worked shorter office hours now that we had children, and today he planned to work from home entirely. I had some time for one more thing.

I opened a browser window using my personal computer and stared at the search bar for a minute, thinking. Then I typed *strange stone under the street* and hit enter. The search window filled up with a lot of nonsense, links to metaphysical sites selling crystals, a Mexican restaurant selling street tacos, a couple of design firms advertising different types of decorative stone for sale. Nothing related to the mystery stone.

I cleared the search bar and tried *granite glass stone*. Nothing relevant, though the same design firms appeared again. I tried another dozen search terms and got the same non-result. Finally I leaned back in my chair and ran my hands through my hair, scratching my scalp lightly. This all assumed the stone wasn't unique, and I had no evidence of that aside from a gut feeling that anyone who had made such a beautiful object wouldn't have stopped with just one.

I drummed my fingers on the desktop. Then I typed *stained glass granite stone hidden in city*. Same result. I was about to shut the computer down when my eye fell on the fourth search result, the one just above the bottom of the screen, and read the words *hidden under the pavement like the others*.

Immediately I clicked on the link. It went to a message board that looked like twenty-year-old software, the background a deep midnight blue, the headers an eye-watering yellow. Across the top of the page were the words SPOTTERNET and a funny-looking symbol that looked like a stylized eye with a tail that curled beneath it. Below the name and logo was a smaller header, still in that awful yellow, that read SIGHTINGS in all capital letters. It felt like the website was shouting at me.

I turned my attention to the post the search engine had caught. It was a few short lines: *Found one! Corner of Sunset Boulevard, if you can believe it, where they were doing construction, hidden under the pavement like the others. I couldn't leave it there without someone noticing it, so I brought it home.*

Fascinated, I read the replies. Most of them were other users yelling at the original poster for moving the stone, but a few wanted more details, and three posts down I found the description. It looked nothing like the stone we'd found; it was perfectly square, and instead of glass, it had been painted with an intricate pattern in black and white. But I was sure this stone and ours were related.

I navigated to the home page and poked around there for a bit, then clicked on more of the topics. It didn't take much digging to discover the site hadn't had any activity for over a year. I found no page with information about whoever sponsored the site, and the Members page was password protected.

Eventually, when I felt I'd exhausted the possibilities of the site, I texted Viv and Judy the address with the message *Take a look and see what you think.* Judy was better with computers than I was, and Viv would either find something out through persistence or give it to Jeremiah. Probably this was something Lucia and her team of investigators had already discovered, but I hated not taking action.

I shut down my computer and pushed away from the desk. My phone lay near the keyboard where I'd set it, though my pockets were deep enough to fit it. I picked it up again and, on a whim, flicked through the photos to the one I'd taken of the stone. It looked unreal in the picture, not like itself and not like a Hollywood prop, more like a photorealistic painting. Looking at it didn't prompt any visions. That seemed like a sign to stop thinking about it and join my family. But I carried the memory of the stone with me, on and off through the rest of the day.

CHAPTER 4

Friday was grocery shopping day, and I took all three children with me. Duncan needed new sandals, having accidentally torn the straps of his old ones, and they were all well behaved on car rides so long as my errands were short and happened before lunchtime. Well, Alastair was well behaved in general, but Duncan's behavior wasn't predictable. He no longer threw tantrums when he got bored the way he had when he was Jenny's age, but too long an excursion he found boring turned him sullen.

For once, though, Duncan and I were in agreement, and he picked a pair of sandals I approved of in record time. Back at the land yacht, I removed the tags and helped him put the new shoes on before getting everyone buckled in. The day was overcast, not as hot as the rest of the week had been, but muggy and uncomfortable with an oncoming storm. I looked forward to the rain. Summer rain was one of my favorite things, especially if I was in a position to sit inside and listen to it drum on the windows.

"I want ice cream," Duncan said. "Can we get ice cream? I was good in the store."

"You were, and I appreciate it," I said. "Groceries first, then lunch, then I think we could have ice cream. Alastair, what do you think?"

Alastair was already head-deep in his book. "Sure," he said in the distracted tone he used while reading.

I shook my head in amusement and started the car, but had to wait for traffic to pass so I could pull away from the curb. I glanced at the rearview mirror and caught sight of someone in a red Camry two cars back, also waiting to pull out. For a moment, our eyes met, and then the woman looked away. I checked over my shoulder, checked the side mirror, and turned on my blinker before easing away from the curb and smoothly accelerating. I wasn't amazed anymore at how well the land yacht handled despite its size.

The grocery store was a mile or so from the shoe store, an easy drive, and at this hour on a Friday, the roads weren't very busy. I parked and got the kids out and Jenny settled into the shopping cart. A car drove past us, looking for a parking spot. Another red Camry. I'd read somewhere about popular colors for cars, but now I couldn't remember if red or black was more common.

Some shopping trips were harder than others, with Duncan and Alastair forgetting to keep their hands on the cart so they wouldn't run off when they saw something interesting. Today, my luck continued to hold, and I had the boys help pick items off the lower shelves and put them carefully in the cart. On a whim, I bought a bouquet of mixed flowers for our dining table and let Jenny hold it while the cashier rung us up.

The overcast was heavier than before, the clouds hanging low and pendulous as if sagging with the weight of water they held, and I pushed the cart faster. After settling the children, I rapidly loaded bags into the back of the land yacht and finished just as the first raindrops spattered my head. Ducking my head into my shoulders, I hurried to put the cart in the cart return and ran for the car, flinging myself into the driver's seat and slamming the door.

"Well!" I said with a laugh. "Just in time!"

I checked my rearview mirror, pressed the starter, and then looked again. Another red Camry was parked on the other side of the aisle, backed into a parking space so the driver was facing us. And it was the woman I'd seen outside the shoe store.

I paused, then tilted the rearview mirror to give me a better angle. It was definitely the same woman. She wore enormous black-rimmed sunglasses despite the rain, and her hair was pulled back sharply from her face now, but I still recognized her.

A shiver ran through me, not a chill but a tingling sensation that briefly numbed my skin. I turned around and looked at the children. Alastair was reading again. Duncan thumped his fist against his booster seat, gazing out the far window. Jenny's eyes were red-rimmed the way they got when she was tired. Then I looked at the Camry and its driver. She wasn't watching us, but every now and then she glanced our way.

I closed my eyes and let myself fall into the oracle, asking a wordless question. The answer returned the same way, without words or images, just the unshakable knowledge that I shouldn't let this woman follow me home.

The knowledge frightened me in its implacability. Then I got a grip and calmed myself. This wasn't the first time the oracle had steered me away from danger. It was just the first time the danger it helped me avoid was human.

I put the car in gear and backed out slowly, pretending I hadn't noticed anything out of the ordinary, but keeping an eye on the woman in the Camry. She sat up straighter when I began to move, and although I couldn't hear the other car's engine over my own, I saw the car shift forward slightly as if she had put her foot on the brake to keep from inching out.

I drove through the parking lot, and the Camry fell in behind me. At the exit to the main road, I turned on my signal and edged over to make a right-hand turn. The Camry followed, though the driver didn't use her signal. It didn't matter, but I held a grudge against people who didn't signal turns, so that was one more mark against her.

At the next corner, I turned left instead of right and headed for the freeway. The Camry stayed close and followed me onto the on ramp. I accelerated to freeway speed, the hiss of the land yacht's wheels on the wet road rising in pitch, and continued to use my turn signal to indicate lane changes. The Camry didn't stay right behind me, instead hovering on my left rear bumper, but it was clear the driver meant to keep me in sight.

"Mommy?" Duncan said. "Where are we going?"

"Just taking the scenic route," I said, my tone light and unconcerned. The windshield wipers flicked back and forth, back and forth as rain struck the glass fast enough to sound like dice rattling in a cup. I turned on my blinker again and changed lanes. "You're not in a hurry, are you?"

"I guess not." Duncan still sounded skeptical. I risked a glance at him and saw his eyes flash silver just before I had to look back at the road ahead. He said nothing, and when I glanced back again, he was looking out the side window and his lips were pressed hard together.

Instinctively, I said, "Duncan, tell me what you saw. It's important."

I expected him to lie about having seen anything, so he surprised me when he said, "Don't take this exit, take the next one."

"Thank you, Duncan." I changed lanes again, still using my signal. The Camry didn't move to follow me, but it was still only a car's length away. We passed an exit, and I sped up so I was going slightly faster than the speed limit.

"Mommy, what's wrong?" Duncan's voice quavered, and I recognized the sound of a child trying not to cry. "Something bad is happening, isn't it?"

"What's he talking about?" Alastair said.

"It will be all right. Hold onto something," I said as the next exit loomed before me. Without signaling, I shot sideways into a space between two cars and rocketed up the exit ramp, ignoring the honking of the car just behind me and the delighted shouts of my sons. I didn't have attention to spare to see what the Camry did, because the light at the top of the ramp was green, for a miracle, and I turned left and sped away from the freeway.

"Wow, Mom! That was so cool!" Alastair said.

"We got away, right?" Duncan said. He sounded more shaken than Alastair did, and I wished I dared stop to comfort him.

"Everything is all right," I said, and drove home, checking behind me all the way.

Jenny was dozing when we arrived home, and I was tempted to let her sleep, but she'd wake from her unscheduled nap hungry and cranky and that was worse. Controlling my impatience, I roused her gently and then settled everyone in for peanut butter and jelly sandwiches before going into our small front room, never used except to entertain guests we didn't care about, and calling Malcolm.

"Somebody tried to follow me home today," I said when he answered.

Malcolm's cheery greeting, which I'd overridden, cut off sharply. "Followed you? A driver, you mean?"

"Yes. I happened to notice her waiting outside the shoe shop, and then I saw her again when we left the grocery store. The oracle confirmed I shouldn't let her find out where we live, and it told Duncan where I should evade her." I drew in a shaky breath. Now that the immediate crisis was over, my nerves had taken over. "It was frightening."

"There was only one?"

The intensity in Malcolm's voice calmed me. "I didn't see any others, and I didn't feel warned a second time about not going home. So I'm sure she was alone."

Malcolm was silent for a moment. Finally, he said, "I wonder how the driver found you in the first place. She couldn't have followed you from our home, not if she was trying to discover where you live."

"Yes, and why now? We don't have an extravagant lifestyle that might make kidnapping a threat, and I don't know of anything we've done that might make someone go looking for revenge." I was proud of how my voice didn't shake on the word "kidnapping."

"We have safeguards in place against that, Helena. Don't be afraid."

"I know. And I'm sure the oracle is a protection." I sank down on one of the overstuffed chairs and rubbed the bridge of my nose. "But... well, what about that stone?"

"The mystery stone?" Malcolm sounded puzzled. "You gave it to Lucia."

"Yes, but those people who dug it up, they don't know that. What if they are trying to get it back?"

"Then they will discover exactly how much hell I'm capable of raining down on them," Malcolm said. "If you weren't the one involved, love, I'd almost welcome them trying. It would give me a better chance of identifying them."

"I assume that means Campbell Security hasn't found them." My husband's security company provided services to the Wardens as well as to its mundane clients, and over the years I'd gotten used to calling on them to solve problems related to the oracle and the magical world.

"They didn't leave us much to work with. And Lucia's people haven't had any luck, either." Malcolm sighed. "Until this call, I'd begun to suspect we were chasing ephemera."

"The woman in the Camry was definitely real. But whoever she was, or whatever group she's with, they can't be omniscient or they wouldn't have needed her. That's good, right?"

"It does narrow the possibilities," Malcolm said. "We—"

I heard Alastair shout, "*Mom!*" and jerked upright. "I have to go," I told Malcolm, and hurried back to the kitchen nook.

"We'll discuss it further tonight. Love you," Malcolm said, and disconnected.

I entered the kitchen nook, where the smaller dining table was, to find Alastair trying to mop spilled milk with a kitchen towel that wasn't very absorbent, judging by how it was mostly pushing the milk across the table. Jenny had peanut butter and grape jelly smeared all over her face. Duncan was stolidly eating his sandwich and ignoring the milk that dripped over the table's edge.

I took the towel from Alastair and said, "Thank you for trying to help, but let's get some paper towels instead, all right? Duncan, scoot back so milk doesn't get on your shorts. Jenny—oh, never mind, you're happy."

Jenny giggled. I'd never seen a three-year-old so pleased with the mess she'd made.

Once everything was cleaned up, and Jenny was in bed, and Alastair and Duncan were in their rooms for quiet time, I lay on the couch in the great room and closed my eyes. Driving the land yacht the past couple of years had made me a more confident driver, but I wouldn't have pulled that stunt if I hadn't had the oracle buoying me up—and if I hadn't had the kids to think of. The shakes had passed, and now I could be angry. How dare those people interfere in my life?

"Mom?"

I opened my eyes. "Alastair, it's quiet time." Malcolm and I had instituted this practice when Duncan was three and decided he was too grown up for naps; I didn't care what they did for that hour so long as they did it quietly in their bedrooms.

"I know, but I saw something." Alastair sounded worried, and he was rubbing the soft upholstery of the couch arm, pressing hard and working his fingers back and forth like kneading dough. "I don't know what it means."

I sat up and guided him to sit beside me. "Tell me."

"I was in a house, in a big white room," Alastair said. "Like, all the furniture was white, and the walls and doors too. And there were a lot of windows, like ours." He gestured at the wall of windows that looked out over our vast backyard and the swing set near the back fence. "Only they didn't show a yard, they showed water. Lots of water. And it was night, and the moon shone on the water."

"Could you tell what time of year it was?"

Alastair shook his head. "There was a man, though. He didn't look old like the Kellers, but he was a grownup. And I heard him say, 'It's humanity or its enemies. You have to choose.' He wasn't talking to me, I know that, but I didn't see anyone else in the room."

I put an arm around his shoulders and hugged him. "Is that everything?"

"I guess," Alastair said, shrugging. "But I've never had a vision like that before. They always show what I'm supposed to do. This was like watching a scene in a movie without knowing what movie it is."

"I agree, that's strange," I said. "Give me a minute." I drew in a breath and blew it out slowly to dispel the last of my anger, and then fell into my deep-rooted sense of the oracle, asking for enlightenment.

Images flashed past, and impressions fleeting enough to be gone before my conscious mind registered them. Taken all together, though, they filled me with a sense of quiet peace, like walking in the woods far from the noise of civilization. I saw, once again, the forest road, only now I flew along it as it curved, and I realized it followed the slope of a mountain. Then I reached the gap in the forest, made a sharp left turn through branches reaching to tug at my hair and clothes, and emerged into a small valley. A house lay at the bottom of the valley—

—and with that, my sight cleared, and the impressions faded entirely. I inhaled again, this time because I'd forgotten to breathe while the visions gripped me.

Alastair was watching me curiously, but without fear. I clasped his hand briefly. "I don't know what your vision means," I said, "but I don't think it was intended for you. I think you were supposed to share it with me."

His shoulders relaxed. "I didn't know what it wanted me to do."

"It's all right. Thank you for telling me." I patted his shoulder in reassurance. "Go back to reading. There's still more than forty minutes of quiet time left."

Alastair nodded and ran upstairs. I lay back down and squeezed my eyes shut. Alastair's vision was related to what I'd been seeing, the prophecies that were building toward the answer to a puzzle. Humanity or its enemies? But the monstrous invaders I'd destroyed were gone, their reality sealed beyond any chance of opening to ours again, and as far as I knew, they were the only enemies of humanity there had ever been.

I ran back over the relevant prophecies in memory, searching for more information, and succeeded only in increasing my tension. My oracular gift had never behaved like this before, and I felt impatient with it. Why I couldn't see the whole future, I didn't know, and while I didn't think that meant the oracle had failed, I also didn't like feeling poised on the edge of a true revelation. It was like being unable to call up a word that was right on the edge of memory.

I considered reaching for more prophecies, but decided I needed a rest as much as the kids did. Besides, if that woman had been connected to the stone, it would help my prophecies to know what Malcolm had learned. I'd discovered in the past ten years that more information made my spontaneous visions more comprehensible, like knowledge gave me greater context for what I saw. And I was still angry enough at being followed to need some release so I didn't take my anger out on anyone else.

By the time Duncan came downstairs—on the hour, exactly, just like always—I'd played four levels of *Legend of Kerigon* and felt more relaxed. "How come I can't play video games during quiet time?" Duncan asked.

"Because Mommy doesn't get video game time like you do. Here, get me past the next boss." I handed him the controller and sat back to watch. I'd grown up with video games as a part of my life, but I'd never been good at them. Duncan played like the controller was an extension of his brain.

Jenny ran into the room and climbed onto my lap. I braced myself against tears, but she didn't cry out the way she did when she had a vision, just settled in to be cuddled. I put my arms around her. She was almost too big to fit comfortably on my lap, with long legs like Alastair had and a bony butt, but her affection warmed my heart. "Did you sleep well?" I asked.

Jenny nodded. "No bad dreams."

"That's good."

The big red "Level Complete" sign flashed in the center of the screen. "Can I play another?" Duncan asked.

"Maybe one more." It wouldn't hurt him to have a little extra screen time. I watched the figure on the screen dodge enemies and use his staff to trip them. I suspected the staff was what had prompted Jeremiah to choose this game; he was a wood magus and therefore a skilled staff fighter. I liked that this game didn't involve gory bloodshed. The children would learn about the sometimes brutal realities of life eventually, just not today.

Though I wasn't sure those particular brutal realities, the ones involving violence, were likely to be part of my children's lives. With the invaders gone, and their reality sealed away from ours permanently, there wasn't any reason for the children to train with knife and gun the way Malcolm had from a young age. Already fewer Wardens opted to receive an aegis, which was a splinter of wood or glass or steel or some other substance that would allow them to tap their own magic and become magi, on the grounds that the danger of death from having a semi-physical object implanted in their hearts was no longer worth the risk. It was a different world now.

Again, the screen flashed its big red letters at me. "All right, enough," I said, extending a hand for the controller. "Go tell Alastair to put his book away, and I want you all to run around outside for a bit and get some exercise."

"Can we go to the zoo today?" Duncan asked.

"Not today. It's too late. But I heard about this zoo and nature preserve in Washington we could visit on Monday, if you're willing to ride in the car for a few hours. There's an aquarium, too."

Duncan's eyes lit. "With a tide pool?"

"I think so." Duncan was passionate about two things, video games and marine biology. I could get him to do just about anything with the promise of handling a sea anemone. "Sound fun?"

"Yeah!" He raced out of the room and pounded up the stairs.

I hugged Jenny again and then encouraged her to climb down. "What do you think? You want to see some animals?"

Jenny nodded. Then her eyes flashed silver. I sucked in a startled breath and reached for her. But she didn't scream or flinch. She simply held still for a few seconds. Then she said, "Daddy can't come."

Casually, not wanting to scare her, I said, "Oh? Why is that?"

Jenny gazed at me with the solemnity of a small blonde owl, her brown-blue eyes enormous. "Lucia needs his help. There's a bad man who tries to run away. Daddy has to catch him."

I kept my tone level and mildly interested. "Did you see the bad man, honey?"

Jenny shook her head. "Lucia is mad, but she's not mad at me. She won't let anything happen to me."

"That is absolutely true." Lucia liked the boys in an abstract way, but she and Jenny had formed an unexpected bond. I probably should have been resentful of their attachment, since it meant Jenny trusted Lucia's word at times when she didn't trust mine, but I couldn't imagine anyone more suited to protecting my sometimes fragile daughter. "That wasn't scary, was it? The pictures you saw?"

She shook her head again. "I don't like the scary pictures, but sometimes it's okay."

"You're very brave, Jenny. Go put your sandals on."

When she was gone, I turned off the console and the television screen, belatedly realizing I should have checked to see if the game's progress had saved. Oh, well. Duncan never minded playing a level again. Then I tapped the remote against my leg. I didn't want to get my hopes up, but that vision had been so mild, and Jenny hadn't been scared...maybe Judy was right, and this was something Jenny would outgrow. I hoped she'd outgrow her fears before they marked her permanently.

CHAPTER 5

I hovered near the Tidal Touch Zone exhibit, keeping an eye on my children while not interfering in their exploration. Point Defiance's aquarium had turned out to be every bit as pleasant as the website promised, and I liked how peaceful the place was despite the number of visitors. I couldn't imagine how busy it would be on the weekend.

My phone rang, and I dug it out of my purse. "Malcolm, hi. Any news?"

"We found him," Malcolm said. "With Jenny's warning, Lucia started looking for him well before he attempted the bank robbery, and we picked him up before he could do any damage."

"I'm so relieved. Though we're sad you aren't with us, of course."

"I miss you all. I'll be home before you return, and then I was thinking you and I should go out to dinner."

"On a weeknight? How decadent, Malcolm Campbell!"

He chuckled. "Just taking advantage of summer. I can call Ysabel and see if she's available on short notice."

Our neighbors' daughter Ysabel Martinez was our regular babysitter, and I trusted her as much as I trusted Viv to watch our kids. "All right, if Ysabel can do it, I'd love to go out with you."

"Wonderful. I'll see you soon. I love you."

"Love you, too." I lowered my phone and sighed, feeling as smitten as a girl with her first crush. Wasn't love supposed to, not fade away, but become more of a commonplace? Yet I was as excited to be with Malcolm as I had been the first time we'd kissed. All right, that had been a bittersweet moment, so maybe I meant the second time we'd kissed. No, I'd been dating someone else...all right, the *third* time...

I checked the time on my phone display. "Time to head home," I announced.

"Aw, mom," Duncan said, not turning away from the tide pool.

"Yes, aw, mom," I said. "Daddy's going to see if Ysabel can stay with you tonight, won't that be nice?"

Duncan scowled, but he got up from where he was crouched over an anemone bigger than his head. "Ysabel makes me go to bed early."

"She does not, and you forget she also lets you show her how to play video games." The secret was that Ysabel was a video game master who played competitively, but she never made Duncan or Alastair feel inferior. "And we'll order pizza for you, how's that sound?" Might as well make this day truly festive.

Duncan shrugged. "I guess." But he nudged Alastair, and I didn't think he was as reluctant as he sounded.

Back in the land yacht, I settled Jenny comfortably so she could sleep most of the way home and started a movie for Alastair and Duncan to watch. I'd been skeptical of the nearly three-hour drive being worth it, but the kids had had fun, and I didn't mind the time it took so long as that was true.

As I put the car in reverse, the world spun around me, and I pressed hard on the brake. Once again, I was on the road through the trees, moving backwards, but faster than before. Scenery swept past, from trees to buildings to fields, and then I was on the 5 and receding from a road sign. I blinked, and the vision ended.

I shifted back into Park and watched the kids in the rearview mirror. Jenny was already dozing off. Alastair and Duncan had their attention fixed on the tiny seatback screen. The opening music to *How to Train Your Dragon* filled the air. I rested both hands on the steering wheel and closed my eyes. "Enumclaw," I said. I'd heard the name before, but only as a mention in the evening news now and again. I had no idea where it was.

And yet that was where my vision was guiding me.

I pulled up the map application on my phone, just to see. Enumclaw wasn't far, not even thirty miles from here. Not far at all. But—

I glanced back at the children, feeling horribly indecisive. I didn't think the visions were leading me into danger. Whatever I was supposed to learn at the end of that forest road, it didn't involve the rogue magi I'd taken the mysterious stone from, at least not directly. But trusting the oracle wasn't the same as voluntarily going into the unknown with my kids in tow. I wasn't sure I was that kind of brave, or maybe I meant foolhardy.

I considered my options. I could take the children home and return later with Malcolm, but that would have to be much later, and suppose the most recent vision meant I was meant to go immediately? I could call Malcolm and have him meet us here—no, he was busy with Lucia's captive, and that would still mean waiting until very late, which would make the kids cranky.

Or I could follow the vision's urging, and go now. The oracle never led me into danger, and it was even more protective of the children than it was of me, something we'd learned over the years as the kids' visions had stopped them running into traffic or riding bikes into dangerous territory. I closed my eyes again and let the question sink deep into my bones: *yes, or no?*

A calm feeling rose within me in response, soothing my fears. I once more put the land yacht in gear and backed out of the parking space. Forty-five minutes, and I would have answers. I hoped I knew which questions to ask.

I navigated through Tacoma and turned eastward, toward the mountains. Traffic was light at this hour of the afternoon, and I made good time along the freeway. Cities turned into open land, forested and then nothing but fields. The Cascade Mountains drew ever nearer, with Mount Rainier looming to the southeast. I hadn't ever been this close to it, and its height surprised me.

When we reached the outskirts of Enumclaw, I slowed, not just because the speed limit changed, but because I wasn't sure I remembered the path my vision had given me, particularly since I was driving it in the other direction. Then I saw a dry cleaner's I remembered, and from there, landmarks emerged, one by one like signposts guiding me along. I navigated the streets of the city, feeling increasingly eager. It was like being in vision again, only this time in command.

Eventually, we left the city behind, and I followed the road that led into the mountains. At late afternoon, the sun was at our backs, filling the air with golden light that cast strange shadows through the trees. After a few turns of the road, we left even that direct light behind. The road was as shady and cool as I remembered seeing it so many times before. I had the odd sensation of déjà vu, of memories overlaying the present. Turn after turn was as familiar as the route to my own house.

We passed only a few cars going the other way, and it was easy to imagine being the only people in the world right up until someone in a speedy little roadster whipped around us and raced away into the distance. I ground my teeth. Speedy little roadsters made me nervous with their unpredictability. Still, that one was gone.

Then, in the distance, I saw the gap in the trees to the left I remembered so well. I slowed as I approached. It was narrower than I'd realized in vision, with trees growing close on either side so the gap looked like a tunnel into the woods, and the road leading into it was barely more than a track, as if few people used it. Turning sharply, I drove off the road and through the tunnel.

Branches scraped along the sides of the land yacht, and Alastair let out a yell. "Mom, don't hit the trees!"

"I won't, honey, it's fine. They're just really close." The tunnel went on for some distance. I sped up, wanting to be out of there quickly; there wasn't any danger, but it was unsettling.

Then both boys cried out in fear, and I came to a stop and turned around in my seat. They were clinging to each other, their eyes wide with terror. "Mom," Duncan said, "Mommy, you just drove through a tree trunk."

I whipped back around. The tunnel still grew close to the road, but it was unblocked. "What are you talking about? Boys, it's fine."

Alastair shook his head. "There are trees in the way."

I looked again at the tunnel, suspicion dawning. "I think this is an illusion," I told them. "It's all right. I bet we get through it soon." I drove on, faster now, wondering when the illusion would end. It hadn't occurred to me that there might be magical protections on whatever this place was, but if these were rogue magi, it made sense they wouldn't want to be found. My fears resurfaced at the thought of rogue magi, and I suppressed them. I had to trust that everything would be fine.

I alternated watching the track ahead with watching the boys in the rearview mirror. Jenny had awakened, but she was silent, which I was grateful for. I didn't need her screaming over a frightening vision when I wasn't in a position to comfort her.

Then the land yacht came out from between the trees, and we bumped down a dirt path that showed signs of use by heavy vehicles, rutted and worn. Ahead lay a valley carved out of the evergreen forest, narrow at both ends and widening in the middle. At the bottom of the valley, a Tudor-style half-timbered house three stories tall faced the gap we'd emerged from, so unexpectedly familiar from my visions I slowed to gape. A couple of outbuildings, one the size of a large shed, the other big enough to be a small house itself, stood near the big house, and a small white gazebo occupied a very overgrown garden between the house and the larger outbuilding.

About halfway down the hill, the dirt road became gravel, and the dull thud of the tires became a lighter, hissing crunch. I followed the road to a gravel circle a short distance from the house, facing its three-car garage. It looked like a miniature parking lot, so I stopped there and turned off the engine.

"Mom? Where are we?" Alastair asked.

"Wait a minute," I said.

One side of the garage was open, and within I saw a maroon Jeep with mud-spattered sides. Legs in blue denim protruded from beneath it, and as I watched, their owner slid out from under the Jeep and sat up. He caught sight of my car and froze. Then he stood, wiping his hands on a rag he then stuffed into his rear pocket, and walked toward us.

"Stay there for now," I told the boys, and got out of the land yacht. Trusting in the oracle was one thing, but instinct told me I should put some distance between a stranger and my children.

The man—young man; he might have been barely out of his teens—

seemed as wary of me as I was of him. He stopped about fifteen feet away from the land yacht and examined me, wiping a smear of engine oil off his brown face. "Are you here to see Emily, or Cassie?"

For about half a second, I considered lying. Claiming to be expected by either of those women might get me information. But it wasn't a lie that could last long. "No, nobody's expecting me," I said. "I...um. Is there an illusion covering that entrance?"

The young man blinked. "Of course. Why wouldn't you know that? You couldn't have gotten in otherwise."

I decided not to explain my innate gift yet. "My name is Helena Campbell," I said, "and believe it or not, a vision led me here."

The young man didn't show signs he recognized my name, and he didn't react at all to that extraordinary statement. "Oh. What for?"

I hadn't been prepared for blasé curiosity. It took me a moment to remember what had started all this. "Hang on," I said. I returned to the car and unhooked my phone from the onboard system, then flicked through the gallery until I found the picture of the stone. I showed it to the young man. "Do you know anything about this?"

Again, he showed no sign that this was an odd beginning for a conversation. "I've never seen that one. Is it Felicia you wanted to talk to? She's the one who creates binding stones."

Awareness was gradually dawning. He wasn't surprised because he assumed I was like him, part of what I guessed was a second organization of rogue magi centered on stones like this one. He might have been associated with the ones who'd threatened to shoot me, but when I looked at his open, curious face, I had a hard time believing it.

Again, I considered letting his misapprehension lie, but I was so confused now I was afraid of increasing my confusion by having to keep track of the lies I told. "I don't know who to talk to," I said. "I'm not part of your group. I'm a Warden."

The words left my lips before I could hold them back. Distantly, I was aware that revealing my connection to the Wardens was potentially dangerous, if these were rogue magi who'd kept their existence secret from the rest of magery. Too late now. "We found this stone in Portland," I said to the young man's politely uncomprehending face, "and took it from some people who were digging it up. That's as much as I know about it."

The young man scowled. "Savants," he said, with as much bitterness as if he'd said *Nazis* instead. Then he hesitated. "Wait a minute. What do you mean, not part of our group? You're not an adept?"

That had been the word the plump man had used. "No. I've only heard of adepts once before now."

"But if you're not an adept, how did you find the entrance? And what's a Warden?"

"What's a—?" I stared at him. "How can you not know what Wardens are?"

"I don't know. Why don't you know about adepts?"

I realized just how long a conversation this could be, and instead said, "Are you the only one here?"

"No." The young man glanced over his shoulder at the house. "You'd better come inside."

"Let me get the kids." I turned to unlock the doors. "Everybody out," I said, unfastening Jenny's car seat. "Come on."

When I turned around again, the young man's expression of surprise made me want to laugh. Finally, I'd startled him. "You brought kids with you?" he said, making it sound like I'd violated the Geneva Convention.

"It wasn't a planned trip. We were at the aquarium when the vision happened." I set Jenny down and took her hand. "Sorry, I didn't catch your name."

The young man ducked his head in embarrassment. "Sorry. It's Milo. Milo Eaton. Come on, I'll see where everyone is."

He led us through the garage rather than going around to the front door. I made sure Alastair and Duncan knew to stay close behind me as we skirted the Jeep and an enormous blue pickup truck with a hard top and a winch attached to the front. Milo opened the inside door, which led to a small mud room and then a laundry room with a couple of baskets of dirty clothes leaning against the industrial-size washing machine. Past that, we entered a kitchen bigger than my own, with a white-tiled floor and cabinets of pale ash. A center island surrounded by bar stools held its own sink and still had enough room for a full-size cutting board.

Two steps down from the kitchen, an enormous great room lined with picture windows on two sides looked out over the far side of the valley, which continued to slope downward until the forest swallowed it up. Furniture made an informal division of the room, with sofas and a love seat surrounding a glass-topped coffee table on one side and a couple of recliners facing a super-sized flatscreen TV on the other.

"Wait here," Milo said. "You can sit if you want." He hurried away down a dark hall leading off the great room.

"Wow, look at that," Alastair said. He pointed at the coffee table, where sat a ceramic pot holding the tiniest tree I'd ever seen. "It's a bonsai. I read about them. You shape them with these really tiny scissors, and they can live for a hundred years!"

I walked over to look at it. It was beautiful, with spreading limbs that made it look like something off a Japanese wall hanging. "It's— Duncan, don't touch, that's not ours."

"They have *Legend of Kerigon*, Mommy!" Duncan exclaimed. "I bet that man plays it. He's probably not as good as me."

"Don't be arrogant, Duncan." I put my hand on Jenny's head as she wrapped her arms around my legs. "Jenny, it's all right. Don't be scared."

"I'm not scared, I'm hungry," Jenny said.

I checked my phone display. It was later than I'd thought. Malcolm wouldn't be worrying about us yet, but I didn't have a lot of time. "We'll eat something when I'm done talking to these people."

Footsteps sounded on the tile, and soon Milo returned with three other people. The white woman was about my age, with dark brown hair and very thin eyebrows. She regarded me with a neutral expression that suggested she didn't want me to know how curious she was. The Black woman was shorter and more petite, dressed for a much hotter climate than the Pacific Northwest even in summer, and lines of paint in half a dozen colors streaked her fingers and the inside of her left arm. The man was younger, though not as young as Milo, and very tall, with long reddish hair pulled back in a short braid and a face like a hatchet, all sharp planes and angles. He looked fierce, but I judged that was because his eyebrows were angled too, giving him the look of a bird of prey.

"This is—sorry, I forgot your name," Milo said.

"I'm Helena Campbell," I said, not offering to shake hands.

The white woman glanced at Duncan, still hovering near the television, then back at me. "Couldn't find a babysitter?"

Irritated at her sarcasm, I said, "You don't have a name?"

The woman's thin eyebrows drew down in the center. "Cassie Leighton," she said. "This is Gabriel Roarke and Felicia Curtis. Don't let that boy touch anything."

"He has manners, don't worry," I said, though I wasn't nearly so confident that Duncan could keep his hands to himself when it came to video games. "My children are well behaved. Alastair, Duncan, come here, please." I sent up a brief but fervent prayer that Duncan wouldn't choose now to become obstinate. Fortunately, both boys ran to my side, and our two little groups faced off. Cassie didn't look thrilled at our presence. Gabriel was impossible to read. Felicia kept glancing at the kids like she expected them to run wild. And Milo looked nervous, his gaze darting from Cassie to me and back again.

"She said she had a vision, but she's not an adept," Milo said. "I didn't think there were any magical people in the world who weren't adepts."

"Unless she's a Savant, and you've just let her into our stronghold," Cassie said.

"I'm not a Savant. I'd never heard of Savants until just a few minutes ago." I wished Jenny wasn't clinging quite so hard to my legs. "I found a special stone, and visions related to it led me here. Are you saying there are more of you?"

"I think you'd better do the talking," Gabriel said. "Since you're the intruder."

I hesitated. My certainty that these were rogue magi was fading—and yet what else could they be, if they could work magic like that illusion? "Look," I said. "If you're rogue magi, don't worry, the Board isn't going to punish you or anything. I don't know why you're hiding, or why you call yourselves adepts, and I don't care. But if something is going on related to these strange stones, I can help."

Now all four of them looked puzzled. "Rogue magi?" said Cassie.

An idea struck me. "I don't suppose any of you is a glass magus? The glass aegis is for discernment—you could see if I'm lying, or trying to confuse you."

Cassie's eyes narrowed, and she said, "What's an aegis?"

Chapter 6

Her words struck me like an electric whip, numbing me briefly. "What's...that's impossible. You can't do magic without an aegis. Aren't you magi?"

Cassie's thin eyebrows arched nearly to her hairline. "I've never heard of any of that. Gabriel?"

"It's not elf magic, definitely," Gabriel said. His voice was smooth and low and sounded as if it belonged to someone much older than he was. "And she's no adept. Which means—"

"It means something very strange is going on," Cassie said. "Milo, go get Emily. I think we should all be present."

"Let's sit," Felicia said. "There's toys in the corner cupboard." She pointed at the television, next to which was an antique cabinet that didn't match the rest of the furnishings. "Unless you think the kids won't be bored listening to the grownups talk."

I resisted the urge to tell her Alastair was probably smarter than she was. "Alastair, keep an eye on Jenny. Go see what's in the cupboard." I wanted to ask why a houseful of adults had children's toys on hand, but for all I knew this was some sort of commune and they had a passel of kids somewhere in the house.

Cassie had already taken a seat on the sofa, with Gabriel beside her.

They didn't touch, but I had the sudden strong feeling that they were romantically involved, lovers or married or something. It probably didn't matter, but I filed the notion away for later use. I sat opposite Gabriel, and Felicia took a chair nearby. Then we all sat there, silent, though I was dying to start asking questions. Whoever this Emily was, Cassie wasn't likely to talk without her present, and it was clear the others took their cues from Cassie.

I glanced over at the children, who'd pulled out Tinker Toys and alphabet blocks and were playing one of their favorite games, City. It meant making the biggest city they could out of available materials and was both the only game they all were willing to play together and the only game I could count on occupying them for at least an hour. I hoped we wouldn't need an hour.

Through the windows, I saw Milo approaching the patio that ran the length of the great room. An older woman accompanied him, not as old as my friend Harriet Keller, but white-haired, with long, dangling earrings that caught the light and fractured it. They entered via the porch door, and the woman approached me immediately.

"I'm Emily St. John," she said with a smile. "And you're the woman who isn't an adept. I must say, I didn't see you coming."

"Did you think to look?" Cassie asked. She didn't sound accusatory, just curious.

Emily shook her head. "No reason to believe there were other magical people in the world—at least, Milo says you call yourself a Warden, which implies organization." She settled gracefully on the couch beside me. "Well. Who should speak first?"

"You're the guest," Cassie said, tilting her head so her chin pointed at me. "Go ahead."

I opened my mouth and closed it again. "I don't know where to start. And I have so many questions. This isn't like telling someone with no knowledge of magic, because I have no idea what you already know."

"Assume we know nothing," Gabriel said. "That's probably closest to the truth."

I shook my head slowly, feeling suddenly very weary. "All right. I guess at least none of us will protest that magic is impossible."

I took a moment to collect my thoughts, then began at the beginning, more than seven hundred years ago, when a parasite reality had latched onto ours and let billions of monsters through, all of them intent on draining our world's magic. How humanity had responded by developing the aegises that allowed a man or woman to tap into their own body's magic, something impossible for an ordinary person to do, and using those aegises to develop and train magi to fight the invaders.

The five strangers listened, unmoving and silent, as I explained about the rift in magery that had come about because of the use of harnessed invaders to fight their own kind, how the Nicollien and Ambrosite factions had prompted the rise of Neutralities, and how some of those Neutralities were more powerful and unique than others. I talked about the oracle that had resided in Abernathy's Bookstore and how I had been its custodian until the end of the Long War. "You remember, about ten years back, those strange terrorist attacks? What they called bioterrorism? Those were actually invaders. And the oracle and I stopped them."

Felicia shifted as if she wanted to ask a question. She had pulled her legs up and tucked her bare feet beneath her bottom and looked relaxed, if you didn't watch her eyes.

I finished by explaining as best I could about how the oracle and I were one entity now, but didn't mention that my children were oracles, too. I didn't feel a sense of menace from these people, but that didn't mean I would casually risk my children's safety. Then I said, "If you didn't know any of that—"

"We didn't," Cassie said.

"Then I really don't understand how you can work magic. Without an aegis, a person's magic is dormant, running through us like blood. It's just not possible to do magic any other way."

Cassie glanced at Emily as if inviting her to speak. Emily shifted her weight, making her earrings tremble. "You're right," she said. "Humans can't tap their own magic. So we don't try. Magic, for us, is a matter of encouraging the world to be different than it is. Making trees appear to be in several places at once, or bringing an object from here—"

She nodded at the bonsai in its pot. Instantly, it was at the other end of the table. I gasped, and Emily smiled. "To there," she concluded.

"Magi can't do that," I said. "They need warded stones—that's amazing."

"At any rate, we use the world's magic rather than our own," Emily said.

I stared at her. "But—how did you all learn to do magic that way? How would anyone ever figure out that was possible?"

Cassie leaned forward. "I guess it's my turn to tell a story. Though what you've said makes me wonder...never mind. A story. It begins a little over a thousand years ago, which means it predates the arrival of your parasite dimension. But maybe there's something in common— you'll have to tell me."

I refrained from saying something snappish about Cassie's method of telling a story. "Go on."

"A thousand years ago, there was a connection between two realms. Our world, and what people now call Faerie." Cassie paused, giving me a look that said she expected me to scoff or deny the possibility of such a place, but I'd seen the inside of the invaders' hell-dimension and the idea of Faerie didn't even trip my weird-o-meter. "Faerie's inhabitants were called by many names, depending on where in the world you encountered them, but for a number of reasons, most of them were called elves. And yeah, they looked like Tolkien elves, tall and—" She glanced at Gabriel, who sat impassively beside her. "Anyway. Whatever you're picturing, that's how they appeared to humans."

I nodded. "All right. You're thinking now that Faerie might have been another reality connected to ours, like the invaders'."

"Yes. But that's not important now. Most elves either kept to themselves, or mingled peacefully with humans. Some of them even interbred with us. But there was a faction within Faerie whose intentions weren't benign. They enjoyed playing tricks on humans, kidnapping them or putting them outside time, sometimes demanding tribute or even sacrifices. And because elves *are* capable of tapping their own magic, they had power over humans."

"You mean, before humans figured out how to do magic your way."

"Yes." Cassie leaned forward. "This particular antagonistic faction of elves was predominant in the British Isles and Ireland—I don't know, maybe you've heard some of the stories that come out of Britain and Ireland about the fey folk. Tam Lin, or True Thomas. No?"

I shook my head. "Sorry."

"It's not important. The point is, the legends humans have about elves, or fairies, mostly persist because of how that faction of elves behaved. Those elves manipulated and oppressed humans. And eventually, humans got fed up and fought back." She smiled, one side of her mouth curving up in a not entirely pleasant expression. "They learned from elves that magic was possible, and figured out how to make the world's magic work at their bidding. Tradition is—I mean, tradition as in the information passed down over a millennium—that tapping one's own magic is an elf thing, so what you say about aegises is mind-blowing."

She cleared her throat. "Anyway. Even though humans had gained the ability to fight back, not all humans, not even the majority of humans, could use magic, and most of humanity was still vulnerable to elves. So a small group, the first adepts, set to work on magic that would stop elves from entering our world at all. They created a magical barrier that blocks all the...we call them slips. They're like membranes that are thin at certain points to allow passage between the worlds. The barrier prevents anyone crossing a slip in either direction, and just to be extra cautious, it kills any elf that comes in contact with it."

"That's astonishing," I said. "So why are there still adepts today, if the barrier makes it unnecessary for humans to use magic? I assume that was the point of developing it, fighting the elves."

"There are many things magic is good for that aren't fighting elves," Gabriel said. "Your magi still exist even though the...Long War...is over, right?"

"Okay, fair point." I returned my attention to Cassie. "I have this feeling like that's not the end of the story, though. Who are the Savants, and where do they come in?"

Cassie's smile became real briefly. "This is where our stories are similar again," she said. "Magic is thin on the ground in Tempus—that's what we call this world, to distinguish it from Faerie—and there's never really enough to go around as far as some people are concerned. And so, about, oh, fifty years ago, there were a couple of adepts who proposed we break down the barrier so we could enter Faerie and harvest its magic. Their claim was that humanity, or at least the adepts, were powerful enough to defeat anything the elves could throw at us, and there was no danger in opening Tempus to Faerie once more."

"Harvest its magic. That sounds sinister."

"That's how Savants think, in terms of us against them. Most adepts didn't agree. Either they feared Faerie and wanted nothing to do with it, or they didn't believe we had a right to pillage someone else's world regardless of how its inhabitants had treated us. But enough wanted to attack Faerie to fracture the adepts and produce the Savants as a splinter group." Cassie's lips thinned in a scowl. "If a difference of opinion was all it was, there wouldn't be a problem. There's no governing council of adepts the way your magi seem to have, and adepts tend to work alone or in small groups, so a few of us believing differently can't hurt anything. But the Savants are well organized, and they have extensive resources because they used magic to become wealthy, and...well."

I nodded. "So, if the Savants want to bring down the barrier, what does that mean for the rest of us? Are they capable of doing what they intend?"

"Who knows?" Emily said. "Those few adepts interested in stopping them have to act as if the Savants can't control what happens if the barrier is gone, because the consequences of elves entering Tempus after a millennium of being trapped are too dire to ignore."

"There's more," Cassie said.

I glanced her way again. She looked grimmer than ever. "I can't imagine what could be worse," I said.

"Maybe not worse. Complicating, certainly." Cassie clasped her hands on her knee and studied her fingers. "Our group, the five of us, have been working on a way to make the barrier impregnable. Prevent the Savants from ever taking it down. You won't understand the details, but it's enough to say that the original adepts who built the barrier were more concerned about stopping elves than in preventing humans from accessing Faerie. We wanted to change that. But what actually happened was that three months ago, I passed through the barrier into Faerie."

She said it so simply I almost didn't understand. "Through—but I thought that was impossible."

"So did we," Cassie said. "But the important thing is what I found. Everything we know about Faerie says what a beautiful place it is, and yet when I entered, I found...corruption. Darkness. It felt like a long-abandoned house, decrepit and falling apart. I wish I could explain it better, but basically, there's almost nothing left of the Faerie of our stories."

Enlightenment struck. "The barrier," I said. "You said it was made to kill elves who touched it—it corrupted all of Faerie."

"You're quick," Cassie said, sounding grudgingly pleased. "Yes. We're sure now it was the barrier that did this. Which means those elves trapped inside have had a thousand years of contamination. And a thousand years to build resentment of humanity. What do you suppose will be their reaction if the barrier disappears and there's nothing stopping them returning to this world?"

"I know I'd be pissed off," I said. "But...am I wrong, or does you having passed through the barrier mean the Savants are more likely to figure it out? Or, at the very least, put you at risk if they learn you've succeeded?"

Gabriel shifted, and now he did take Cassie's hand. Cassie continued to watch me. "Both true," she said. "And the Savants know what I've done. They can't find this place, which is well protected—"

"Except Helena found it," Milo said.

"I doubt the Savants have my advantage," I told him.

"Which is...what?" Cassie asked.

I ignored that for the moment. "I encountered Savants in Portland, digging up a strange stone that was buried under the pavement. I'm sure they were Savants, because they reacted to me as if I were an adept. What do the stones have to do with your story?" I pulled out my phone and showed the picture of the stone to each of them in turn.

Felicia put her hand over mine and drew the phone closer to peer at the picture. "That looks like Andrea Teichert's work," she said. "You said they dug it up? How deep was it?"

"Um...maybe a foot deep? Does it matter?"

"Not to you." Felicia sat back. "Binding stones anchor the barrier, provide it with magical energy to maintain itself. We bury them deep so they can't be easily retrieved, but the magic they contain works against the world's magic, like magnets with opposite poles, and the pressure eventually raises them. That one would have been buried forty years ago. If it worked its way to the surface this quickly, the Savants must have figured out how to accelerate the decay."

She'd addressed Cassie with that last sentence, but it was Emily who replied. "That means we no longer know how many stones they have to loose to unravel the barrier."

"There's nothing we can do about that," Cassie said. "Not when we have a worse problem." She looked at me. "You're so insightful, tell me what the problem is."

That one was so easy I didn't even resent her slightly dismissive tone. "The barrier is damaging an entire world," I said. "Could even be on a path to destroying it. And you're not in the business of genocide."

Cassie nodded. "Which means we and the Savants have the same goal, if for different reasons: remove the barrier. The thing is, the Savants *don't* know what I discovered about Faerie's corruption, and they can't be allowed to learn the truth. I don't know if that corruption has weakened the elves, leaving them vulnerable to an assault, but we can be damn sure the Savants will assume that to be true. Knowing that will only make them more determined on their goal of subjugation."

"This is astonishing," I said. "So, the binding stones keep the barrier going—and if the Savants destroy all of them, they can bring the barrier down?"

"They might not need to destroy all of them, just a critical number," Felicia said. "But Cassie is right that we don't have any control over which stones, or how many, the Savants unearth. I've been making as many new ones as I can, as fast as I can, but that's still just a temporary measure."

"We have to figure out how to destroy the barrier without aiding the Savants or freeing vengeful elves to destroy humanity," Cassie said, again with that lopsided smile. "Easy enough, huh?"

"Maybe easier than you think," I said. "How can I help?"

"You?" Cassie seemed surprised, which surprised me.

"I've had any number of visions pointing me here," I reminded her, "and encountering those Savants can't have been coincidence. The oracle has always been concerned with helping humanity, and this is just the next step."

All of them looked skeptical, even Emily, who I'd judged to be marginally more sympathetic to my presence. "We already know what the Savants intend," Cassie said, "and, no offense, but visions can't tell us how to proceed."

"Maybe. But visions aren't my only resource. I—"

Jenny screamed. I swore and rushed across the room to hold her close, whispering calming words even as I was uncomfortably aware of five virtual strangers staring at me. I didn't care if they thought I was a terrible mother, or if they believed Jenny was one of those children who loved to shriek for no reason; all I could think was that she had had a terrifying vision when I wasn't in a position to openly help her, not if I didn't want to give her secret away.

"It's all right, you don't have to talk about it," I whispered. "The pictures can't hurt you."

"Scary people," Jenny whispered back. "All stretched out. Like drawings. And they're angry."

"Okay, they're not here, right? And nobody will let them hurt you. Mommy, and Daddy, and Lucia, and...who else, honey?"

Jenny sniffled. "Aunt Viv and Uncle Jeremiah and Aunt Judy and Uncle Mike."

"That's right. You tell us what you see, and we make sure it can't hurt you." I turned her to face me so I could pat her back. "It's all right."

She stiffened. "Mommy," she whispered, "that man. All stretched out. But he's not angry."

I awkwardly turned to look behind me. Both Cassie and Gabriel had risen from the sofa. Cassie looked uncomfortable, the way someone looks when they've witnessed some private thing made public. Gabriel's expression was remote, and his features looked even more angular than before. Some tiny observations clicked into place.

I returned to my seat, still holding Jenny. "Sorry about that. She sometimes gets scared," I said. "Now, what was it you were saying? That visions can't tell you what to do against the Savants?"

"I imagine, if they brought you here, they must be useful," Cassie said, sounding not a little condescending, "but they didn't tell you anything about us, or about the barrier, so I'm not sure how practical they are."

"More practical than you know—but then, it's not like you have any reason to believe me. They reveal much of what's hidden." I smiled. No need to tell them it wasn't my vision I referred to. "For example, you haven't been totally forthcoming, have you? Because Gabriel isn't human. He's an elf."

CHAPTER 7

Cassie's mouth fell open. Gabriel looked even more remote and alien than before. He slowly resumed his seat. "Remarkable," he said. "A vision told you that?" He tugged on Cassie's hand, bringing her to sit next to him again.

"The oracle knows all sorts of secrets, and that's the one I judge will convince you I can do what I say," I said. "If what you've told me is true, then the Wardens have a stake in what happens. We protected humanity from monsters for centuries, and it sounds like the invaders weren't the only monsters around. No offense, Gabriel."

Gabriel smiled. "None taken. And I'm impressed you haven't asked the million questions I'm sure you're curious about."

"Well, some of them are pretty personal." I rubbed Jenny's back in a gentle circling motion. "But...yes. I do wonder how you got here, if the barrier kills your kind."

Gabriel and Cassie exchanged glances, and now I was sure they were married, or at least long-time partners, because they were the sort of glances Malcolm and I used when we were silently arguing over who got to perform an unpleasant task. Finally, Gabriel said, "I left Faerie over a thousand years ago, before the barrier was erected. I was part of a clan war—it's a long story, but to protect myself, I took myself out of time.

Put myself in stasis, you might say. My clan's enemies played a trick on me, pushed me through a slip into Tempus. And I stayed in stasis until about thirty years ago, when some adepts discovered me and worked out how to free me."

"And didn't kill you," I blurted out.

"Not all adepts hate elves," Cassie said. "There were always some of the fey folk who were friendly to humanity. A small minority, but still a group that mattered. Gabriel was lucky he was freed by people who knew that."

I stared at Gabriel, suppressing the urge to pour out more questions. He smiled in a way that said he knew what I was thinking. "Elves do live much longer than humans, Helena. Me, I'm only fifty-four, but I can expect to live at least another eight centuries. That still means I'm the only living elf left in Tempus. Any other elf who was trapped on this side of the barrier is long dead."

"So, where do your loyalties lie?"

I regretted saying it the moment the words left my lips. Obviously the four human adepts trusted Gabriel, so he couldn't be aligned with any faction, human or elven, that wanted to hurt humanity, and it was an insulting question. But it was the one I felt needed most urgently to be answered.

Gabriel's smile fell away. "I want to see Faerie restored, of course," he said, "but I've lived in Tempus as long as I did in Faerie, and my priorities aren't what my kin would say they should be. Even if the barrier were gone, and if Faerie was no longer corrupted, I wouldn't want to go back."

"I'm sorry, that was rude."

"No. It's an obvious question. For all you know, I'm suffering from a major case of Stockholm Syndrome." Gabriel smiled again. "I had to choose—resent the life that was stolen from me, or make a new life here. And resentment doesn't do anything but eat you away from within."

"So, you have visions that can help," Cassie said, clearly determined to bring the conversational train into a station she controlled. "Where does that leave us? How sure are you that your Wardens will accept our guidance? Because we adepts are the ones with the knowledge. And the Savants are our problem."

"I hope you're not suggesting some kind of power struggle," I said, stung by her abruptness. "Obviously, you know more about the situation than we do. But the Wardens are more organized, and we might have better resources because of it. We need to work together, not fight over who's in charge."

"This can't become a matter of one person being in charge," Emily said in her calm way. "Adepts stay independent because when one of us takes control, the resulting cult of personality distracts from our ability to work magic. The world can sense disunity."

"But that's not how it works for us," I said. "I mean, I don't want to disregard your experience, that's not what I'm saying. It's that we Wardens can put focused effort into solving the barrier problem, and I think we should do that by working with you adepts—which means *somebody* among you needs to step up, or we'll waste all that energy following a hundred different directions."

"You know you just don't like being in charge, Cass," Felicia said. She was watching Jenny, and to my surprise, Jenny was watching her closely, regarding her with wide eyes.

"I don't," Cassie said. "For good reason."

"You shouldn't worry," Emily said. "You aren't likely to fall into the same trap twice."

I kept my mouth shut, though my curiosity had spiked again. But that cryptic little exchange really did seem like none of my business.

Cassie turned to me again. "All right," she said. "How should we do this? I'd rather we didn't bring a lot of strangers here. The protections on this place are robust, but it's impossible to disguise the movement of many people in the surrounding area."

I startled. "Oh! Well...I suppose we should start with you all meeting Lucia Pontarelli. She's sort of the chief Warden—we don't have chief Wardens, it's not totally accurate, but she handles matters that come up in the Pacific Northwest. She'll need to hear the whole story, and then she will probably have some ideas about what to do. How to find the Savants, for one—"

"Their headquarters is in Seattle," Gabriel said.

"Ah. That's...really close to here."

"Hence the need for protections," Cassie said. "Our being here is coincidence, though. We didn't set up here for the sake of watching the Savants, we came because it was the best location for studying the barrier."

I nodded. I still didn't know how they could be so blasé about being within fifty miles of a dangerous enemy, but it wasn't my problem. "Anyway, that meeting is the first step. Then everything else will have to proceed from it."

"You must be important to the Wardens, if you can act so decisively in their name," Emily said.

I briefly recalled the things I had done as Abernathy's custodian and as the oracle. "I've earned their trust. And Lucia is an old friend."

"I want to see Lucia," Jenny said.

I patted her head. "Soon enough, pumpkin." I moved her to sit on the couch and stood. "Boys, let's put the toys back now, it's time to leave."

"They don't have to," Milo said. "I can clean up."

"Their mess, their responsibility," I said, but politely so Milo wouldn't feel embarrassed. "Jenny, go help, please."

Jenny was still staring at Felicia, but at my words she slid off the couch and ran to where the boys were putting blocks away. Felicia turned to watch her. "She's cute," she said.

"She likes your hair," I said, feeling embarrassed. "I have a friend who wears hers in lots of braids like yours, and Jenny finds it fascinating. I hope you don't think it's rude."

"Nothing rude about admiring something you like," Felicia said. She picked at a stripe of paint on her finger, scraping at it until the green pigment flaked away.

"I still can't believe you brought your children," Cassie said. "Oracle or not, weren't you afraid we might be terrorists or something?"

A vision struck hard and fast, leaving me with only a deep-seated knowledge and the desire to act on it. "All my children are oracles as well," I said. "And the oracle protects them. I wasn't afraid because I'd seen enough to know we were all safe in coming here."

"Those little kids?" Milo said. He sounded astonished rather than disbelieving, which made me wonder what he had seen to be so casually accepting of strange things.

"It's genetic, it seems, or at least it is now," I said. "I wonder sometimes what might have happened if I'd had a child before becoming the oracle, if he or she would have been changed as well. But it's not an issue. Children, please say 'thank you' to our hosts."

"Thank you," chorused Alastair and Duncan. I bit back a smile at Cassie's astonishment. My children weren't ill-behaved hoodlums, thank you *very* much.

Cassie recovered quickly, to her credit. "I'll give you my number, and you can text me. Though I'll want to set the meeting time, since I can't set the place."

That didn't seem either irrational or arrogant. I entered her number into my phone and gave her my number as well. "Thank you. And— thank you for being open about all this. You might have chosen not to let a stranger in on your business."

"It doesn't take a vision to see potential," Cassie said, with an unexpectedly friendly smile. "We're not desperate, but I admit we're at an impasse. Someone else's perspective might be the difference we need. But tell your Lucia Pontarelli we won't give up what we've accomplished."

"I will." No sense explaining that Lucia wasn't likely to care about other people's feelings if they got in the way of what needed doing. Cassie would learn that for herself soon enough.

This time, we went out through the front door, passing a small sitting room entirely given over to a baby grand piano, sleek and black. I guided the kids down a short path made of head-size stones with grass growing between them, through the overgrown garden that didn't look like anyone had made an effort to tame it in a thousand years, and across the gravel to the land yacht. Once I got everyone strapped in, I hooked up my phone again and called Malcolm on the hands-free as I drove away. I didn't want to sit in what was effectively the adepts' front yard and have a long phone conversation where they could see me. Despite our mostly friendly interaction, they might assume something sinister.

Malcolm picked up after one ring. "Helena, why are you in Enumclaw? I thought you'd be most of the way home by now."

"Don't worry, everything's fine. A vision—kids, we're

approaching the illusion, close your eyes if you're scared!—sorry. A vision took me here, and...Malcolm, the most unbelievable thing has happened."

"What kind of vision? And what do you mean, illusion?"

I pulled back onto the mountain road and accelerated to cruising speed. "Let's just say we're going to want a very long evening out while I explain it," I said. "But the short version is—the Wardens aren't alone in the magical world anymore."

"Unbelievable," Malcolm said.

We were at our favorite steak house, nothing fancy, but they cooked steaks Malcolm and his refined palate approved of, they were close to our house, and the booths were big enough and well-spaced enough that we could talk about anything without being overheard. It was where we always went when we needed some time away from the kids for serious discussion.

I forked up a bite of poached salmon and chewed slowly. "You mean astonishing," I said when I was finished. "Because I know you believe me."

"Yes. That's a better word." Malcolm seemed suddenly conscious of the steak in front of him, emitting waves of delicious beefy aroma as it slowly cooled. He cut a piece off, but held it halfway to his mouth rather than eating it. "Doing magic by encouraging the world to change—do you realize how unprecedented that is?"

"Probably not as well as you do, since I wasn't born a Warden." I ate more fish and rinsed it down with water. I'd opted not to include alcohol with my meal, feeling overwhelmed enough by the day's revelations without adding a fuzzy head to the situation. "Any of what I learned is enough to blow my mind. Adepts, Faerie, Savants...can you believe we coexisted with them for over seven hundred years and never encountered them? Or they us?"

"I'm sure most Wardens will see it as a triumph of our ability to stay hidden," Malcolm said. "Which will unfortunately provide fuel for those on the side of *remaining* hidden from the world."

"I don't want to have that discussion now. Don't you think Faerie's plight is more important?"

Malcolm frowned, and I was sure he was going to repeat what he'd said a hundred times before—that the world would benefit from magic being practiced openly. It wasn't that I disagreed with him, because I didn't. Not exactly. But I'd said it to Judy, I'd said it to Lucia, and I'd said it to Malcolm himself: my children couldn't have a normal childhood if the world knew they had the oracular gift.

Instead, Malcolm said, "You haven't told Lucia yet?"

"I wanted to discuss it with you first. Besides, this is Lucia's fencing night, and you know what she's like when she doesn't get to blow off steam. I'll tell her in the morning."

Malcolm nodded. "I think you should suggest we use our house for this meeting, if Lucia agrees to it. The Gunther Node is intimidating, and those adepts are already giving up secure ground."

"*You* just want to be sure you're invited," I teased.

"You catch on quickly." Malcolm noticed his laden fork and ate the piece of meat impaled on it. "I can make a case for Campbell Security's involvement, if the solution to the Faerie question requires a more... active intervention."

"Intervention? Do you think things might turn violent?"

Malcolm shrugged and cut more steak. "The adepts said nothing about the kind of threat the Savants posed, but the ones you encountered had guns. I don't think it's much of a stretch to imagine their resources might include more weaponry."

I shuddered. "You're right. I hate to think about it, but it makes sense to assume the most dangerous possibility."

"Don't take this as criticism, love, but I can think of a dozen questions I wish you'd asked."

"I know. I'm amazed I learned as much as I did, given how surprised I was at all their revelations. But time enough for more questions when we meet with them." I drank more water and patted my lips with my napkin. "It seems pretty clear that Faerie is another parasite reality like the invaders', or maybe not the same. The invaders definitely wanted us all dead, and the adepts made it sound like most elves were fairly benign. And, of course, Gabriel Roarke wasn't antagonistic."

"My understanding of how all the realities work is that we brush up against others dozens of times over a millennium," Malcolm said. "Very few of them stay in contact with us for more than a year. It takes intent to make those connections longer lasting. I imagine if those adepts hadn't created the barrier, Faerie would have eventually drifted away."

"It sounds like they were desperate, though. And I bet they didn't know about other realities."

"No. And I wouldn't criticize the decisions of the dead." Malcolm laid down his fork and knife. "What does the oracle say?"

"I haven't had time to meditate on the subject." I chewed my lower lip in thought, fiddling with my unused second fork so it rocked back and forth. "And I'm not sure what questions to ask. I feel I already have a fair idea, given the number of spontaneous prophecies the oracle provided to lead me to Enumclaw. I think I should see what comes of this meeting, learn more information before seeking out another vision."

That reminded me of something I hadn't told him. "Malcolm, Jenny had another vision that frightened her. I think she saw elves. At least, she saw men she was scared of, and then she recognized Gabriel as one of them. I put the rest together."

Malcolm's lips thinned in a frustrated scowl. "This can't go on, Helena."

"Yes, but there's nothing we can *do*," I retorted.

"We can't let her suffer. I don't understand why the oracle is silent on this. It's protective of the rest of you, but not of the smallest and most vulnerable?"

I put my hand over Malcolm's, which was rigid with anger. "I don't understand it, either. I have to hope there's a reason, and that eventually we'll know what that reason is. And until then, we can only comfort Jenny and try to help her see the good in her visions—"

"There's nothing good about scaring a three-year-old child with things she can't do anything about!"

"I mean the good that comes of acting on them. Malcolm, I know it kills you to be unable to protect her. You put your life on the line to defend all of us. But Jenny needs you to be her father more than she needs Malcolm Campbell the steel magus. Please."

Malcolm closed his eyes briefly. Then he put his other hand over our joined ones. "I know," he said. "I wish this was something I could fight. But you're right, all we can do is ride out the storm."

"And make the best use of what she sees, so her pain isn't for nothing. If Jenny saw elves, that tells me the barrier *is* coming down. Maybe sometime soon."

"She might have seen the past. You've had plenty of visions about earlier times, even a few regarding earlier centuries." Malcolm threw his napkin down on his plate and waved down our waiter for the check.

"All right, that's true, but with two groups, three if the Wardens get involved, wanting to destroy the barrier, doesn't it make more sense for her prophecy to be about the future?"

"Did you have something in mind?" Malcolm watched me curiously.

"I...don't know. I suppose I was thinking, if Jenny's vision means elves entering our world, maybe our strategy ought to be about controlling how they enter, or what they're capable of when they get here. Minimizing damage, or something like that."

"I see. Prepare for the worst?"

I stood when Malcolm did. "It seems safer than assuming the best is inevitable."

"You know Lucia," Malcolm said. "Preparing for the worst is practically her motto."

CHAPTER 8

As if I'd used up all my good parent points yesterday, Tuesday morning was a nightmare. Jenny woke screaming at three a.m. and took an hour of cuddling to finally fall back asleep, and then Malcolm's alarm didn't go off, leaving us scrambling to manage breakfast so he wouldn't be late to the office. All the children picked up on our irritable mood, with even the usually-placid Alastair grousing at Duncan, making Duncan storm off in a huff, which set Jenny crying. In desperation, I finally sent the boys to their rooms with instructions to stay there for half an hour while I snatched a minute or two to brush my teeth and put my hair in a ponytail.

Feeling marginally more human and possessed of a little self-control, I carried Jenny to her bedroom and sat with her on her bed. "You don't need to cry," I said. "Alastair and Duncan aren't mad at you."

"I don't like it when they fight," Jenny sniffled.

"I know, but we're all going to calm down for a bit, and you and I are going to pick up your toys." Jenny had a tendency to pull out several toys at once but only play with one, as if she wanted the rest to see what they were missing out on. Unfortunately, she was terrible at putting any of them away unless someone watched her, like cleaning was a performance art. So I sat on the edge of her bed with my elbows on my knees and made encouraging noises as she packed her doll clothes into their trunk and carried each of her vast collection of miniature cars, one by one, to the plastic box where they lived.

My phone rang when Jenny was almost done. I glanced at the screen and winced. Lucia. I'd forgotten I'd meant to tell her this morning about meeting the adepts, but she couldn't be calling about that, and she never called just to have a pleasant conversation. I let it ring for a couple of seconds before picking up. "Hi, Lucia."

"Have you seen anything else regarding this bank robber? Would-be bank robber, I should say." Lucia also never bothered with small talk.

"Nothing spontaneous. Why?" I nodded encouragingly as Jenny showed me one of her little cars. I only recognized the most well-known vehicles, but Jenny knew the make and model of every one, thanks to her enthusiastic father.

"He's not being forthcoming about his motives, and I don't like it. It feels off. Like the proposed robbery was a front for something else."

"I can ask the oracle, if you want."

"Not yet. If you don't know anything already, that tells me whatever he's hiding isn't urgent." Lucia sighed. "Sorry to interrupt your morning."

"No, it's all right—actually, I was planning to call you. Here, talk to Jenny while I let the boys out of prison." I handed the phone to Jenny, saying, "Say hi to Lucia, okay?"

Thirty minutes' time out had been enough to cool the boys down, and I found Alastair reading and Duncan coloring pictures in his knights and dragons coloring book. I took a minute to hug each one, then, feeling balance had been restored, retrieved my phone gently from my daughter. "Sorry about that."

"Prison, Davies?" Lucia sounded amused. "And here I thought you had the perfect family."

"That's just what we put on our recruitment posters. Look, Lucia, something's happened, and it's big. Do you have some time?"

"I'll make time, Davies. You've never wasted it before." I heard faintly the metallic scritch of Lucia's desk sliding an inch, which told me she'd put her feet up on it and was ready for a story.

I settled on the floor in the hall outside the children's bedrooms where I could be available in case of a crisis. Jenny had wandered into Alastair's room and was pulling out books to look at, which ought to keep her occupied for a while, at least until Alastair realized what a mess she was making. "It's related to that stone I found, and the visions I've been having since then."

Lucia didn't interrupt while I talked, telling her the bare facts of my encounter with the adepts and what I'd learned from them. I was sure she would come up with any number of questions when I was done, so I didn't fret over maybe leaving out a detail or two. I finished with, "You're better equipped to know how we can help than I am. I was hoping we could set up a meeting at our house, get an idea for how to proceed."

Lucia said nothing for a moment, which told me she had a lot more questions than usual and was lining them up in the right order. Finally, she said, "How many adepts are we talking about? A few dozen, a few hundred, what?"

"I didn't think to ask. They made it sound like it was enough that they could have had a governing body if they wanted."

"That's the other thing that worries me. Meeting with these five could be pointless if they don't have the authority to impose a solution on the others." Lucia sighed. "I dislike working with amateurs."

"I understand, but it seemed like nobody is in a position to argue." I shifted my butt, which was getting sore from sitting in one position on the floor, soft carpet or not. "And even if they were, if Cassie Leighton is the authority on the barrier, and it sounds like she is, who'd want to argue?"

Lucia chuckled. "You're not that naïve, Davies."

"All right, true, people argue whether they have a right to or not. But you get what I mean. If it's a matter of authority, Cassie's group has claimed it. And I don't think we Wardens ought to get involved in adept politics by reaching out to the rest of them proactively."

"I agree with you, don't worry." Another chuckle. "Still, I don't think we can act unless I know more details about the threat these Savants pose. That will have to be central to whatever discussion we have."

"What about the barrier?"

"Davies, I've got so many questions about that I'm not sure where to begin. These adepts think about magic in a totally alien way, and it might be there's nothing we can do to help protect *or* destroy the barrier. But we'll talk about that too. And don't think I missed that you want to host this meeting. That was Campbell's idea, wasn't it?"

"It's still a good idea."

Lucia snorted. "I thought he'd take it easier once the Long War was over. No more nights in the field, for one."

"You know Malcolm isn't made for sitting on the sidelines, Lucia."

"I do. And neither are you, much as it occasionally disturbs me that both of you go looking for trouble. If you're going to throw yourself into danger, you really should learn how to fight. No, don't argue. Call this Cassie Leighton and see when she wants to meet. I'll be ready." She hung up with no more comment. I listened to dead air for a second or two until Alastair's shout alerted me to the pile of books Jenny had made on his floor.

"Alastair, hush. I'm sorry, it's my fault Jenny did that, and I'll clean it up," I told him, gathering a stack of illustrated nonfiction books.

"You have to put them away right so I can find them again," Alastair, budding librarian, said. Instead of putting books on shelves, I handed them over one at a time and watched in secret amusement as Alastair shelved them according to his personal system. I didn't think he owned enough books to require a system, but it made him happy, so I never commented.

Malcolm returned home at lunchtime, as I was pouring juice into cups. "Sorry I'm late," he said, loosening his tie. "You're not in a rush?"

Tuesdays were my day to go into the office to handle corporation business. "I have a meeting with a prospective grant recipient, but that's not until three."

"Anyone I've heard of?"

"I don't think so. Castellan Children's Network? They fund programs for disadvantaged youth in Washington State. Merle met one of their board members at a luncheon or something and was impressed with their outreach, so I'm meeting with the executive director today." I handed out juice cups, then took a bite of my own tuna fish sandwich.

"Sounds promising. I'll go get changed." Malcolm kissed my cheek, my mouth being full of tuna fish, and left the kitchen. I leaned against the center island and took another bite. The oracle made enough money that disposing of it was tricky. My corporation—that still felt weird even after nearly ten years—was as legitimate as possible so only a minimum of magical trickery was necessary to keep from coming to the attention of the IRS. And I enjoyed being able to donate to causes I cared about.

At one o'clock, I walked into the Campbell Security main building downtown and was waved past security. I'd mentioned to Malcolm how strange that felt, and wondered if they should be so casual about my comings and goings. "What if I became a double agent, or something, and wanted to sabotage the company?" I'd said, and Malcolm had replied, "If you were a double agent, we'd have a lot more problems than just the possibility of you blowing up the building." Which hadn't been completely satisfying an answer, but Malcolm was as suspicious and security-minded as they came, and if the possibility didn't worry him, I wouldn't let it worry me. And it was convenient not to have to stop at the front desk every time.

I had an office on the sixth floor, bigger than I needed—though that wasn't really true, because I met with potential funds recipients there and it needed to look official as well as comfortable. It had a smaller antechamber where my receptionist/secretary/research assistant, Merle Garvold, had his desk. He was on the phone when I entered, but acknowledged me with a wave. I waved back and continued on to my office, where I sat at my oversized executive desk and stared out the window. I loved my family, but it was really nice to have some alone time.

Eventually, Merle came in and leaned casually against the door frame. "That was Mr. Castellan," he said. "He's on the road on his way here. I told him where to go at reception for a visitor's badge."

"Thanks. I'm interested to speak with him. You said such glowing things about the foundation."

Merle shrugged. "I hope I didn't steer you wrong. Ms. Laurent's description of their program was intriguing, but I'm not a glass magus to know if she was overhyping it."

"I trust your instincts." Merle was, in fact, a skilled wood magus who spoke seven languages and had a degree in international relations and a master's in communications. He didn't need a glass aegis to ferret out someone's hidden motivations.

"I'm going to get coffee, you want some?" Merle asked.

"Please."

When he was gone, I pulled out the paperwork I had on Castellan Children's Network. They funded several programs for children of all ages and all socioeconomic statuses, including some educational set-ups and, of course, the program for helping disadvantaged youth. It looked good on paper, but, Merle's instincts aside, I wasn't going to make a final decision until I'd spoken with Castellan himself.

There wasn't a lot of business to take care of, and I tried not to feel guilty that I spent the hour before my meeting playing phone games. I'd had a rough morning, and I deserved a break. But I was happy to put my phone away when Merle buzzed my desk with the announcement that Michael Castellan was there.

I rose to greet my guest when he entered. Michael Castellan was an attractive man maybe a few years older than me, with sandy blond hair and heavy eyebrows of the same color and a square, masculine jaw. I assessed his suit in the seconds it took me to walk around my desk and offer him my hand: expensive, but not obscenely expensive, the suit of someone who wanted to make a good impression without bragging about his personal wealth. That was a mark in his favor.

"Helena Campbell," I said. "Welcome, Mr. Castellan. Won't you sit?"

Castellan nodded and sat in one of the armchairs near the window. I sat opposite him. "Would you like water, or coffee?" I continued.

"Water would be nice, thanks," Castellan said. His voice was a smooth baritone, a voice that could have belonged to a TV newscaster. I nodded to Merle, who stood in the doorway waiting on instructions, and Merle disappeared and returned moments later with a couple of bottles of water. Castellan accepted his, but didn't open it, instead setting it on the table adjacent to the chairs.

As soon as Merle closed the door, I said, "I hope you had a good trip. You're in Seattle, yes?"

"In Redmond," Castellan said. "It's a fine day for a drive, and of course your invitation made it even more worthwhile."

"Well, my associate Mr. Garvold said such interesting things about your foundation. Castellan Children's Network champions a lot of causes." I opened my water bottle and took a drink, hoping Castellan would take the gesture as invitation.

Sure enough, he opened his own bottle, but instead of drinking, he said, "As do you, Ms. Campbell. I looked into your operation—I hope you don't mind."

"Of course not." He wouldn't find any of my corporation's true secrets.

"You donate widely and generously, but never to the same organization within three years. There's no common theme to your donations— that is, you don't concentrate on schools, or on environmental issues— but you do seem interested in organizations with proven track records." Castellan sipped his water, then added, "And, of course, most of your causes are sited within the Pacific Northwest."

"I like supporting local groups," I said.

"I didn't mean that as a criticism. Far from it, particularly since my organization meets that criterion and we might benefit from your pref- erence." He smiled and sipped again. "What can I tell you about the foundation?"

I felt the world shift around me, and swiftly I raised my bottle to my lips as the vision gripped me, hoping I didn't look like someone having a petit mal seizure. Images flashed before my inner eye, visions of Castellan in several different settings, outdoors, a living room done all in white, a cavernous warehouse. And a creeping sense of wrongness filled me, growing stronger with every image, until finally I saw Castellan with his back to a bank of windows. The image flickered as if flipping between television channels, showing Castellan with his hands outstretched, then shouting and waving a fist, and then holding a gun and smiling a very nasty smile.

I blinked, then made myself cough, long and loud. "Sorry," I said when Castellan made noises of concern. "Just...went down the wrong pipe." I swallowed more water to give myself time to think. Those last flickering images—I'd seen that effect once before about four years ago, in trying to prophesy about someone who'd turned out to be a sociopath. Whoever Castellan was, he wasn't just a philanthropist, unless I was wrong and philanthropy was delivered with small arms these days. The other images niggled at me, giving me the sense that I'd seen them before, though I was certain that was untrue.

"Mr. Garvold was very interested in your program for disadvantaged youth," I finally said. "I understand you've had remarkable success. Aren't those programs usually plagued with a high overhead and recidivism, or whatever it's called when the youth you try to help fall back into bad habits?"

"That's true," Castellan said with a smile. "I believe our success is due to three things."

He began listing the things, but I stopped listening. I'd remembered why those images, or some of those images, were familiar. I hadn't seen them, but Alastair had. A room, all in white, with a lot of windows overlooking a vast body of water. And a man in that room, going on about a choice between humanity and its enemies. Castellan. Who was based in Seattle, or near enough to as made no difference. He had to be a Savant.

I nodded politely in what I hoped were the right places. This couldn't be a coincidence. Castellan wasn't here looking for money; he knew I'd interfered with the Savants unearthing that binding stone, and he wanted...what? Information, possibly? It chilled me to think I'd let a Savant inside my defenses, though I didn't know how I could have guessed what he was. Whatever else I did, I dared not let on that I knew the truth of his identity. As long as Castellan believed he had the upper hand, I had control.

"That's remarkable," I said when it sounded like he was winding down. "So, if I were to donate to your foundation, what would the money be used for? More staff?"

"We'd like to experiment with a different kind of community outreach," Castellan said. "But I don't feel we should take money from existing programs to pay for that experiment. Though maybe that doesn't appeal to you, with how you prefer programs with a proven track record."

"I do, but I think in this case, your track record extends to your new endeavors." Was he probing for more information? The whole conversation sounded so innocuous, I couldn't imagine what Castellan could gain from it.

"That's a nice compliment, thank you." Castellan smiled again. This time, it seemed sinister, though he didn't look any less friendly than before. "Our foundation is interested in promoting the interests of humankind, starting with its most vulnerable members."

That sounded sinister, too, but I was sure it was my secret knowledge about Faerie that made it so. "What an interesting way to put it," I said.

"I feel certain that's something you care about, Ms. Campbell." Castellan set his water bottle on the table again and leaned forward slightly. "Your pattern of generosity reveals how much you care about helping others. I hope we can be partners in that endeavor."

I swallowed. "You've impressed me, Mr. Castellan," I said. "I'll give serious consideration to donating to your cause."

"That's all I can hope for," Mr. Castellan said. "Your consideration, I mean."

Suddenly all I could think of was getting him out of my office. I wasn't so sure anymore that I was being as careful as I thought. Even my silences might tell him something. "You'll have my decision by the end of the week," I said, rising and extending my hand to shake his, though it took all my self-control not to flinch at his touch.

"That's very decisive of you," Castellan said, clasping my hand and releasing it. His grip was firm, his skin warm and smooth, and I couldn't help thinking that the people who said you could tell a man's character by his handshake were full of crap.

"It's easier when it's just me directing the corporate giving program," I said with a smile. "Thank you for your time, Mr. Castellan."

"No, thank *you*," Castellan said. For just a moment, our eyes met, and I felt another chill go through me, for his gaze had nothing human about it. Then he blinked, and the moment was gone.

I walked with him to the inner door and said goodbye, giving Merle the covert signal to meet me in my office the second Castellan left. I didn't wait for Merle; the instant the inner door closed behind my guest, I had my phone out and was calling security downstairs. "I need someone to tail Mr. Castellan—yes, the man who was just here—I don't know, they may have to go all the way to Redmond, so someone who's got a full tank of gas." To Merle, who entered at the tail end of that conversation and looked mystified, I said, "I need a full workup on Michael Castellan. And I mean *full*. I want to know the color of his bedsheets. But no giving our investigation away. It's important, Merle."

Merle, to his credit, didn't say anything, just left my office and shut the door behind him. I leaned my hands on my desk and breathed deeply, two, three, four. Then I picked up my phone again and called, not Malcolm, but Cassie Leighton. The call went to voicemail. "It's Helena," I said. "We need that meeting as soon as possible. I think the Savants are closer than we realized."

CHAPTER 9

I set water bottles on the coffee table in our great room and was struck by a sense of familiarity. The last time I'd hosted this kind of gathering, it had been a handful of genetic sports I'd invited to my home, hoping to encourage them to put their talents to use helping the Wardens. A few people, maybe no more than a million, scattered throughout the world had natural magical abilities like me due to a genetic difference, and almost none of them were Wardens—or hadn't been until I reached out to them to help me fight a battle only they could win.

It was a bittersweet memory; of the seven of us who'd gathered here that night, two were dead, and Ines Varnado and Mangesh Kapoor lived far enough away I hardly ever saw them. Victor still lived in Portland, and we saw Greg Acosta, who'd retired from police work last year, at least once a year, every summer at our Fourth of July barbecue. But nothing had played out the way I'd imagined that night over ten years ago.

Jun Li was still a poignant memory, even after all this time. I no longer felt inappropriate guilt over being alive thanks to her having given her life to save mine, but occasionally I considered how things might have turned out if she'd survived. Whether we might have become real friends. And that regret tinged all my memories of her.

I walked to the wall of windows looking out over our backyard. Evening sunlight cast long shadows from the boundary fence and the children's playset, and the air looked heavy with it, like the light weighed more the farther the sun sank. It was an interesting fancy I recognized as my brain trying to distract me from my worries about tonight. Not serious worries—at least I wasn't in the position of having to convince anyone that magic was real—but Cassie was a strong-willed personality, and I had a feeling she and Lucia were going to clash even though they were both on the same side and Lucia, at least, was inclined to listen. I hoped.

Malcolm joined me at the windows and put his arms around my waist. "It will be fine. And if it isn't, well, we've survived worse things than a disagreement with an opposing magical faction."

"Sweetheart, the last time we had a disagreement with an opposing magical faction, it was the Mercy, and you nearly died three times."

Malcolm chuckled. "Point taken. I doubt we're in danger of that again."

"I agree. Mostly I worry that there's nothing we can do for each other, adepts and Wardens, I mean." I bit my lip in thought. "And Cassie reacted very strangely when I told her about Michael Castellan. She said he was bad news, and that it was too long a conversation for a phone call, but I got the feeling her reaction was personal. Like they had a history."

"You don't think she'd conceal important information just because she has a past with Castellan, do you?"

"I don't know her well enough to say. I hope not." I turned around in Malcolm's arms and put my own arms around his neck. "She has to know something, though I think if she knows he's a sociopath, she would have mentioned it. Whoever he is, he's buried deep. Merle found practically nothing about him—all the public information fed back into itself, almost as if he doesn't exist. When he tried to dig deeper, he found traps. Like someone was watching for that kind of search. And tailing Mr. Castellan back to Redmond just led to the foundation's offices."

"I instructed Verity not to give away her presence by following him farther," Malcolm said. "As long as Castellan believes we don't know his connection to the Savants, we maintain the upper hand."

"I know. I was just hoping for a secret Savant hideout."

The doorbell rang. I kissed Malcolm and let him go. "This will all be fine," I said. "I'm going to stick to that."

Malcolm brushed a tendril of hair out of my eyes. "Ever the optimist," he said, and left the room.

I walked over to the fireplace, cold and dark at this time of year, and ran my fingers over the mantel. They came away pale with dust. Oh, well. It wasn't like any of my guests were likely to check my housekeeping skills. In the distance, I heard the murmur of voices, and then Lucia entered the great room, followed by Malcolm. "Interesting," she said. "I'm on time, so either your adept friends got lost, or they're positioning themselves to gain the upper hand by being the last to the party."

"I don't think they'd be that cunning," I said, but of course I had no idea how Cassie's mind worked. What I meant was that I *hoped* they wouldn't be that cunning.

Lucia sat in her favorite chair, and again I had a moment's dissociation, remembering Jun seated there, toying with a water bottle. I had no idea why those memories had chosen tonight to disturb me. I sat adjacent to Lucia and clasped my hands on my knees.

The doorbell rang again. Malcolm met my eyes briefly, then left again. Lucia had her gaze fixed on our family portrait, the one I disliked because it looked so posed. Next time we had pictures taken, I would insist on something less formal.

Again, voices sounded, but no one appeared at the end of the hall. My nerves began jangling. I couldn't imagine what Malcolm and the adepts had found to talk about that didn't involve joining the rest of us. But in the next moment, the voices grew louder, and then Malcolm entered, with Cassie, Gabriel, and Felicia following him.

I stood. "Thanks for coming. Please, sit anywhere."

There was a moment's jostling for position as the four of them found seats. Malcolm sat next to me. Cassie and Gabriel sat on the sofa opposite us, and Felicia took the chair facing Lucia. I had expected Cassie to sit there; she had to know who the other person in the room was, and I'd thought she would want to take a position that challenged Lucia. Instead, she'd ended up adjacent to her. I didn't know whether to take that as a good sign or not.

"This is Lucia Pontarelli, custodian of the Gunther Node," I said. "Lucia, this is Cassie Leighton, Gabriel Roarke, and Felicia Curtis." I indicated each in turn, then hesitated. "I admit this is as far ahead as I thought. I'm not sure where this discussion should go from here."

Lucia shifted her weight. "I have questions," she said. "Davies here has told me a lot, but there are still things we don't know about each other. And I'm sure you feel the same. If you'd rather go first—"

"I'd like to know who I'm dealing with," Cassie said. "You're the custodian of a magical nexus of some kind, and you police the Wardens in the Pacific Northwest. How do you fit into the larger organization, which I assume there is?"

Lucia smiled. "You know what Neutralities are? No? There are hundreds of thousands of magical nodes throughout the world, and the largest ones are called Neutralities. Before the defeat of the invaders, the Neutralities were divided into geographical districts around the world. It's been convenient to maintain those districts in the ten years since that defeat. The fiction is that all hundred and fifty-plus of us custodians are equal in status, but in reality, there's a pecking order. I am as close to the top of that order as it gets. The Board used to turn to me to supervise situations that arose between other Neutralities."

"Used to. As in, doesn't any longer?" Cassie's eyes narrowed.

"Those situations don't come up very often anymore. Say, rather, they turn to me less frequently." Lucia smiled again. "It helps that the oracles live within my jurisdiction."

"What's the Board?" Felicia asked.

Lucia turned her gaze on Felicia. "It used to be the governing body that set the rules, the Accords, that all the Neutralities, all the Wardens, had to obey. Now that the invaders are gone, and there are no more factions, they play a diminished role. They still have power and respect, but enforcement of the rules has devolved onto the local Neutralities."

"But you don't respect them," Gabriel said.

Lucia arched one eyebrow. "I didn't say that."

"You didn't have to. I'm good at reading human body language after nearly thirty years' observation. You're not fully committed to following the Board's directives."

Lucia's posture didn't change, but I could guess he'd startled her. "You're the elf," she said, and I was pretty sure she was trying to regain her poise by redirecting the conversation.

"I am," Gabriel said. If he was still reading her body language, he didn't comment on what he saw.

"And married to a human. Interesting." Lucia slowly uncapped her water bottle and took a long drink.

"Elves and humans interbred for over a century before the barrier went up," Cassie said. "There are thousands, maybe hundreds of thousands, of humans living today who have elven ancestors."

Lucia nodded. "Any other questions?" she asked. I didn't know what she'd intended in bringing up the elf subject and not following through.

"That's enough for now," Cassie said. "What do *you* want to know?"

"For starters, how many adepts are we talking about?" Lucia capped her water bottle and held its neck between two fingers so it dangled.

"We're not sure. It's not the sort of thing we keep track of," Cassie said. "Less than five hundred in North America, less than seven thousand in the world."

"Which means seven thousand potentially differing opinions on the subject of this barrier," Lucia said. "Davies says you don't have a governing council. What happens when an adept goes bad, starts using her magic for evil?"

"That doesn't happen often—" Cassie began.

"It happened at least once, to produce the Savants," Lucia said. "Do you police your people at all?"

Cassie stiffened. "That sounds like an accusation."

"Just a question, asked forcefully. It's important, Leighton. I need to know how adepts view their responsibility toward magic and each other." Lucia leaned forward slightly, though I didn't think her words needed any more emphasis.

Cassie let out a deep breath. "As I was saying, it doesn't happen often, and for us, magic polices itself. Using magic to harm others—

using force to impose our will at all—makes it increasingly difficult to convince the world to bend. So someone intent on using magic for evil, specifically against other humans, ends up unable to wield magic at all. But it doesn't take magic to do evil, as I'm sure you know."

Lucia inclined her head in acknowledgement.

"When that happens, adepts near the villain take action. Mostly that means bringing the villain to the attention of local law enforcement, if the evil is something punishable by law. Sometimes it means invoking magic of their own against the villain to stop him or her acting. Rarely, it means violence."

"Even if violence would save innocent lives?"

"You don't understand yet how our magic works," Gabriel said. "Taking a life imposes a spiritual burden on an adept. Taking too many lives means losing the ability to work magic at all. We are very cautious about the actions we take."

"But the Savants I met on the street had guns, and they were willing to kill me," I said.

Gabriel's mouth twisted in a bitter frown. Cassie closed her hand into a fist so tight I saw the tendons standing out. "Savants don't care anything about staying connected to the world," she said. "They kill when they want, and depend on their material resources, their money and political influence, to support their cause. Very few of the ones high up in Castellan's organization can still work magic."

"Michael Castellan," I said. "You wouldn't talk about him before."

"I take it you didn't learn the truth about his organization," Cassie said. "Or you wouldn't be so calm."

She didn't sound accusatory, like we'd failed in not figuring out the truth, so I didn't feel angry. "Everything we tried looped back on itself. Why does he care so much about keeping his company a secret?"

"Because he's the head of Astraeus Resources," Cassie said.

I drew in a startled breath. Lucia leaned forward. "You've got to be kidding," she said. I understood Lucia's shock. We'd all heard of Astraeus Resources—it wasn't as big as the heavy hitters like Amazon or Microsoft, but it was a powerful force in the fields of technology and pharmaceuticals. It suddenly occurred to me that I had never heard the name of its owner or even any of its high-ranking officials.

Cassie shook her head. "Astraeus Resources is itself a front," she said. "If you'd investigated Castellan from that direction, you would have found nothing unusual in its business practices or organization. But it is in reality the heart of the Savant empire, so to speak, and Castellan runs the show while keeping himself entirely out of the spotlight. His name is nowhere on the paperwork, presumably because he doesn't want anyone looking too closely at what he does."

"So he is the leader of the Savants," Lucia said.

"He is our enemy," Cassie said. "He keeps his own hands clean, but he pulls the strings of hundreds of Savants. To our knowledge, he's killed exactly once."

"Someone important," Malcolm said.

Cassie flicked a glance at him. "One of our colleagues," she said, but I heard the hesitation before "colleague" and felt sure what she was about to say wouldn't be the whole truth. "Kieran Nuallan. He was the one who came up with our barrier project. Castellan murdered him a few years back."

"I'm sorry," I said impulsively. "What a terrible loss for all of you."

Cassie looked briefly surprised. "Thanks. It was...it doesn't matter now. The point is, Castellan is dangerous."

"Maybe more dangerous than you realize," I said. "I can't prophesy about him. I can see his past, and places he goes, but as far as his intentions and actions go, it's impossible."

Gabriel leaned forward. "Why is that?"

I hesitated. Even my confidence that these adepts were allies and might become friends didn't stop me feeling reluctant to reveal the oracle's weakness. "There are a few people who can hold many possible futures in mind at once. The oracle isn't capable of determining which one will happen, so prophecies about such individuals either fail outright or flicker through a dozen visions. I've encountered two people with the ability before now. Both of them were sociopaths—maybe that was coincidence, and Mr. Castellan is just immune. But even if he had no wealth or power, that trait would still make him a danger."

"And he does have wealth and power," Cassie said. "If he knows who you are, Helena, it's just a matter of time before he sends his thugs after you. And your family."

A chill shot through me, and Malcolm put his arm around my shoulders and hugged me close. "We have resources," he said. "Castellan will find that a difficult prospect. And I personally have no problem killing to protect my family."

"I believe it," Cassie said, one corner of her mouth twitching in a smile. "But I hope you'll take my warning seriously. Castellan has resources, too."

"I don't take unnecessary risks, and I'm never overconfident." Malcolm smiled in return.

"And he wasn't totally careful," I added. "We know where he lives—he told me Redmond, but that's just the corporate headquarters. His house is on Puget Sound."

Gabriel and Cassie exchanged glances. "We know about the house," Cassie said. "We assumed he'd moved, after our last encounter with him, but I suppose it's like him to assume there's nothing we can do with that information."

I wanted to ask about the encounter, but Felicia was already speaking. "Even without considering Astraeus, the Savants have always had a strong position here in the Pacific Northwest. Lots of wild places for slips to occur means lots of places to investigate the barrier."

"Slips are the places where the worlds are closest, yes?" Lucia asked. "Do they only exist in the wilderness?"

"Yes, and no," Gabriel said. "Slips are organic in nature, and the ones that occur in cities harden and become unusable due to the rigid Euclidean geometry of most human construction—elven construction, too. But a lot of cities were built over slips because of how...if I say 'fertile,' you'll misunderstand, but the concept of fertility is important. Fertile in the sense of being hospitable to civilization."

"And we don't know why, if that's the case, building cities over slips eventually destroys them," Felicia said. "There's still a lot we don't know about magic, even after more than a thousand years."

Lucia shifted her weight again. "Which brings us to the barrier," she said. "Davies explained—"

"Sorry, why do you keep calling her that?" Cassie asked, as if the question was something that had been bugging her for a while.

"My maiden name is Davies, and Lucia has known me since before

Malcolm and I married," I said, feeling awkward about having to explain Lucia's idiosyncratic naming behavior.

Cassie's eyebrows rose, but she didn't say anything else.

"I know the barrier blocks movement between this world and Faerie," Lucia went on, "and that it kills any elf that touches it. But you passed through and returned. What does that mean for the barrier's stability? Is it weaker now?"

Cassie shook her head. "We don't know. It's not really a matter of strength, but cohesion, and I'm afraid since you don't work magic our way, you won't understand the details. And the truth is, even if the Savants figured out what I did, it won't help them in their goal. Only one person can go through at a time, my way, and the elves are alert to anything on the cuivuirskeen—that's the places the slips emerge to on the Faerie side of the barrier. So the Savants couldn't send an army through before they were spotted."

"But you're afraid they'll be able to use that knowledge to destroy the barrier," I said. "Even though you yourselves don't know how that's possible."

"Right," Cassie said. "We don't underestimate the Savants' resources and knowledge. Many of them were adepts once."

"And that brings us back to what *you* have in mind," Lucia said. "You want to bring down the barrier before the Savants do. How does that put you on the side of the angels? You'd still leave our world vulnerable to elves who've had a thousand years to develop an epic-sized hatred of humanity."

Cassie's jaw clenched. "We don't see an alternative. Either the Savants destroy the barrier and rape Faerie of its resources while incidentally starting a war with elves, or we bring down the barrier in a way that prevents that happening—"

"And still start a war with elves," Lucia said.

Cassie glared at her. "Or we make the barrier impregnable, and destroy an entire race through inaction. There are no good solutions here, Ms. Pontarelli."

Lucia tapped her fingers against the arm of her chair. "What will happen when elves enter our world? Regardless of how it happens? They're not going to be quiet about their presence, are they?"

"Hence what I said about starting a war," Cassie retorted.

"I mean," Lucia said in a slow, deliberate way, "their presence here is going to be open. Which means Wardens and presumably adepts are going to have to fight openly, as well. Magic can't be kept secret under those conditions."

"I don't understand your point."

"That wasn't directed at you." Lucia looked at Malcolm. "Stirlaugson's not going to like this. I don't suppose she knows about the adepts?"

"Not yet," Malcolm said. "I admit I was going to leave that to you, once you'd met with Cassie and the others and had a better sense of the situation."

Lucia scowled. "Thanks tons, Campbell." She turned her attention back to Cassie. "You might as well know there's a difference of opinion among Wardens. A lot of us have been talking about the possibility of making magical abilities public. Ever since the end of the Long War, magi haven't had as much to do, and they've been able to think about uses for their magic that could benefit everyone. But there are just as many Wardens who are afraid of going public. Fears of backlash, or of being rounded up and interned by the government. Laverne Stirlaugson, head of the Board, is also head of that faction. She's going to insist on any solution being a quiet one."

"Does she have the power to do that?" Cassie asked.

"Only so far as we Wardens let her." Lucia's scowl deepened. "You can leave her to me, but it's important you know we're not as unified as I made it sound."

Gabriel said, "Helena. Where do you stand?"

I jumped. He was regarding me with his steady gaze, his hatchet face more forbidding than ever, and I wondered what I'd done to draw his attention. "I just want my children to have a normal life," I said. "I don't want them followed and pestered by people wanting visions and prophecies. I can see benefits and drawbacks to each argument, so I'm not firmly on one side or the other, just—just on the side of my children."

Malcolm's arm closed around my shoulders again. "That is, fortunately, a problem for another time," he said. "The more pressing issue is whether the Wardens can do anything to assist your group."

"Do you want to?" Cassie snapped. "Given that our solution isn't great?"

Lucia was unmoved by her hostility. "What about replacing the barrier?" she asked. "Putting up a different one that doesn't contaminate or kill elves?"

"We tried that first," Gabriel said, "or at least tried altering the barrier first, to remove the contaminating factor. It resists any changes we try to impose on it, which is what's keeping the Savants out, so that's a mixed blessing. Then we tried putting up a second barrier beyond the first, as a buffer, but the knowledge of how the barrier was created has been lost, and while that might eventually be possible, it won't happen in time to stop the Savants destroying the first one."

"Again, it's a mixed blessing," Felicia said, "because if we knew how the original barrier was created, we'd know how to take it apart, and this conversation would be irrelevant."

Lucia nodded. "So it really is a matter of choosing between war and genocide."

"Are you always this succinct?" Cassie said, somewhat sarcastically.

Lucia ignored this too. "All right," she said. "I'm convinced. Now, what will it take to bring this barrier down?"

CHAPTER 10

Lucia called me on Friday, beginning the conversation with the abrupt, "I told Stirlaugson about the adepts. She's on the warpath."

I balanced a basket of dirty laundry on my hip and tucked my phone between my shoulder and chin. "Why is that? Let me guess. She thought you should have told her sooner what was going on."

"Got it in one, Davies." Lucia's voice sounded distant, as if she was on speaker. "She went into great detail about how this is something that affects all Wardens, not just ours, and how I shouldn't take on more than I'm responsible for. It all comes down to her feeling marginalized again."

"But she's not! You talked to her as soon as you understood the situation. There's no point running to her with every weird thing that happens." I tossed the children's underwear into the washing machine with more than usual force.

"Stirlaugson isn't as rational as she lets on, you know that. I'm calling to warn you that she's in town and likely to show up at your house, since I know she won't give you advance warning."

I sighed. "It's not like I don't appreciate her position. She still has responsibilities as head of the Board. And she doesn't try to control me even though I know she really, really wants to."

"You're more generous of spirit than I am." I heard a couple of sharp claps over the connection. "Sorry, I have to run. Good luck." The phone went dead.

I put my phone in my pocket and finished sorting the laundry. It was my favorite chore, something that calmed me. All that organizing and bringing order out of chaos, no doubt. Distantly, I heard voices raised, but the kids didn't sound like they were fighting, so I didn't hurry toward the noise.

Having looked in Duncan's room and assured myself that he and Alastair were playing some kind of racing game and that Jenny was peacefully lining up toy cars, I went downstairs for a little quiet time for myself. Any time the three of them were willing to play together was a miracle I wasn't going to question.

I was halfway down the stairs when the doorbell rang. I wasn't expecting anyone, so either it was another salesman ignoring the NO SOLICITING sign, or Lucia's warning had come none too soon. I checked my phone display anyway. Laverne Stirlaugson stood just where the video pickup would see her clearly, dressed the way I always saw her in a bland business suit. She was always very conscious of our security measures, at least. And in truth, I didn't hate her. She had always been my staunchest ally when it came to protecting the children. But I had the feeling she still saw me as property of the Board, and that made our encounters uncomfortable.

I opened the door and said, "Hi, Ms. Stirlaugson, it's been a while."

"I was in town and thought I'd drop by," Stirlaugson said. "Do you have a minute to talk?"

That was politer and more direct than I'd expected. "Sure. Come on in. The kids are all playing upstairs."

"Those peaceful moments are a blessing, aren't they?" Stirlaugson smiled. "When my children were young, it sometimes felt like being in a war zone."

"I know what you mean." I gestured for her to sit in our small front room and hoped she didn't know it was reserved for guests we didn't want to stay long. "Would you like coffee, or water?"

"I won't be here that long, thanks." She'd grown her hair out a few inches since I'd last seen her, and it now made a dark brown corona around her head, softening her features. "And I'm sure you know why I've come."

"Lucia said she'd spoken to you about the adepts." I decided not to expand on this statement. I'd learned to control my nervous tongue around Stirlaugson since the days when I'd felt I owed her something as the one responsible for my fate with regard to Abernathy's.

"She did. I wanted to get your side of the story."

"My side?" I stammered. "Um...it's not really different from Lucia's."

"I mean," Stirlaugson said, "you were the first to encounter these people, and it was the oracle that led you to them. Did the oracle also confirm their trustworthiness?"

"Their...I'm not sure I understand."

Stirlaugson leaned forward in her seat. "These people intend to draw the Wardens into a conflict that is none of our business. How sure are you that they aren't the enemy?"

"I didn't feel menace from them, if that's what you mean."

"And yet you have no independent confirmation of their story."

I blinked. "I don't know what that would look like. And I'm not sure why you're so quick to assume they lied to me. To us."

"This is an independent organization that supposedly works magic in a way impossible to us." Stirlaugson's voice was low and confident. "They are in conflict with others of their kind, or so they say. And both groups are apparently interested in unleashing a terrible destructive force on this world—a force that would bring the Wardens out of hiding. It's not impossible that the adepts you encountered took advantage of your meeting to enlist the Wardens in their cause."

I started to protest, but she wasn't wrong—the adepts did want our help, and they had suggested ways that could happen. "I don't think—"

"What's more, you only have their word for it that the Savants' motives are what the adepts say they are." Stirlaugson leaned forward a little further. "How much did you and Lucia promise?"

"We haven't promised anything," I said, uncomfortably aware that this wasn't totally true. "We talked about how we might support them.

And I've met the Savant leader, Michael Castellan. He's immune to the oracle's prophecies, he lied to me about his identity and the name of his corporation, and he's tried to follow me home—those aren't innocent actions."

"*You* deceive others about the nature of your corporation, Ms. Campbell. I know the kinds of protections you have on your family. Why is it not possible that the adepts are the villains, and the Savants are simply defending themselves?"

Again, I wanted to protest. But she had a point. Much as I trusted my instincts with regard to Cassie and her people, I had only spoken to them a few times, and I *didn't* know that they were telling the truth. Except—

"That's possible," I said. "But the oracle guided me to the adepts. *With* the children in tow. It wouldn't do that if the adepts were a danger to them. You know that."

Stirlaugson sat back. "That is a point in their favor, yes. Ms. Campbell, my responsibility is to magery as a whole. You and I both agree that revealing magic to the world could result in irreparable harm to the Wardens. We have no guarantee that the world would not react badly. This new organization is a threat to us even though they may not intend harm."

"So, what do you want me to do?"

I'd sounded more hostile than I meant, but my momentary consideration of the adepts as unfriendly had shaken me. But Stirlaugson didn't react. "Keep me informed of any developments. If that barrier comes down, the Wardens will need to be prepared to deal with the fallout." She stood. "I hope your family is well. How is Jenny?"

"She's fine," I said curtly. I knew Stirlaugson meant well, and that she was genuinely concerned about Jenny, but I still couldn't help feeling she saw us all as tools as well as people.

"I'm glad to hear it. Thank you for letting me stop by." Stirlaugson inclined her head, proud as a queen, and let herself out without waiting for me to open the door.

I leaned against the front door and cursed, quietly. Stirlaugson had sounded reasonable. She *always* sounded reasonable. And yet every time, her "reasonable" approach came back to the same thing: the oracle belonged to mankind, and it didn't matter that the oracle was a person now. People. She was polite about it, but it was clear she preferred the days when she could come to Abernathy's with an augury request and deal with me just as a necessary intermediary.

A scream from upstairs alerted me to the fact that peace was at an end. I bolted up the stairs to find Alastair and Duncan wrestling over one of the toy cars and Jenny sobbing with her arms over her head, blocking the noise of their shouts. I waded into the conflict, retrieved the object of contention, and in firm tones sent Alastair to one corner and Duncan to the opposite one. Then I sat and held Jenny until her weeping subsided.

To their credit, when the noise abated, Duncan and Alastair looked more ashamed than angry. They'd each independently decided, a year or so back, that their fights shouldn't involve their little sister, and I tried not to feel too guilty at how I played on that decision. "Jenny was having a good time until this fight started," I said. "And I'm sure you were, too. But sometimes we forget that fighting doesn't make anyone happy. Now, Jenny, what car were they fighting over?"

"Mazda MX-5 Miata roadster with a hardtop," Jenny replied promptly. She took it out of my hand and ran it over my leg with a "vroom, vroom" sound.

"I assume she's right," I said. Malcolm was delighted that she'd shown an early interest in cars. I guessed he wanted her to be Marisa Tomei's character in *My Cousin Vinny*. "Let's all go outside and run around for a bit, and then you can have video game time."

All three brightened, and I relaxed. More good mom points for me. I wasn't always that calm and reasonable.

I chased the kids around the backyard for a little while, laughing at their shrieks of pretend fear, then settled in a chair on the patio while they clambered over the playset. My mind returned to Stirlaugson's words. Now that she'd brought it up, I was disturbed at how readily I'd accepted the adepts' story. The oracle hadn't indicated they were dangerous, but it also hadn't weighed in on whether they were trustworthy. And the oracle, while protecting us from overt harm, didn't prevent every possible bad thing from happening. I felt I was supposed to use my own wisdom and understanding to assess not only the prophecies received, but the choices life presented me with.

At the same time, though, I couldn't help remember my encounter with Castellan. He had frightened me, not just because of the oracle's reaction, and that hadn't been my imagination and hadn't been a predisposition to fear Savants, because Cassie hadn't told me about Castellan murdering her friend until after I'd met him. No. I might not know everything about adepts and Savants and the barrier and elves, but I felt sure I'd taken the right side. And, having decided that, I was determined to do what I could to help, even indirectly.

SATURDAY WAS our monthly dinner with the Kellers. Everyone came, Malcolm and I, Viv and Jeremiah, Judy and Mike, and Harriet Keller cooked us a meal fit for the gods. She and Harry were in their eighties and showed no signs of slowing down, though Harry depended on his walker these days and Harriet was thinner than she'd been when I met her.

Tonight's dinner was barbecue, real traditional barbecue Harriet had set to cooking twenty-four hours before, with corn on the cob and mashed potatoes so rich with butter and salt they melted on contact with my tongue. I'd learned over the years, though, to always leave room for dessert, and Harriet's strawberry meringue roulade was like a bite of heaven.

By the time the last scrapings of roulade had been eaten, and we were all sitting around the Kellers' living room with our tiny cups of after-dinner coffee, I felt so relaxed I couldn't bring myself to worry about anything, certainly not the abstract threat of elves.

But Harry Keller clearly didn't feel the same. "I can't believe there used to be elves in the world," he said. "You don't suppose Tolkien had some kind of inside line?"

"Unlikely," Jeremiah said. "He was drawing from legend, sure, but the elves he wrote about just suited his narrative. Not a lot of use for tiny sprites in Middle-Earth when the Fellowship is fighting orcs."

"And there still is one elf in the world," Malcolm said.

"Yes," Harry said. "Who looks human enough that no one's ever questioned his identity."

"humans poisoned Faerie, inadvertently, but still," Judy said. Her voice was slower than usual, as if she was in the same food coma I hovered on the verge of. "Those elves have to be angry."

"I wonder if they look different now," Viv mused. "Like, are they all white with black veins like an undead monster from a Japanese horror film."

I shuddered. "I hope not. Cassie didn't say. I'm not sure if she saw elves when she went through the barrier."

Viv sat up. She seemed as sprightly as ever, though she'd had two helpings of roulade. "We could find out."

"You mean, scrying?" I said. "That can't be a good idea. And it might not be possible."

"I don't see why not. It would give us more information. And more information is always good."

"No one was ever able to see into the invaders' reality," Malcolm pointed out.

"Then we won't see anything," Viv replied. "But we *definitely* won't see anything if we don't try. What do you think, Harriet?"

Harriet had the distant expression she got when she was considering a problem. "Scrying is difficult enough when you have a focus. No focus, *and* we'd be trying to see into a different reality..."

"There's Noden's Scope," Harry said. He was reclining with his head flung back and his eyes closed the way *he* got when he was considering a problem.

"That's for medical examinations, dear."

"Yes, but fundamentally it works by building up a picture from a single germ cell. If we consider what those adepts said about the barrier as that cell, it might be enough for the Scope to latch onto." Harry raised his head and looked, not at Viv, but at me. "Would you be willing to participate?"

"Me?" I swallowed, suddenly very alert. "What kind of participation?"

"You're the one who's had the most contact with the adepts," Harry said, "and you've heard more of their story than anyone else here. Don't worry, the Scope isn't invasive. You'd just provide your knowledge as a point of origin."

That made no sense to me, but I was willing to trust Harry's word. He might not be capable of wielding magic anymore, but he still had all the knowledge of a glass magus of more than sixty years' standing. "I guess," I said. "What do I do?"

Harry pushed himself off his recliner and took hold of his aluminum walker. "Viv, you'll need to carry what I choose," he said, and Viv joined him at the drinks cabinet that held, not liquor, but glass objects in a wide array of colors, shapes, and sizes.

When they returned, Viv set down her burden on the glass prism the Kellers used as a coffee table when they weren't using it in glass magic. Among the objects were a familiar pyramid of deep blue glass as well as a lot of things I hadn't seen before: a pink and white spiral coil that looked like one of those old-fashioned lollipops the size of a baby's head, an ordinary glass measuring cup with Pyrex stamped on its base, and a beautiful glass pen with a gently twisted nib and a peacock pattern all along its sides.

Harriet picked up the Pyrex cup and disappeared into the kitchen. I heard water running, and the sound of a cabinet opening, and soon Harriet returned. The cup was now two-thirds full of water, and in her other hand she held a spiral-bound artist's sketchbook, a big one as long as her arm. She set both items at the end of the prism table.

Viv held the pink and white coil in one hand and ran two fingers over its end, which looked tucked in like it was keeping the coil from unraveling. Then, as I watched, it did unravel, peeling away from the rest of the coil like tape coming off a roll. Viv pinched the loose end, which squished and deformed as if it really was candy, until she pinched off a chunk about an inch and a half long. "Is that too much?" she asked Harry.

"Too much won't matter. It's too little that will fail. We try to get it as close to ideal as possible to avoid waste." Harry peered closely at the lump of pinkish glass. Viv's squishing of it had made the stripes blend together. "That should be fine."

Viv nodded and dropped the chunk into the cup, where it sank to the bottom. Tiny bubbles collected along its sides and fizzed upward, but slowly, like Alka-Seltzer dissolving in slow motion. I watched, fascinated, until Harriet said, "Viv?"

Viv nodded. She picked up the blue glass pyramid and held it flat on her extended palms. Her breathing became slow and regular, like she was concentrating. A blue glow began deep within the pyramid, a small round light that reminded me of the way an Abernathy's augury had looked. Gradually, it grew in size until the whole pyramid glowed a deep, rich blue. I had seen blue like that off the coast of Kauai, a color so perfect it seemed impossible for it to exist in nature.

Harriet gingerly took the pyramid from Viv's hands, moving like the thing was hot and she wanted as little contact with her skin as possible. Then she slowly turned the pyramid over and lowered it point first to rest against the prism table. Letting out a deep breath, she removed her hands. The pyramid didn't fall down, didn't so much as wobble.

Without speaking, Viv and Harriet extended the first two fingers of their left hands and each rested them on a corner of the pyramid's bottom, diagonally opposite one another. Nothing happened. I held my breath, waiting for a brighter glow or a flash or something. But the pyramid didn't so much as pulse with light.

Then I realized it was sinking into the prism.

I'd seen the table's glass flow like water before, but this time, it didn't react despite the pyramid's movement. Whatever was happening, it wasn't the pyramid displacing the prism's glass. It looked more like a computer animation, or a drawing, something that could defy the laws of physics or whatever governed the movement of liquids and solids.

The pyramid's appearance wasn't distorted by the prism, either; it was as clear and sharp-edged beneath the surface as it was above. The prism might as well have been air. Gradually, more of the pyramid sank under the pressure Viv and Harriet were applying, until Harry said, "Stop." The two women lifted their fingers. The pyramid's base was perfectly even with the top of the prism.

Harriet shook out her hand and then opened the sketchbook, tearing out a blank sheet of thick, rough-textured paper. She laid it over the pyramid's base, obscuring it completely. Viv picked up the Pyrex cup and swished its contents. The lump of glass was still visible at the bottom, and it didn't move with the water, but faint swirls like pink glittering sediment obscured its outline.

"All right, Helena, this is how the Scope works," Harriet said. "I'll want you to describe what the adepts told you about Faerie in as much detail as you can remember."

"They didn't tell me much."

"It doesn't take much to activate the Scope. I'll spare you the details —all that matters is that your memory and imagination provide a germ to build up from." Harriet handed me the glass pen, which was cool and smooth to the touch. "As you speak, dip the pen into the water and then rest it point first at the center of the pyramid, on the paper. It doesn't have to be the exact center, but the pen should be as vertical as you can manage. Then let go."

That seemed easy enough. I cast my mind back to listening to Cassie describing Faerie, the words she'd used, and said, "She said it felt like corruption. Like something decaying. A house unoccupied for centuries."

On the word "corruption," I dipped the pen's nib into the cup Viv held and then moved it to what I thought was the pyramid base's center. The liquid clung to the spiral nib without dripping. When I said "a house unoccupied," I lowered the pen until the nib barely touched the surface, and then I let go.

The pen hung there in midair, quivering with pent-up energy. Then it moved in a graceful swoop across the paper. And as it moved, a bright blue line sprang up, as if the blue of the pyramid was bleeding up through the paper wherever the water touched. It was like watching an ice skater leap and spin as she drew pictures with her blades. I was so fascinated by the pen's movement I didn't at first take note of the picture it drew.

Then Judy gasped, and I focused my gaze on the paper. The pen had drawn a forest, reaching all the way to the edges of the pyramid so the image looked like we were seeing it through a square window. The trees didn't look unusual at first, just ordinary evergreens, but then I became aware that the needles bore flowers like cherry blossoms. A path led between the trees, delicately sketched so the tiniest pebbles were visible.

I couldn't see the sky, but the way the branches hung gave the impression of a storm blowing them.

With a jerk, the scene deepened and sprang into motion. The ink lines vanished, becoming real trees and flowers and dirt, and the branches lashed the air in an unheard wind. Unheard, because despite the clarity of the picture, it was perfectly silent, like a movie on mute.

"Astonishing," Malcolm said.

"Yes, but it doesn't tell us anything," Viv said. "I was hoping to see people."

Far down the path, deeper into the picture, the movement of the branches changed. Now it looked like someone was pushing his way through them. I clutched Malcolm's hand in mingled excitement and fear.

Then the man emerged. He was a dark shape for a moment, and then, as he drew closer to us, his features became clear. He resembled Gabriel in how sharply etched the bones of his face were, but where Gabriel's face looked like it had been carved by someone in love with stark angles, this man was beautiful. His cheekbones were sculpted to match perfectly the line of his jaw, his dark eyebrows defined his brow ridge, and if he hadn't been too pale, he might have been a supermodel.

Too pale. I didn't know why I'd thought that. I looked more closely as he continued to approach. Yes, the paleness of his skin was unnatural to my eyes, tinged blue and gray. Maybe that was the weird light that didn't look like any storm light I'd ever seen before, but he looked alien, or possibly undead. He wasn't white and veiny like Viv had suggested, but he gave off an aura of wrongness that made me want to hide so he couldn't see me.

"That's not how I picture elves," Jeremiah said in a low voice, though it didn't look as if sound carried past the window.

"I think—" Viv began.

The elf nearly filled the window now. He stopped and tilted his head, his eyes shifting like he was looking around. Then his gaze focused on me. His lips moved soundlessly, and a look of rage came over his features. And the window swung wildly as he leaped toward it.

CHAPTER 11

I gasped and leaned back. Swifter than thought, Malcolm grabbed the paper and crushed it, destroying the image. I waited for an elven scream, but everyone was exclaiming, talking over each other, and eventually my heart slowed.

"I apologize for ruining the scrying," Malcolm said.

"No, don't," Harriet said. "That was unsettling. I've never seen Noden's Scope do that before."

"Probably because cancer cells don't attack," Harry said. He ran a gnarled hand through his thick white hair and said, "That was damned unsettling."

"Could he have reached us?" I asked.

"I don't see how," Harry replied. "The Scope is just a window on some other place. There's no actual connection."

"And you said that barrier kills elves," Mike said. "Even if the elf could get through, shouldn't the barrier protect this world?"

"Unless we just found a way around it," Judy said.

The room fell silent. Finally, Harriet said, "I don't know anything about the adepts' barrier to be able to judge, but I do know about scrying, and I really don't think we made a literal connection to Faerie. But we can't take the chance that I'm wrong."

"So how do we find out?" I asked.

"There are other kinds of scrying," Viv said. "Probably the quickest way would be to go to one of those slips the adepts mentioned and see what happens when someone scries through the barrier. If there *is* a physical connection, it would be obvious really fast."

"That could be dangerous," Malcolm said. "If that scrying bypasses the barrier, and there are elves on the other side, we might be giving them access to our world."

"So we take precautions," Mike said. "Make sure there are more of us than there are of them. And that we're armed."

"Guns might not work," Jeremiah said. "The legends talk about elves only being vulnerable to cold iron, which might just mean steel, but suppose it's a particular kind of metal?"

"Can we not talk about killing elves before we know if they're dangerous?" Viv said.

"That one looked like he wanted to rip our eyes out," Judy said. "I think we should be cautious."

"Look," I said, raising my voice above Viv's objection, "this is all irrelevant. We don't know how to find a slip or what the barrier looks like. I'll call Cassie in the morning and see what she says. Maybe they know about scrying, and they've done all this before."

"Very sensible," Harriet said. She rested her thumb against the center of the pyramid's base and pushed. The pyramid sank deeper by about half an inch, then popped up so its edge was above the level of the prism. Harriet picked it up by its edges and pulled it free with no effort, leaving a pyramidal hole that the glass rolled back into, not like a liquid, but like sand filling the bottom of an hourglass. In about ten seconds, the prism table looked just as it always did.

Viv gathered up the rest of the objects and put them away in the cabinet, except for the measuring cup, which she took into the kitchen. When she returned, the cup was empty, and she held the lump of glass, colorless now, between thumb and forefinger. "Can I keep this?"

"Sure," Harry said. He leaned back in his favorite recliner and regarded me closely. "You don't look so good, Helena."

I realized there was a sheen of cold sweat over my forehead. "He looked like he was coming after me."

"I felt like it was me he wanted," Jeremiah said. "Is that how it was for everyone?"

Everyone nodded or murmured an assent. "Weird," I said. "Maybe it's just that the scrying window was so small."

"Or maybe," Malcolm said, taking my hand, "an elf's perception is different from a human's."

"Either way, it's not something we can use at the moment," Mike said. He looked thoughtful, as if despite his words he was trying to work out what he could do with that information.

"Yes, and I'm unsettled enough I think I want to go home and reassure myself Sophia is all right," Judy said with a grimace. "Sorry, Harriet."

"That's all right, dear, I was trying to work out how to get you all out of here," Harriet said with a smile that made us laugh.

In the car on the way home, I said, "I'm not sure that accomplished anything but scaring all of us."

Malcolm shrugged. "If it turns out the Wardens have a way around the barrier, that's important. Being able to access Faerie without encountering the barrier could mean negotiations."

I sat up straighter. "I hadn't thought of that. I don't know if the elves are interested in negotiating. That one certainly seemed furious."

"We don't know unless we try. At the very least, it might prevent an elven incursion that would complicate the politics of the situation." Malcolm gripped my hand briefly. "Though it does raise the question of who would do the negotiating."

"Not Ms. Stirlaugson. I feel like that would be a disaster." I ran my fingers over the line where the window met the door. Malcolm's Camaro was more comfortable than I remembered the Mustang being. "Lucia, possibly."

"Not one of the adepts?"

"I don't know them well enough to say. I mean, they've known about elves and Faerie for centuries, but don't you think it's telling that they couldn't figure out a solution that didn't just push the problem off on future generations?" I sighed. "Maybe I shouldn't criticize."

"I don't think you're wrong. They don't seem to have a better plan, certainly, and there aren't enough of them to influence world government policies. Which this will almost certainly become an issue for."

I tensed. "You mean, making magic publicly known."

"I know how you feel about that, Helena. But this isn't something that can stay secret forever. Elves, I mean. That barrier will come down eventually, and we have to be prepared for it."

"I want the children protected."

"So do I. But that protection might look like public knowledge."

I turned my head away so I was looking out the window at the dark streets swooshing by. "I have trouble believing that's true."

Malcolm was silent for a moment. "I don't want to argue about this," he finally said.

"Then why don't you understand my position?" I sat up and faced him. "Malcolm, what happens when everyone knows they're oracles and some bastard decides he wants his own personal seer? How are we supposed to protect them from kidnappers or even governments without locking them away forever?"

"Helena—"

"I don't want to hear it." I turned away again. "I know you care about their safety. That's not the point. I don't believe the benefits outweigh the disadvantages here. And I wish you'd take my concerns seriously."

"I—" Malcolm was silent again. "You're right," he said. "I see so clearly how my perspective benefits them that I've disregarded your fears. I'm sorry."

It was so not what I'd expected to hear, not after all the times we'd had this argument, I was struck mute. "I don't know why you'd do that," I finally said.

"Because I'm confident in my ability to shield the children, and you, from anyone who might try to use your power for himself. But that's like asking you to depend on my strength by sacrificing yours." Malcolm took my hand again. "That would be terrifying."

I blinked away tears. "It's not that I don't trust you."

"I know. And I think we haven't approached this the way we should. Like a team." He squeezed my hand lightly. "I love you. I don't want you to be afraid. But that can't happen if all I ever do is tell you your fears are groundless."

"Malcolm," I said, and let out a deep breath. "Thank you."

"We'll figure this out, I promise," he said, making the turn into our driveway. "But not tonight. It's already been overwhelming."

I nodded. "All I want is to sleep beside you and forget about elves and barriers and oracles for a while."

Malcolm gave me a provocative smile. "Sleep beside me?"

"Well," I said, "we'll sleep eventually."

I STARED at the oracle's computer screen, dumbfounded. Monday mornings were my busiest time, since I usually took Sundays off, and the requests tended to pile up. But I hadn't expected this one. It was a single line, straightforward in its question:

Are the adepts a threat to magery?

I hadn't told anyone but the people closest to me about the adepts, so hearing them referred to by a total stranger stunned me. For a moment, I wondered who had spread the word, Lucia, or Stirlaugson, or someone else they'd told, or my friends? But I didn't dwell on that long. It wasn't like the adepts were a secret, and it didn't matter how the word had gotten out.

I read the line again and realized the oracle hadn't given me an answer, not the first time and not the second. Gone were the days when Abernathy's had communicated its refusal to answer through red light. Now, I just knew when a question didn't have an answer—or wasn't something the oracle wanted to reveal.

I considered the matter a few seconds longer, just in case, and finally typed, *The oracle has no answer.* I continued *The question isn't simple* and then deleted those words, one backspace at a time. That wasn't the oracle's wisdom, and I couldn't explain why I thought it was an unanswerable question without violating what I thought of as the terms of my responsibilities.

I sent the reply and then paused before moving on to the next request. I didn't believe the adepts I'd met were a threat to me, but that wasn't the same as all adepts and all of magery. Which was my guess as to why the oracle wouldn't answer that question; it required more subtlety than the oracle was generally willing to give to strangers, and even if there was an answer, the subtle ones were always horrifically expensive.

By the time I'd finished giving prophecies, my neck and shoulders ached and I was ready for something that wasn't staring at a screen. I stretched, shut down the computer, and spun idly in my chair, rotating half an arc before coming up against the edge of the desk and pushing off in the other direction. There had been forty-one requests. Seven of them had had something to do with the adepts. None of them had mentioned the barrier, instead focusing on questions like "who are the adepts?" or "what do the adepts want from magi?" but the oracle still hadn't answered any of them.

I picked up my phone where it lay next to the keyboard. No calls, no texts. I'd called Cassie the previous day and left a message, but she hadn't called back, and I was starting to get antsy. Maybe I hadn't left enough details to entice her to respond quickly; I'd explained that we'd gotten an unusual reaction from scrying into Faerie, but not how the elf had seemed to attack and not the possibility that we'd found a way around the barrier.

My finger hovered over her contact, but I didn't tap her number. I was reluctant to seem too eager, and I wasn't sure why. This could be something important. But I didn't like feeling so involved in the adepts' problems, possibly because of what Stirlaugson had said. It wasn't that I didn't trust them so much as that my loyalties were with the Wardens, and I wasn't sure yet where the line was.

I stuffed my phone into my pocket—I'd chosen these shorts for how deep the pockets were—and tidied my desk before leaving the room. If Cassie didn't call by noon, I'd call her again. Until then, I was going to enjoy spending time with my family and not dwell on the memory of that enraged, alien face.

The house was unnaturally quiet when I emerged. I found Malcolm and Jenny in her room, building something with her Duplos. "Where are the boys?"

"Play date with Jasper and Elliot down the street," Malcolm said. "Everything go all right?"

"I had some requests about the adepts. Is that weird? I hadn't thought the news had spread." I sat beside the blocky structure—a garage, I realized, because there were small metal cars parked in and around it. "It made me feel like someone had violated secrecy, though of course there's no reason to keep the existence of the adepts secret."

"No, but I understand what you mean. I doubt anyone has gone out of their way to reveal it, but the more people who know about the adepts, the more likely the information will get out." Malcolm sat back and fiddled with a couple of linked blocks. "Can you tell me what the oracle said?"

"I couldn't if there had been prophecies, but I don't think it's against the rules to say none of the requests were answered. I don't know why not."

"And yet the oracle revealed things about them to you."

That hadn't occurred to me. "You're right. And maybe that's part of my unease. The oracle didn't conceal the adepts from me, but it won't tell others about them? I don't know what that means, either."

"It may not—thank you, Jenny—mean anything," Malcolm said as he accepted a small truck from Jenny. "But if you want my opinion—"

"Always."

"That in itself might be worth turning to the oracle in search of an answer. Finding out why the oracle won't answer requests about the adepts from anyone but you."

I nodded. "I'll give it a few more days. It could just be that I don't know enough about the adepts to receive a prophecy for someone who knows even less. Or maybe the questions so far have been too complex for an answer." I stood. "Anybody want a snack?"

"Me, me!" Jenny exclaimed.

Malcolm got to his feet and swept Jenny up dramatically so she giggled. He put his free arm around my waist and kissed me. "I regret having to go in to work this afternoon," he murmured. "I can think of ways to spend quiet time."

"Malcolm Campbell! So frisky!" I kissed him back.

"What's frisky?" Jenny asked.

I laughed. "You'll understand someday."

After Jenny's snack, Malcolm and I tidied the kitchen, and then

Malcolm left to pick up the boys from their play date. Jasper and Elliot didn't live far away, but our boys were still young enough I didn't like the idea of them walking that distance alone. I'd never told Malcolm, but despite the precautions, magical and mundane, we had in place, there was a part of me that feared kidnapping. It was a totally irrational fear, which was why I never brought it up, but I wished I had more certainty that the oracle, if nothing else, would protect them from that kind of threat.

I was setting out the makings of ham and cheese sandwiches when my phone rang. I set down a jar of mayonnaise and checked the display. Cassie. "Hi," I said. "Thanks for returning my call."

"Sorry it took so long, but we've been busy," Cassie said. I waited for more details, but apparently that was all I was going to get. "Is it true you were able to scry into Faerie?"

"It seems so. Is that something you adepts have done?"

"No. Our scrying is limited to Tempus, because we do it by generating a connection between two earthly points. Make them believe they're one. It didn't occur to any of us that Wardens might have a different approach."

"Make two points believe they're one?" I asked.

"It's complicated—is that really something you care about?"

"It's not that," I said. "We have something similar called an ansible. I'm sure it works on different principles, but...anyway, you're right, that's not the point now." I made a mental note to mention this conversation to Rick Jeong at the Gunther Node, who had become the premier authority on ansibles after the death of Darius Wallach. This was the first time anything had suggested that adept and Warden magic might have enough in common to learn from.

"The thing is," I said, "we saw an elf, and apparently the elf saw us. The scrying we used isn't supposed to work both ways, though I guess it might be that it's never been used in a situation where the thing being looked at is able to look back. We're concerned that our method of scrying might bypass the barrier's protection."

Cassie was silent for a moment. "I'd like to say that's impossible," she said, "but since I know practically nothing of your magic, I won't make assumptions. We should investigate further. Could you repeat the scrying at a slip?"

"Not me personally, but yes, that was actually the idea we had."

I heard the back door open, and the sound of young voices raised in the kind of conversation children think demands shouting. "Just a minute," I told Cassie, then "Kids, mommy is on the phone, can we turn the volume down, please?"

Alastair and Duncan raced past, no longer shouting. "Sorry," I said. "Sometimes they fill the house with their noise."

"I'm impressed at how calm you always are with your children," Cassie said, sounding amused. "You're not just demonstrating self-control in front of strangers?"

"There's some of that, yes. Parents want to look good as much as anyone." I let Malcolm take the butter knife I'd been holding but not using out of my hand. "I'm not sure how calm I am at other times. But the kids are well-behaved, for the most part, and that makes it easier."

"I see. It's something I think about, having children, but with the Savant threat becoming more present, Gabriel and I aren't sure it's a good time." Cassie cleared her throat like she hadn't meant to say anything so personal, so I didn't follow up on that conversational thread. "Anyway. We can arrange to show you a slip whenever it's convenient. There's one just over the state border in Washington, northeast of Camas. It's the one closest to both of us."

"I'll need to talk to Viv—she's the glass magus who'll do the scrying —and Lucia might want to be there. It could be a day or two."

"Why does it not surprise me that Lucia Pontarelli wants in on this?" Cassie's amusement was sharper now. "I know, she's your boss—"

"She's not really my boss. She's just good at organizing things." In a sense, the oracle was Lucia's boss, but I didn't feel like explaining that.

"I believe it. Just so she doesn't feel the urge to organize *us*." Cassie chuckled. "We'll make the preparations on our end. Let me know when you're ready, and I'll send directions."

"Thanks."

I hung up to discover Malcolm had nearly finished making sandwiches. I hurried to cut bananas in half for small hands to manage.

"That was Cassie," I said. "They can take us to a slip to experiment with scrying."

"I intend to be there," Malcolm said.

"It's not going to be dangerous." I wasn't nearly so certain of that as I sounded, but I didn't want Malcolm feeling like he had to be my body-guard. "And I'm not sure I should go. It's not like I can assist with the scrying."

"No, but the oracle functions better with more information, and this qualifies as a great deal more information." Malcolm took a bite of his sandwich, which he'd loaded with pickle slices and spicy brown mustard. "And I am curious enough I don't want to be left out. *And* there's no reason not to prepare for the worst, so unless you're willing to go armed…"

I shook my head. "I've come to terms with the fact that I'm not a fighter, not in the sense of being able to punch or shoot someone."

"You fight in other ways, love." Malcolm hugged me. I wrinkled my nose ostentatiously at the smell of dill pickle coming off his breath, and he laughed.

CHAPTER 12

The following Thursday, Malcolm steered the land yacht along the road paralleling the Washougal River. I'd let him drive in case the oracle felt like chiming in with a spontaneous prophecy, but now I felt glad I'd made that decision for other reasons, because the drive was beautiful. The river ran low and fast, surrounded by trees, making me wish wading was an option. The car's robust air conditioning kept us comfortable, but the sun heated the window glass, reminding me that it was another unnaturally hot summer day.

On the other side, a cliff wall covered in chicken wire loomed up, with long-limbed shrubs clinging to its base. I didn't know what the chicken wire was for, though I'd seen similar setups on the coast and guessed someone was concerned about erosion. It gave the cliffs a comical look, like cafeteria workers the size of office buildings in hair nets big enough to drag the ocean floor for fish.

"Almost there," Malcolm said, glancing at the onboard map. I sat up and looked ahead to where a side road branched off the two-lane road I couldn't bring myself to call a highway. This was as far as the map could take us. Cassie had said she would meet us at the end of this road and lead us the rest of the way.

In the back seat, Viv stretched and yawned. I heard her big Tinker Bell bag make a dull clink as her movement shifted it and its glass contents. Jeremiah, beside her, said, "This is pretty far out of the way, but there are still houses. I wouldn't call it wilderness."

"I guess Cassie's definition of wilderness isn't the same," I said. Two cars passed us going the other way. "She said slips couldn't exist in a city, so maybe that's the key."

Malcolm made the turn onto the side road. Immediately, the land yacht's smooth ride roughened, bouncing us along the irregular surface of the unpaved road. I put a hand on the door to steady myself. On we drove, gradually rising until the cliffside had vanished and we were surrounded by trees that grew within a foot of where we passed. Their emerald leaves brushed the windows with the faintest scratching sound I could only hear because my head was so close to the door.

The road took a few winding turns, growing ever narrower, until I started to worry that we'd have to reverse all the way back to the main road. Then, as abruptly as a cork popping out of a bottle, we shot through the narrowest gap yet and into a clearing big enough for ten land yachts. It was unexpected enough I gasped.

The only other vehicle in the clearing was the big blue pickup I'd seen in the adepts' garage. Gabriel was sitting in the driver's seat with the window rolled down. Beyond him, I could barely see Cassie, and Milo sat behind Gabriel. They watched us come to a stop a short distance away, then got out. Instead of approaching us, they walked around to the rear of the truck and opened the topper and the tailgate, and Milo climbed inside.

I looked at Malcolm. "I guess we...go talk to them?"

Malcolm turned off the engine. "It's why we're here. But I feel reluctant, too. As if we're intruding on something personal."

"No sense waiting around," Jeremiah said. He opened his door. A second later, Viv followed him, lugging her clinking bag. I shrugged and got out.

By the time we all gathered at the pickup truck, Milo was handing out long poles—no, they were tree trunks, about four inches in diameter and still with their bark on. They were each at least seven feet long, but

Gabriel handled them easily despite how they swung and bobbed. Cassie held a coil of hairy rope made from some natural fiber. "Glad you found the place," she said.

"This is Viv and Jeremiah," I said. "Viv will do the scrying. Jeremiah is a wood magus, in case..." I felt stupid explaining my fears that we might need more backup than Malcolm provided. "I hope we didn't keep you waiting long."

Cassie shook her head. "It's no big deal. Follow me." She set off into the trees beyond the truck. Milo slammed the tailgate and topper shut and took up the other end of the tree trunks, stabilizing them. He and Gabriel didn't move, so I hurried to follow Cassie.

The spaces between the trees were narrow enough we had to go single file. Cassie kept a brisk pace, but not so fast I couldn't keep up with her. We all made enough noise I didn't think we'd see any wild animals, but I didn't have attention to spare to look for them, either. Well, Jeremiah the wood magus probably sounded like a squirrel himself, and Malcolm didn't know how *not* to be stealthy.

I heard water ahead, and started looking for the river before remembering it was on the far side of the road and we were unlikely to see it. Instead, after a minute or so, the trees opened up, and Cassie and I stood on the banks of a stream much smaller than the Washougal that cut deeply into the ground. The bank on the far side was about a foot lower than where we stood. Despite its small size, the stream smelled deliciously cool and wet.

"It's just the other side of the stream," Cassie said, pointing.

I looked, though I had no idea what I was looking for. The trees seemed to grow as thickly in that direction as everywhere else. Then I realized the space beneath the trees about twenty feet away was more brightly lit than where I stood, as if the forest was thinner there and more sunlight could reach the ground.

Cassie leaped across the stream—it was more of a hop than a leap— and waited for me to follow. The stream really wasn't that wide, but the ground on either side was slightly slippery, and I took care not to land heavily. Malcolm followed, putting a hand on my elbow. "Should we approach in any particular way?" he asked.

"The slips aren't special, or sacred, or anything," Cassie said, "just close to Faerie. You'll notice a difference, but it's not a big one. There's nothing you can do to accidentally damage the slip." She moved on through the forest. I glanced at Malcolm, then once more followed her.

It wasn't long before we reached the area where the trees were thinner. It couldn't really be called a clearing, just a place where there was space enough between the trees to pitch a few tents. I walked from one side to the other, looking for the difference Cassie had mentioned. At first, I didn't see anything strange. Then I tripped over a root, not falling, just putting a little hop in my step, and in searching the ground for what had tripped me, I noticed the grass.

I'd seen the ground as we walked, and it was typical forest floor: scruffy growth here and there, mostly around the bases of the trees, a lot of fallen twigs, some pebbles, but primarily raw earth. If there was ever grass, it grew at the beginning of spring, not midsummer. Yet this ground was covered in fine, perfect grass the color of fresh new peas, and here and there white flowers the size of my thumbnail bloomed, each with five petals and the tiniest dot of yellow where they joined. It looked like something my kids would draw, too perfect to be natural.

I dropped to one knee and brushed my fingers through the soft grass. It tickled like Duncan's beloved sea anemone. "Is this what you meant?" I asked Cassie.

"Ever heard of fairy circles?" Cassie said. "Slips don't all grow in perfect circles, but they're close enough. This one's shape is less noticeable because of the trees."

Gabriel and Milo had joined us, awkwardly maneuvering their poles through the trees and setting them down atop the strange grass. Gabriel removed a hatchet from a loop on his belt. With a couple of expert blows, he chopped one of the three poles into unequal thirds. Milo picked up the pieces on each end, leaving Gabriel with the middle section. I watched Milo carry the lengths of wood off to one side, then returned my attention to Gabriel just as Cassie handed him her coil of rough, hairy rope.

I opened my mouth to ask a question, realized any question I might come up with was inane, and closed my mouth again. Gabriel was lashing the short piece of wood to the long poles to make a rough doorway, swiftly and expertly as if he did this all the time. I did come up with a question then. "Isn't that dangerous? I mean, if that's going to be a doorway to the barrier, doesn't Gabriel risk touching it?"

"It helps if you imagine this as an actual door, with something filling the space within the frame," Gabriel said, not looking up. "I'll set this upright, and then Cassie and Milo will open it—you'll see." He tied off the second rope and took hold of the crosspiece that formed the lintel, lifting it until the door frame was vertical, the lintel a few inches over his head. Then he switched his grip so he had one hand on each of the tied corners. With a little effort, he pulled, and the doorposts sank into the earth.

I took a step forward in astonishment. Despite the grass, the earth was hard and compacted, and yet Gabriel had driven the posts in as if we stood on soft loam. Gabriel let go of the frame and stepped back. It didn't so much as quiver.

Gabriel rubbed his hands on his jeans and stepped back farther. "The rest of you should give Cassie and Milo room."

I retreated quickly to stand near Gabriel. Malcolm and Jeremiah moved more slowly. Viv stood still for a moment until Cassie approached the doorway, then backed up, her attention still fixed on the wooden frame that led from nowhere to nowhere. Her bag, slung over her shoulder, clinked once and then was still, like it knew this moment was serious.

Cassie and Milo stood side by side, Cassie on the right, Milo on the left. "Put your left hand on the post at head height," Cassie told Milo, and mimicked his gesture with her right hand on her post. Cassie then clasped Milo's free hand and brought it up to rest on her left shoulder. He was a few inches taller than she was, so when she put her left hand on his right shoulder, their arms made a downward-sloping line.

"We do this differently than most adepts," Cassie said without turning her head, "because we have an elf to choose wood that's reso-nant with the slips. But the end result is the same. Milo, go ahead and center yourself."

She fell silent, and for a moment, the slip was unexpectedly loud with woodland noises: birds singing to one another, the wind gusting through the tops of the trees, and the little stream flowing with a cheery gurgle nearby. The air beneath the trees wasn't as warm as it had been on the open road, but it still felt like velvet caressing my face, velvet that smelled of soil and green leaves and fresh water.

"Now," Cassie said. As one, she and Milo stepped away from each other, hands slipping from shoulders to run down arms until their hands were clasped. The effect was like two people holding a giant, invisible balloon as it inflated, separating them. Their clasped hands loosened, sliding farther until their fingertips were barely hooked together. Milo and Cassie stood poised like that for what felt like forever. I found I was holding my breath. It felt as if we were all waiting for something momentous to happen.

Then, in an abrupt movement totally at odds with the smooth sliding and separating, Cassie and Milo flung their hands apart, stretching their arms wide while still holding the doorposts with their other hands. Now it looked like two halves of a door opening wide, like an old-time saloon door when the new sheriff comes to town.

And light flared within the doorway, bright yellow-tinged light that made me flinch and throw up a hand to shield my eyes. I blinked away pained tears and tried to focus. Slowly, my vision swam back into clarity. A shimmering golden glow that sparkled with tiny flecks of light filled the doorway, undulating gently like a wave pool, if wave pools were vertical. It wasn't totally opaque; I could see trees through it. But it was so bright it was easy for me to focus only on it.

"Wow," Viv said, stepping forward. "It's so...*gaudy*."

"Viv," I said.

"Seriously, Helena, it's—I mean, *look* at it. It looks like a Mardi Gras float was in a glitter explosion." Viv set her bag down a few feet from the doorway. "That is the barrier, right?"

"It is," Cassie said. "And gaudy is a good word for it. There's no way that could be mistaken for anything natural."

"We don't know if it always looked that way," Milo said. He let go of the doorpost and wiped his hand on his jeans as Gabriel had. "People didn't write down descriptions of it until the fifteenth century, and about all we know is it used to be more orange. Maybe."

"Even I think it's awful, and you know how much I love glitter." Viv knelt and began rooting in her bag, sending up more muted clanks.

I walked toward the barrier, my eyes focused on the waves of glittering gold. My first impression had been wrong; they came at irregular intervals, not with the smoothness of ocean waves, but like an interference pattern, undulating in all directions. At times, the surface was almost flat, and then ripples crisscrossed it so it looked like corrugated cardboard spray painted gold. My mind told me there was a pattern there, if I could just find it—

A hand gripped my upper arm. "Don't stare at it too long," Cassie said. "You'll end up mesmerized."

"You mean, hypnotism?" I blinked and turned my head away.

"Not in the psychiatric sense. More like...you lose interest in doing anything else. Moving, eating, that sort of thing." Cassie glanced once at it and then looked away as if emphasizing her point. "It's why we don't open doors to Faerie alone. There are stories of people dying because the barrier entranced them and there wasn't anyone around to break the trance."

"That's disturbing." I fixed my gaze on the lintel, where the effect of the waves was unnoticeable. Where the barrier met the lintel, it looked like a sheet of gold lamé fabric tacked to the wood. Viv was right; the whole thing was as gaudy as a high school theater set. I didn't feel any particular emotion while looking at the barrier, though the slip itself had a peaceful aura to it. I'd half expected to sense menace from the thing that was poisoning Faerie.

"Is it okay if I touch it?" Viv asked.

"You won't feel anything," Cassie said. "The visual effect is a warning, we think. So elves don't stumble into it by accident."

"You think?" Jeremiah said.

Cassie shrugged. "Not all adepts were in agreement about creating the barrier. Some of them wanted to cross into Faerie and start killing elves. The adepts who created the barrier did it in secret, and most of what we know about the barrier from that time comes from other adepts who spoke to the creators. And those creators never revealed what they did to create it, or even whether what they ended up with was what they intended."

"If it can't be touched, how does it prevent people crossing?"

Malcolm walked over to stand beside me and put an arm around my waist.

"Without the barrier, crossing is just a matter of walking through the door," Gabriel said. "How it works is complicated even for us, and I can't explain it. But you can think of the barrier as a deflector, maybe. The door is a portal between worlds, and the barrier shunts anyone who tries to enter the portal to elsewhere in the same world. But not very far away—Milo, why don't you show them? I think I'm just confusing the issue."

Milo nodded. He adjusted his Baltimore Orioles baseball cap to a different angle and strode directly at the door and its eerie glittering contents. Without stopping, he walked through the door. Nothing seemed to happen except that now he was on the far side of the barrier, his body obscured by it. He turned around and walked back through. This time, I saw it—the tiniest twitch of his whole body, as if he'd jumped through the doorway.

"Weird," Viv said. "So it basically teleports you from one side to the other, but it's a microscopic movement you probably don't notice."

"Exactly," Gabriel said. "But an elf who comes in contact with the barrier—again, we don't know precisely what happens, and I'm not interested in testing it myself—they stick to the barrier, and it supposedly unravels their magic. And then it unravels their body."

"Ew," I said. "So does that mean those adepts back then didn't hate elves? Because they could have made the barrier invisible instead of being a warning."

"Some of us think so, yes," Cassie said. "But, again, it could just be this was a side effect, and they did intend it to kill elves without warning. We don't know."

Viv had risen from where she knelt near the door and was now standing right next to the golden barrier, both her palms raised to lie flat against it, or at least that was how it looked. "It's also like a seal," she said, her voice distant. "It's holding the portal shut, but it's quivering. Like the seal is under pressure. Is that normal?"

Cassie and Milo exchanged glances. "When I went through," Cassie said, "it felt like sliding sideways through a narrow hallway that was parallel to the slip and perpendicular to it at the same time. Like the space was distorted. I didn't see anything like a seal. How can you tell?"

"Glass magic is meant to perceive what's hidden," Viv said. She stepped back from the barrier, lowering her hands. "But it doesn't grant any special awareness. I can see the seal, but I can't tell whether it's close to breaking or if this is just how it always looks."

"Will you attempt to scry beyond the barrier?" Gabriel asked.

"Sure." Viv knelt again. This time, I took a look at the contraption she'd built. Most of it was a glass mirror about three feet in diameter, with two silver handles attached to it on opposite sides so it looked like a weird dinner tray. On the mirror's non-reflective side, Viv had placed flattened glass pebbles, the colored kind used in floral decorations. I walked closer to get a better viewing angle and discovered they were arranged in little piles by color, amber, green, blue, and deep red like a ruby.

Viv balanced a final green pebble on its pile and sat back on her heels, staring at the barrier. "I think that's it," she said, and picked up the mirror by its handles. The glass pebbles didn't slide or fall over.

"What is that?" Milo asked.

"Each pebble represents an aspect of the door and the barrier and the portal," Viv said. She rotated the mirror so it was vertical. The pebbles clung to its surface as if magnetized. "I chose them based on my own connection to all that. That gives them resonance. The idea is to convince the scrying mirror that the barrier isn't there so I can see past it."

"But it won't remove the barrier, right?" I asked.

"The point of this is to determine if the Wardens' type of scrying can bypass the barrier, so it has to have the possibility of affecting it somehow. But from what I've seen, a simple scrying won't remove that seal." Viv grinned. "Whether it weakens the seal further isn't something I'm willing to swear won't happen."

"So we have to be prepared," Jeremiah said. He gestured, a complicated movement involving both hands, and his staff appeared out of nowhere.

"Wow," Milo breathed. "How did you do that?"

"Magic," Jeremiah replied, perfectly straight-faced. Then he smiled, and said, "Actually, it's stored in a pocket dimension offset from our reality by a fraction of a degree. There's not enough room there to keep much, but it beats walking around Portland with a wizard's staff."

Malcolm had his gun out and was looking it over. I caught the looks on Gabriel and Cassie's faces and said, feeling defensive, "He's not going to shoot unless it's necessary."

"Sorry," Cassie said, glancing away from the gun. "It's not something we ever do. The idea of using firearms is so alien. But you do things differently, I know."

Malcolm nodded. "I understand." He held the gun firmly, with his finger away from the trigger, his attention fully on the barrier as if despite everything he expected something to burst through it.

I watched Viv instead as she carried the scrying mirror to the barrier. She stopped half a foot from the glowing surface and braced herself, her feet shoulder-width apart and her knees slightly flexed. She still held the mirror vertically with the non-reflective side and the pebble piles pointed toward the barrier, but now the mirror was close against her chest so her elbows were bent sharply. I took a few steps so I could see her face, at least as much of it as was visible from the side. She looked calm but intent, just as she always did when she was doing magic. Looking at her, I had trouble remembering she hadn't been a magus her whole life.

Viv glanced at me and smiled. "Don't worry, Helena," she said. "Let's see what's on the other side."

She extended the mirror away from herself until it reached the barrier, pressed up against the constant movement. The mirror didn't do anything to disrupt the barrier, and I let out the breath I'd been holding, feeling stupid. Then Viv let go of the handles, and the mirror stayed there just as if the barrier were an ordinary wall and Viv had hung it up like a picture.

All three of the adepts took a step forward. I realized Malcolm was at my side when he put his hand on my elbow and drew me back, putting himself between me and the doorway. Jeremiah flanked Viv on the other side, his staff held ready.

"It's not showing anything," Viv said, sounding disappointed.

The second she stopped speaking, the mirror flashed brightly as if a stray sunbeam had hit it, though the light through the clearing was indirect. "It's—" I began.

Milo stood in front of the mirror, then walked from one side of it to the other. "It's not a reflection. I can't see myself." He returned to stand in front of it and waved. From where I stood, I could clearly see he was right—the mirror wasn't reflecting him.

"We're seeing into Faerie," Gabriel said. "Look at how broad the clearing is on that side. It's the cuivuirskeen."

Now everyone but Gabriel crowded close to the mirror. At first glance, Faerie didn't look any different from the forests of Washington. Then I noticed the strange little flowers blossoming on the ends of the fir tree branches, how they bobbed in a breeze that wasn't blowing on our side. I became aware that I was hearing that distant breeze just as Malcolm tensed and pushed past Cassie, leveling his gun at the mirror. "Something's there."

"You can't just shoot things," Cassie said, sounding irritated.

"I have no intention of shooting anything that isn't dangerous, and by dangerous I mean an active, attacking threat," Malcolm said, his gaze not wavering. "And the odds are whatever it is can't get at us. But I intend to take precautions."

I stayed behind Malcolm, peering over his shoulder. At first, I didn't see anything but the moving branches. Then I saw it—a moving shadow, low to the ground, creeping from tree trunk to tree trunk. It was impossible to judge its size, but it was definitely getting closer.

"I think—Jeremiah!" Viv protested.

"Time for you to back up," Jeremiah said, moving Viv out of the way. "Malcolm?"

"It sees us. Did you mean this to be a two-way vision, Viv?" Malcolm asked.

"Yes. It's the only way to confirm if there's a physical reaction." Viv sounded distant again, and I turned to watch her. She'd retrieved her illusion-piercing lenses from the bag and held them to her face. "I can't see it. It's not invisible, whatever it is."

It hadn't occurred to me that creatures of Faerie might be under illusions. I looked back at the mirror and couldn't see the shadow anymore. "Is it still there?" I asked, whispering as if the creature might hear and attack.

Malcolm nodded. "To the right."

I still didn't see it. I took a step away from Malcolm. In an instant, the barrier flashed dark blue, thick and still sparkling. A deep snarl echoed through our clearing. And something flew through the barrier, knocking the mirror away and launching itself directly at Viv.

CHAPTER 13

I screamed and flung myself at Viv, pushing her out of the way without thinking that this stupid move would only put me in the path of the creature. Then it hit me, slamming into my shoulder and knocking me down. Malcolm shouted, but didn't shoot, probably because the thing crouched over me, its growl a low rumble that made my chest vibrate. I squeezed my eyes shut and flung my arms across my face.

"Don't shoot!" Gabriel shouted. "Put down the staff. Just back away slowly. It's not going to attack."

I opened my eyes and peered over my crossed arms. The creature's head was inches from mine, and its lips peeled back from sharp fangs, but it didn't move. It was breathing heavily, but that didn't interfere with its ongoing growl.

Then it ducked its head and licked my forehead.

"Ew," I said reflexively, though it hadn't been an unpleasant sensation. The creature's tongue felt dry and rough like a cat's, and its breath smelled of fresh-cut grass, clean and a little sweet. I lowered my arms to get a better look at it. My first impression was of a cat, pointed ears and long, lashing tail and rounded flanks. But it was the biggest cat I'd ever seen, easily the size and weight of a German shepherd, and its ears were huge and tufted at the tips. Its short purply-black fur looked ragged and dirty, giving me the impression of a wild animal. But despite the growl, it didn't seem hostile.

"Helena," Malcolm said, "don't move."

"It's not dangerous," Gabriel said. "It's a caracal. They used to cross the border all the time and interbreed with wildcats on this side of Faerie. There are places in northern Africa and India where their smaller descendants still live."

"Wildcats are dangerous," Malcolm said, his voice tense. He held his gun at his side as if waiting for a clear shot. Beyond him, Jeremiah stood braced to attack, his staff at the ready.

"Yes, but the caracals of Faerie aren't any more wild than housecats here." Gabriel approached slowly. "I don't want to scare this one."

"It doesn't look like a pet," I said. "Look at its fur." Though I was looking at its eyes at the moment. They were golden brown and slanted, and regarded me with as much interest as I had in it. We stared at each other, not blinking, until my eyes were too dry and I couldn't help myself. The caracal tilted its head in a gesture that looked like curiosity. Then, to my shock, it shifted its weight and lay down across my chest, crossing its front paws below my throat, and lowered its head to lick my chin once before settling its head on its front legs.

My heart thumped hard, once, and a surge of compassion swept through me. Without a second thought, I scratched behind its ears, and it leaned into my touch, just like an ordinary cat. "Gabriel," I said, somewhat breathily because the thing weighed a ton and my lungs were straining to compensate, "what's going on?"

"Like I said, they're not wild animals," Gabriel said. He knelt beside me and petted the caracal's head. "This one looks like someone's lost pet. He—" He swiftly lifted the caracal's tail and released it a second later. "*She* has definitely been alone for a while. The cuivuirskeen are well away from civilization, and I wonder if she wasn't deliberately abandoned, because I can't imagine a caracal getting that far away from her owner by accident."

"Isn't anyone going to address the important issue?" Cassie demanded. "How did that thing get through the barrier?"

Everyone fell silent. Gabriel's hand on the caracal's head stilled.

Finally, Viv said, "I don't know what caused the change, but something about the scrying neutralized the barrier briefly. Part of the barrier, I mean. I'll need to examine it again, but I'm sure whatever it was didn't remove the bit that is deadly to elves."

"But it looks normal again," Milo said, gesturing. I craned my neck to look at the barrier. Sure enough, it was back to its old gaudy golden self. "That blue color must have been part of the change."

"Give me a minute," Viv said. She retrieved the mirror, which had fallen facedown on the grass next to the barrier. All the glass pebbles had fallen off and lay gleaming on the ground like treasure. Viv set the mirror aside and opened her bag again. She removed objects wrapped in silk scarves that obscured their contours, though Viv didn't seem to have any problem identifying the ones she wanted. Soon, she had four or five fabric bundles to her right, next to the barrier.

The caracal on my chest closed its eyes and began purring. The sound made my heart melt. It had been a couple of years since our cats Cyrus and Xerxes had died of old age, and I hadn't wanted another pet despite the kids' pleas. It had been too hard to say goodbye to our Persian friends. But this warm, cuddly creature reminded me of how nice it was to have the love of a furry animal.

Gabriel picked up the caracal with some effort and set her beside me. Malcolm instantly helped me to my feet and steadied me while I brushed myself off. He'd put away his gun, but his attention was all on the cat. "That was terrifying," he murmured.

"I know, but look at how sweet she is. I think she was lonely." I knelt beside her to pet her stiff, dirty fur, and the purring intensified.

"Helena," Malcolm said, his voice a warning.

"We can't leave her here, Malcolm. She's a pet. She can't survive on her own."

"It was doing fine for itself. Look, it's not too thin the way it would be if it was starving." Malcolm knelt next to me and stroked the fur over the caracal's flank. She made a deeper, growling sound and rolled over to present her belly more fully, a clear request for more petting. Malcolm's expression changed in an instant from stern to warily pleased. He stroked her fur in a slow, contemplative way.

"Well, that's not good," Viv said.

I kept scratching under the caracal's chin as I looked up at Viv. She held an ordinary metal triangle by a string at head height. In her other hand, she held, not a metal stick for ringing the triangle, but a doctor's reflex hammer, one made entirely of glass. When she had everyone's attention, she struck the triangle with the hammer. It made no sound, not even the dull *tink* I'd expected, but the barrier shivered as if sound waves had struck it anyway, sending up ripples across the golden surface.

With those ripples, the color of the barrier changed. Not much—the ripples turned it the faintest green, and the original color returned once the ripples faded—but it was still noticeable. Viv lowered the triangle. She was normally the most cheerful person I knew, but she looked unexpectedly grim now.

"I said the barrier acts like a seal, and that the seal was straining like it was under pressure," she said. "I can't tell for sure what the scrying did, but what I do know is that the barrier is weakening."

"Weakening, how?" Gabriel asked. Cassie, standing beside him, closed her eyes and grimaced as if Viv's words had hurt her.

"Maybe the sight of that influenced my perceptions," Viv said, pointing at the barrier. "To me, it looks like fabric, gold lamé or something. But I'm sure whatever I see when I look more closely at it isn't really what it's made of. It's like my mind is telling me something I can understand. Anyway, what I mean is that I see it as fabric, and that fabric is getting thinner. That's what I mean by the seal straining. It's like if you put on a shirt that's a size too small. The fabric stretches, and if the shirt's a lot too small, it tears. The barrier is going to come down eventually."

"Your scrying did that?" Gabriel said.

"Hey, you asked her to try scrying! This isn't her fault," I retorted.

"Fault isn't the issue," Cassie said. "We need to know if anything we do accelerates the process, or if it's a natural decay."

"It wasn't the scrying, not exactly," Viv said, sounding calm and not defensive. "That brought Faerie and our world into contact briefly, but it's more like it made the world believe the barrier wasn't there for a few seconds. I think it was the caracal's crossing over that weakened the seal." She pointed at the caracal, who rolled back onto her stomach and butted her head against my hand for attention.

"So you've found a way to allow people to move back and forth," Cassie said.

"Not elves, but humans. Yeah." Viv shoved the glass hammer into one of her pockets. "Which sounds like the opposite of what you wanted."

"If we can access Faerie before the Savants do..." Cassie's voice trailed off.

"The barrier will go on poisoning Faerie," Malcolm said.

"It's a start," Gabriel said.

"No, it's not," said Jeremiah. He was leaning on his staff, watching Viv collect her things. "Didn't you hear? Every time someone crosses over, it weakens the seal. The barrier. Who knows how many of those crossings you'd get before it all came down? And then the Savants could do whatever they want, and the elves could enter our world...you can't keep crossing into Faerie, not for any reason."

Cassie looked unnaturally pale. "Then it was me," she murmured. "My passage started the decay of the barrier."

"It's not about fault, remember?" I said. "If you hadn't gone into Faerie, no one would know about the barrier poisoning it. And for all you know, the Savants would figure the trick out, and they'd implement their plan and you wouldn't be in a position to stop it."

Gabriel put his arms around Cassie. "Don't blame yourself. That's pointless. We have to move forward, not waste time thinking about the past."

Cassie closed her eyes again. "Sorry. You're right." She hugged him briefly, then stepped away. "So, we know how to bring down the barrier, but not in any useful way. Meaning, we don't know how many crossings it will take. And we still don't know whether that's something we want."

"Leave the barrier up, and condemn the elves in Faerie to a slow death," I said. "Remove it in a way that lets elves enter our world unchecked. Remove it in a way that gives the Savants an advantage." I looked at Malcolm. "Maybe we need to do something about the Savant threat."

"That's impossible," Gabriel said. "Astraeus Resources is far too powerful."

"Well, so are we," I said. "The Wardens or Campbell Security, either one—we may not have a single organization worth a billion dollars, but there are a lot more of us than there are of the Savants. If they weren't a problem, humans could enter Faerie and negotiate with the elves so they don't start a war."

"That is extremely optimistic thinking," Malcolm said. "Astraeus Resources is still an unknown as far as their hidden magical or technological assets go, and they might turn out to be more powerful than the Wardens."

"But she's right that eliminating the Savants would solve a lot of problems," Jeremiah said. "I think we need to put some effort into learning what it will take."

"I agree." Malcolm helped me stand. "Cassie, Gabriel, we should discuss what you already know, and I will set my people to investigating. Now that we know more about what Astraeus is hiding, we may have better luck piercing its defenses. Lucia will do the same."

"I'm surprised you're willing to speak for her," Cassie said. "She strikes me as extremely independent."

"That is an acknowledgement of what she will do when she hears what we've learned," Malcolm said with a smile. "She likes taking action."

Milo was already reaching for the ropes tying the door together. He loosed the first set, making the lintel sag, and the golden barrier vanished in an instant. "Breaking the door is the fast way to close a portal," he said when he saw me watching.

Cassie untied the second rope and caught the lintel as it fell. "But Gabriel still doesn't come near until it's completely disassembled. We don't take chances."

Gabriel did wait for them to put all the poles on the ground before using his hatchet to chop them into manageable pieces. "We can't use the same wood twice," he said. "Nobody knows why. This will all be firewood later this year."

I took a step and came up against the caracal, who'd stood when I did and now leaned against my legs. Standing, she was as tall as my thighs. "We can't leave her here," I said. "Talk about introducing a non-native species. She'll have to come home with us."

"Well, we can't take her," Milo said. "Cassie's cat Merlin would have a fit. He's a Maine coon and used to being the biggest animal around."

"I think she's adopted you, Helena," Viv said with a grin.

"We could try sending her back—but that would just make the problem with the barrier worse," Gabriel said. "But caracals aren't hard to care for. They're just like cats. Enormous cats. They eat raw meat—I'm not sure they can digest cat food. They're trained to bury their waste, so she'll understand a litter box. At worst, you might have to explain to Animal Control why you have what looks like a wild animal in your yard."

"She'll be fine," I declared. "Come on, Midnight."

"You're naming her Midnight? How boring," Viv said.

"You'd probably want to call her something weird like Pumpernickel that has nothing to do with her appearance," I retorted. "Or Snowball or Bianca or something else contrarian. At least Midnight is descriptive. Look at that fur."

"If you're going to be traditional, at least call her Night-Noon instead of Midnight." Viv scratched the caracal's head.

"Night-Noon?" Cassie said, arching a skeptical eyebrow.

"Viv couldn't remember the word 'midnight' when she was seven and she came up with 'night-noon' instead," I explained. "It's very evocative. Okay, Night-Noon, come with me." I patted the caracal's shoulder. She looked up at me with those big golden-brown eyes, and I was sure there was some intelligence behind them. When I started walking, she followed me immediately.

We crossed the stream and headed back toward the cars, with Gabriel and Milo bringing up the rear with their armloads of firewood. Night-Noon leaped the stream as easily as stepping over a sidewalk crack. I turned to point her gracefulness out to Malcolm, but he was scanning the woods, his hand near his gun, and I decided not to distract him. I didn't think we were in any danger, but his caution had saved my life more than once, and I never second-guessed him.

There was a moment's difficulty when we reached the land yacht and tried to entice Night-Noon inside. She didn't like the smell of the car, based on how she backed away from it, head low and ears flattened. Finally, I knelt beside her and hugged her, then lifted her with some effort and put her in the front passenger seat where I'd ridden that morning. She sniffed the upholstery, sniffed the console, sniffed Malcolm's arm, then settled at my feet and started in on her rumbling purr.

"She really is attached to you," Jeremiah said as Malcolm put the car in gear. "Just as well it wasn't me. I'm allergic."

"The house never bothered you when we had Cyrus and Xerxes," I said.

"I'm not severely allergic. Just enough to make cat ownership tricky." He put his arm around Viv's shoulders and pulled her close. "All right. What didn't you tell them?"

I startled and slewed around in my seat to face Viv. "You lied?"

"Of course not," Viv said. "I just left a few things out. I'm still not convinced they're being honest with *us*, so I was being cautious."

"And what were those things?" Malcolm kept his eyes on the road.

Viv bit her lip in thought. "For one, the strain on the barrier happened before Cassie went into Faerie, at least based on the timeline she gave us. Somebody else was putting pressure on it—I'm pretty sure nobody else went through before she did, but there were attempts that strained the barrier's fabric."

"But if that was the Savants, isn't that something the adepts should be told?" I asked.

"Maybe. They said the adepts don't all work together, and I'm not sure it wasn't some other adept, or group of adepts, who did it. Which would suggest Cassie wasn't totally forthcoming with us."

"Unless she didn't know."

"I said I wasn't sure, Helena." Viv shook her head. "The other thing was the scrying itself made a temporary hole. It wasn't just connecting the two worlds briefly—it was an actual hole."

I gasped. "Viv—"

"I know, that's not what I said. I didn't want them to know in case it meant they wanted me to do it again, when they're ready to enter Faerie."

"Do you think they'd be that manipulative?" Jeremiah asked. His arm tightened around Viv's shoulders.

"I have no idea. They're still mostly strangers, and they have motives that aren't ours. But now we know there's a way into Faerie that bypasses the barrier, and we should figure out what to do about it."

"I thought you said it would still kill an elf," I said.

Viv shrugged. "It probably would. That thing is weird. Half of what I saw, I can't describe, and the other half is so strange I'm already forgetting it. Is it bad that I want to dump this all on Lucia and let her decide?"

"We don't have the authority to make decisions on behalf of all of magery," Malcolm said. "Lucia and Ms. Stirlaugson need to be informed. But I intend to do as I said and start a real investigation of the Savants. Helena's instincts are sound, and I'm prepared to treat them as enemies."

Night-Noon shifted her weight and lay down across my feet. I stretched to scratch behind her tufted ears. "I'm afraid no amount of discussion is going to solve the problem of the barrier. It can't stay in place forever, and it shouldn't be dismantled. Doesn't that sound like a no-win situation?"

"Which is why we will take action as best we can," Malcolm said. "But if the oracle has an answer..."

I shook my head. "I've tried, but I haven't received any prophecies. Maybe that means I don't know enough, but it feels like the problem is too complex for a definitive answer."

"So maybe that means asking a different question," Viv said. "You can't see what Castellan intends, but you could find out things about the Savants, maybe. Or whether Cassie and her people are being honest with us."

"Or if the elves are watching the barrier, ready to invade once it disappears," Jeremiah said.

Viv patted his cheek. "You're so pessimistic," she said fondly.

———

WE DROVE to our house first, since Viv and Jeremiah had driven Viv's car Clarence there before we all left for Washington. After a little discussion, I got out too and coaxed Night-Noon to join me. "I'll see about getting her cleaned up and fed," I told Malcolm.

"Then, when you bring the kids home from my parents', she will be a fun surprise."

"This is the most spontaneous thing you've done in years," Malcolm said with a smile. "I love it."

"Oh, good. I was afraid you were humoring me."

"I would never bring an animal into our household if I wasn't convinced we were both equally committed to caring for it." Malcolm's gaze fell on Night-Noon, and his smile widened. "She is beautiful. And I miss having a cat around."

I shut the passenger door and waved goodbye as Malcolm backed out of the driveway. Viv, who'd only gone as far as the sidewalk, watched Malcolm drive away. Jeremiah climbed in behind Clarence's wheel, but Viv walked back up the drive to where I stood. "I'm worried," she said.

"Did you have a premonition?"

"No. That's what worries me." She ran her fingers restlessly through her hair. "These are some really big things about to happen, and you'd think I'd feel something. But my intuition might as well be asleep for all it's given me any hints."

"Maybe it's the same as you said about the oracle not giving any prophecies when I ask about the barrier. Maybe you need to look at it differently."

"I don't know. It's not the same, but—" Viv sighed. "I'm going home, and I'm not going to think about this for a whole day. Maybe that will kickstart my premonitions."

I nodded. "I'm going to see about making a home for this cat. I might even try to bathe her."

Viv grimaced. "She's not going to like that. I predict you're going to get very wet."

"Was that a premonition, after all?"

"No," Viv said. "Experience."

But it turned out Viv was wrong, and there was one caracal trait Gabriel hadn't mentioned: they loved baths. Or maybe that was just Night-Noon's quirk. Either way, when I filled the bathtub with warm water, she sniffed it delicately, like a society lady testing the aroma of a vintage wine, then patted the water with one paw and sniffed that. And then she stepped into the tub with the same grace with which she did everything and sank down until the water covered her back.

I scrubbed her clean and rinsed her twice, all of which she endured with dignity, then toweled her as dry as I could manage and left her lying on the bathmat, licking the last of the water from her fur. I ran out to the garage and pulled down the litter box from the wide shelf that ran around two sides of the garage at just over head height. Good thing I hadn't been able to bring myself to get rid of it, though I really hadn't wanted another cat. There was also a half-full plastic sack of kitty litter, still around for the same reason.

I put the litter box in its old place in the laundry room and filled it, then dug around in the kitchen cupboards until I found Xerxes's old bowl. There were some raw boneless chicken breasts in a package in the fridge, and I cut one into cubes, then, mindful of something I'd read about feeding a very hungry animal who might vomit from overeating, I filled the bowl only half full and put the rest of the chicken into a plastic bag. That and the water dish went in the old familiar place, and to my surprise, the sight didn't make my heart ache.

Night-Noon sat up alertly when I returned to the bathroom. "Downstairs," I said, stroking her head briefly. She stood and trotted down the stairs at my heel, more like a dog than a cat, though no dog would purr the way she was doing. She didn't devour the meat in three gulps as I'd feared, which suggested Malcolm was right and she'd been feeding herself well enough, but she did drink most of the water.

As I was showing her the litter box and making encouraging noises about her using it, the doorbell rang. I left Night-Noon to do her business and checked the video display on my phone. Laverne Stirlaugson stood on my doorstep. Surprised, I stared at the display for a few seconds before hurrying through the house to the front door.

"Ms. Stirlaugson, hello," I said. "I wasn't expecting you."

"I apologize for not calling first, but this can't wait," Stirlaugson said. "May I come in?"

I stood back and let her enter. She didn't wait for another invitation, but immediately took a seat on the nearest sofa. I closed the door and sat opposite her, so full of questions I didn't know which to start with. So I opted to say nothing. She was the visitor; let her speak first, reveal what was so important.

"Have you spoken with Cassie Leighton recently?" Stirlaugson said.

"Yes. A few hours ago." I decided not to explain about the barrier, figuring that might distract Stirlaugson from her purpose.

"What did you tell her?"

Surprised at Stirlaugson's intensity, I stammered, "Um, nothing, really, it was more about her telling us things—why?"

Stirlaugson's jaw tensed, and she frowned. "Ms. Leighton hasn't been honest with us. I hope you haven't given her too much information about the Wardens."

Now I was thoroughly confused. "What makes you say that? I'm sure she and the other adepts haven't told us everything, but that's not the same as dishonesty. I mean, it's not like we've been totally open either."

Stirlaugson had started shaking her head halfway through my words. "Not telling us everything isn't the problem. I've just had a long conversation with Michael Castellan, the man who is supposedly the head of the Savants. Ms. Campbell, you've been lied to."

CHAPTER 14

"You talked to Mr. Castellan?" Unexpected fear shot through me, a sharp jolt that set my heart to beating too quickly. "I told you he's dangerous."

"What you told me," Stirlaugson said, "was that the *adepts* told you he was dangerous. You have only their word for it. It's never a good idea not to get both sides of a story when one is being asked to choose between those sides."

"That's true, but I've spoken to him myself, and I did not get the sense that he's one of the good guys. He might even have sociopathic tendencies." Even as I said that, I felt uncertain. All my previous doubts resurfaced—my fears that I'd jumped too quickly to believe Cassie and her friends, that I hadn't done the right kind of research. Even the woman in the red Camry who'd tried to follow me home—the oracle had revealed she was dangerous, but I'd jumped to the conclusion that meant she was a Savant, and suppose she was an adept instead?

"Did the oracle warn you about him?"

"Yes. Sort of. I saw him in situations I thought were dangerous."

"Situations? Did they prove he was a Savant?"

"I—" Again, I doubted my memories. "They weren't proof, exactly. I couldn't prophesy about his motives. But I'm certain of my conclusions, Ms. Stirlaugson. He wasn't open with me about his identity, and he didn't say anything about his connection to Astraeus Resources. Don't you think if he was on our side, he'd have been forthcoming about that?"

"Mr. Castellan and I had a very enlightening conversation. He explained that he wasn't sure who you were or what the Wardens' organization entailed, and he didn't want to be open with you when there was a chance you were the enemy. Reasonable, don't you think?" Stirlaugson regarded me steadily.

"I guess...Ms. Stirlaugson, did you go to him, or did he come to you?"

"He approached me."

"Doesn't that seem suspicious to you? That he investigated the Wardens enough to know you were the one to talk to?"

Stirlaugson shook her head once. "Since we investigated him, I hardly think his organization doing the same thing qualifies as suspicious. And Mr. Castellan was extremely candid in revealing what he had done to seek me out. He also answered every question I had and asked very few of his own. He struck me as a very forthright person."

"How *did* he find you?" Another jolt shot through me. "He didn't trail you from this house, did he?"

Stirlaugson's eyes narrowed. "No. He said he connected your corporation to Campbell Security, and Campbell Security to the Board. I would say we have not been cautious enough, but it sounded as if that tracing was difficult and required extensive resources, even for such a company as Astraeus."

My uneasiness grew, enhancing my fears that maybe I'd done the wrong thing. "All right," I said, "what did he tell you about himself?"

"For one thing, that his organization is not the Savants, but is in opposition to them," Stirlaugson said. "They know the barrier is weakening, and they want to find a way to contact the elves before it is entirely destroyed, in the hope of making peace."

"So he said Cassie and Gabriel and the others—they're the Savants?"

"What he said was that the adepts you've spoken to have different goals from his, and that their animosity toward him is rooted in profound misunderstandings. He was also open about how not all adepts share his vision, and that he tries to convince them otherwise, but not through violent means." Stirlaugson leaned forward as if in emphasis. "I believe he was telling the truth."

Uncertainty made my head spin. I *didn't* know anything about Michael Castellan but what Cassie had told me—except Cassie had sounded so reasonable—but then, according to Stirlaugson, so had Castellan—and Castellan hadn't accused anyone of evil—

I made my hands relax and rubbed my palms on my knees. "It sounds like one person's word against another's, Ms. Stirlaugson. And each of us were convinced by a different person's word. I don't know what to do with that."

"Mr. Castellan would like to meet with you again, openly this time, and plead his case. He told me Gabriel Roarke, for one, is extremely persuasive, and you could not be blamed for believing him."

I felt unexpectedly sick. "Does he know what I am?"

"If he does, he didn't learn it from me," Stirlaugson said sharply. "The security and privacy of all the oracles is my paramount concern, Ms. Campbell."

That made me feel better. If Stirlaugson was a dupe, she wasn't a foolish one. "So why does he want to meet with me, then?"

"He claimed an interest in your philanthropy, and said he wanted to make an appeal in his true identity for you to support his organization," Stirlaugson said. "He seemed very impressed with what you've accomplished."

That set off a little warning bell in my head. "That's...awfully flattering, considering I'm not a heavy hitter so far as donations go."

"Yes, but you have a record of choosing charities that make the best use of their resources, none of which have a history of corruption or misuse of funds. He informed me that it wasn't your money he wanted so much as your insight. A collaboration to help guide his own charitable giving efforts."

"I guess that's possible." I still didn't feel certain. Stirlaugson wasn't stupid, and her caution verged on paranoia, so if she believed Castellan, she did so after careful analysis. And yet...

I closed my eyes and massaged my temples against the tension building there. "This doesn't feel right," I murmured. "I do not believe Cassie lied to me. And yet I don't want to tell you you're wrong."

"Which is why I encourage you to meet with Mr. Castellan when he approaches you again," Stirlaugson said. "Speak to him candidly, and —*what is that?*"

My head jerked up. "Oh, it's Night-Noon," I said. "Come here, sweetie, let Ms. Stirlaugson look at you." I extended a hand, and the caracal sniffed it once before butting against it to be petted.

"You have a wild animal in your house? Surely that's not legal, Ms. Campbell." Stirlaugson's voice was tight, and she sat back in her chair, well away from the caracal.

"She's not wild, she's a pet. From Faerie—" I stopped, but it was too late. Stirlaugson's eyes widened.

"This is a creature of Faerie? The barrier is down?" she exclaimed. "Why didn't you tell me?"

"Because it's not down, we just—well, we found a way to open the portal without removing the barrier." I felt every word was digging my grave deeper. "But it's not something we want the adepts to know, in case—"

"Ms. Campbell, this is essential information," Stirlaugson said. "If it's possible to pass between the worlds, we could negotiate with the elves with impunity. We could convince them not to wage war on humanity. I cannot believe you would be so irresponsible as to not inform me of this!"

"Ms. Stirlaugson," I said, irritation supplanting my unease, "this all happened less than an hour ago. There hasn't been time to tell anyone. I promise I didn't try to conceal anything. In fact, we were going to tell you and Lucia both so you could work out what to do with the information. I'm not in a position to make policy."

Stirlaugson's lips thinned in annoyance. "Very well," she finally said. "I'll take this information under consideration. How is it done?"

"Opening the portal? It's an effect of scrying." I felt instinctively I shouldn't go into more detail than that. It wasn't a warning from the oracle or a Viv-style premonition, just a feeling, but it was a feeling that worried me. Withholding information wasn't the act of an ally, and Stirlaugson was, if nothing else, my ally. But if she wasn't suspicious of Castellan, I didn't want her to know the details.

"I see." Stirlaugson rose, staying far away from Night-Noon, who was sitting back on her haunches and shedding fine black fur all over my hand. "I'll bring this up with the Board."

"Not with Mr. Castellan?"

Stirlaugson frowned. "The Wardens may choose to work with others, but ultimately, the protection of humanity is our responsibility, not that of a scant handful of adepts with no governing body or consensus on the issue. I don't intend to involve Mr. Castellan unless the Board judges his resources will be valuable. Good afternoon, Ms. Campbell." She let herself out, moving more rapidly than usual.

I continued to scratch Night-Noon's head, my gaze fixed on the door as if I could see through it to Stirlaugson's retreating form. "Meet with Mr. Castellan again," I mused aloud. "Night-Noon, what am I missing? Ms. Stirlaugson sounded so reasonable, but I'm not stupid and I don't feel like Cassie and Gabriel lied to me."

In response, Night-Noon put her front paws on my lap. Then she leaped awkwardly to sit across my legs, purring like crazy. "Oof!" I said. "You are much too big to be a lap cat!"

Night-Noon settled herself so her hindquarters were on my lap and her front paws dangled over the sofa armrest. I stroked her short black fur, which felt softer than velvet now it was clean, and considered what Stirlaugson had told me. If Castellan had claimed Cassie was a Savant, I wouldn't have believed it—it was too easy an answer. Saying she was an adept with other goals was not only reasonable, but true. Everything I'd heard from Stirlaugson was plausible.

So why did I still feel uncertain?

I cast back in memory, looking for answers, and found myself remembering the day all this had started, the day I'd interrupted three people digging a strange stone from beneath the street. They hadn't acted like people interested in sharing knowledge; regardless of whether I'd misunderstood them, I was sure they'd believed I was an adept, and their reactions told me they believed adepts were their enemy.

Then I felt like an idiot. They'd had guns. They'd threatened to kill me.

If Castellan was interested in pursuing his goals through non-violent means, that was a strange way of going about it. And suddenly everything came into focus. Maybe they'd been afraid, and maybe the situation with Faerie was serious enough to warrant violent defense against strangers, but I couldn't bring myself to believe they'd been the good guys in that scenario.

And what had Stirlaugson said about why Castellan hadn't told me the truth in my office? That he wasn't sure if I was the enemy? That made no sense now. Someone with as many resources as Castellan wouldn't hesitate to threaten or kill anyone he believed was his enemy. He'd been cagey at that meeting because he was sounding me out.

Now I felt impatient with myself. I'd known the truth the whole time, that the adepts were right and Castellan and his Savants were their enemies. But I'd let my lingering respect and, well, maybe a little residual fear of Stirlaugson make me question my instincts. That, and a pesky feeling that I should hear both sides of a story before making a decision. That wasn't a bad policy, but sometimes right and wrong were obvious. And this was one of those times.

I gave the caracal a gentle push, which she ignored, and then a stronger push, and finally she climbed off my lap and wandered away, exploring the rest of downstairs. I needed to tell someone that the Savants knew more than they should about the Wardens, and that Stirlaugson might be an unwitting pawn—unwitting, because I was just as sure Stirlaugson would never take chances with the Wardens' safety.

As if responding to my need, the distant hum of the garage door opening told me Malcolm and the kids were home. I hurried to the back door to greet them, reaching it just as it opened and Alastair said, "Mom, Dad says there's a surprise! What's the surprise?"

In my worry over the Savants, I'd temporarily forgotten Night-Noon was a surprise. "We have a new pet," I said. "No, take off your shoes before—oh, there she is."

Alastair stopped with one sandal dangling from his fingers. "A lynx!" he exclaimed. "But they're not pets. We shouldn't keep a wild animal."

Duncan had already pushed past his brother and was extending his hand for Night-Noon to sniff. "He's so big," he said. "Is he a cat or a dog?"

"She's a kind of cat called a caracal, and she's not a wild animal," I said. "Jenny, don't be afraid, she won't hurt you."

Jenny had hung back, pressing against her father's legs, but when she saw Duncan pet Night-Noon's head, she slowly came forward. Night-Noon butted against Duncan's hand, then sniffed Jenny's stomach and butted her there, too. Jenny smiled in delight and joined in petting the caracal.

"But, Mom, a caracal *is* a wild animal, they live in India and they're not black—"

"I know, Alastair. This is a different breed, and she's tame." I reflected with some exasperation that Alastair's intelligence and self-directed education were sometimes really annoying. "We'll explain the details later. For now—her name is Night-Noon, and would you children like to learn how to care for her?"

I led them through the instructions on feeding and keeping the water dish full, showed Jenny the litter box—Xerxes and Cyrus had passed away when she was an infant—and left them to play with the newest member of our family. "Malcolm, Laverne Stirlaugson was here," I said in a low voice, though we were in the front room and well out of earshot of the kids. "She said Michael Castellan approached her. He spun her a tale about how he's really the good guy, and she believed it."

Malcolm cursed. "Did you tell her otherwise?"

"No, because it all sounded plausible while she was talking. It's not like I've ever spoken to the man when we were both being open about who we were. And I wondered if maybe I should have given both sides an equal hearing. But that was stupid thinking, and now I'm afraid. She doesn't believe he's dangerous, and she has tremendous power over the Wardens."

"Did she tell him you are an oracle?" Malcolm's hand closed gently over mine.

"No. She's not stupid, she just believes his lies. I don't think she fully trusts him. But she's willing to give him the benefit of the doubt. And she wants me to meet with him again so he can plead his case."

Malcolm's grip grew tighter. "Ms. Stirlaugson has put us in a terrible position. She may not have revealed everything, but Castellan certainly knows more about us than we do about him.

My investigation just became much more urgent. We need information we can use to defend ourselves. Defend the oracle, certainly."

I nodded. Then another memory surfaced, and I grimaced, squeezing my eyes tight shut. "I accidentally told her about scrying opening a hole in the portal."

"Accidentally?"

"She saw Night-Noon, and explaining about her led to the other thing. Malcolm, this could be bad. If Ms. Stirlaugson tells Mr. Castellan—"

Malcolm released my hand to put his arms around me. "She won't do that. Not immediately, anyway. As you said, she's not stupid, and so long as she doesn't entirely trust Castellan, she won't give away more information than she has to. Besides, I don't see how you could have avoided explaining why we now have a cat from Faerie living in our house."

"That's how I felt, too." I returned his embrace and rested my head on his shoulder, letting the tension drain away. "But I'm going to see what more I can learn from the oracle tonight."

"And I will drive in to the office and set this investigation going." Malcolm kissed me, and I returned his kiss wholeheartedly. "I may be back late, so don't wait dinner on me. I'm sorry I won't be here."

"It's all right. I think Night-Noon will keep the kids occupied while I make dinner." I laughed. "Though I didn't think about establishing a sleeping space for her. I don't want them fighting over whose bed she sleeps on."

"The novelty will wear off soon enough, and then they'll argue over who has to let her take up most of the bed," Malcolm said.

As if the universe knew when not to push, the next few days were uneventful. Castellan didn't contact me. Malcolm's investigation into Castellan's businesses didn't turn up anything immediately, though Malcolm assured me this was normal. "Castellan is as careful as Campbell Security is," he said, "and it will take time to find a way around those defenses." I decided not to worry about it, since worrying wouldn't make the investigation go faster.

I didn't hear from either Cassie or Stirlaugson, which wasn't so much of a worry, given that both of them were probably still dealing with the information they'd gained. Nobody tried to follow me to or from my house, nobody tripped any of the security measures we'd set up to protect the oracle, and nobody sinister approached me on the street.

The kids loved Night-Noon, who joined in all their play as enthusiastically as if she were a child herself. I'd gotten used to Cyrus and Xerxes being laid-back and sedentary in their old age, and Night-Noon's vigor and active nature were delightful, if unfamiliar. The children made up a game that involved being chased by Night-Noon, pretending to trip and fall so she would pounce on them, then giggling hysterically as she washed their faces with her rough pink tongue. I hadn't realized how much I'd missed having a cat around until I sat on the patio watching them all run, laughing whenever Night-Noon broke away from the game to lay her head on my lap for petting.

The oracle remained silent on the subject of elves, barriers, Savants, portals, and adepts. Whenever I attempted a related prophecy, I received incoherent images and a sense of foreboding, the feeling you get when some big event draws near. It wasn't scary, but it left me feeling on edge in moments when I wasn't doing something. So I filled my time with taking care of the kids and chores and fulfilling prophecy requests.

I went in to the office on Tuesday as usual, though there wasn't much to do and I didn't stay long. My phone rang while I was in the elevator going down. "Hi, Judy. What's up?"

"Just wondering if we can switch girls' night to tonight. I know it's short notice, but there's a back to school activity we just found out about that's tomorrow night." Judy sighed. "I can't believe school is starting soon. It feels like summer just started."

"I'm trying not to think about it." We'd just gotten messages from Alastair and Duncan's teachers welcoming us to the new year, though the first day of school wasn't for another two and a half weeks. "Tonight is fine. Same place? Or did you want to take a turn choosing?"

"No, we can do LaserPinz still. If we go a little later, we can do the after dark session." A dull rumble sounded in my ear, and Judy said something that was lost in the noise. "Sorry," she said, more clearly. "I'm just leaving the store, and there's this enormous truck revving its stupid engine practically on top of me. Pick us up tonight?"

"Sure." I hung up just as the elevator doors slid open. My phone rang again almost immediately. I walked to a sheltered corner of the lobby and said, "Merle? Is something wrong?"

"Not exactly," Merle said. "Michael Castellan's office just called, wanting to set up a meeting for the two of you."

A jolt of fear shot through me. I closed my eyes and took a calming breath. "Did they propose a date?"

"No. They asked for you to suggest something 'at your earliest convenience.' I told them you were out of the office and I'd let you know." Merle sounded shaken, which was so out of character for him I felt another jolt of fear.

"I don't want to meet with Mr. Castellan until I have enough information to deal with him on my own terms," I said. "But if I put him off entirely, he'll know something is up." I pinched the bridge of my nose, a gesture that helped me focus. "Don't call back tonight. I'll talk to Malcolm and we'll make a plan."

"Will do," Merle said.

I disconnected again and took a few more calming breaths. Then I dropped my phone into my purse and left the building, walking quickly so no one interested in casual conversation would stop me. I didn't slow down until I got to the land yacht and settled myself behind the wheel. This was the next step in Castellan's plan, I knew from what Stirlaugson had told me. It still felt sinister, as if this was the thing my prophecies had pointed at. Which was probably true. And *that* meant the oracle was preparing me for whatever might come next.

I started the car, but didn't put it into gear. Now was the time to seek out a prophecy—well, not *now*, not when I was about to get on the road, but when I reached home. Then I would talk to Malcolm. Maybe he knew something about Castellan's organization now, and I could use that against the man. Or possibly I needed to speak to Stirlaugson again, to find out what else she'd told Castellan. The idea sickened me, the thought that the head of the Board might be an unwitting ally of our enemy. But there was nothing I could do about that, so instead of worrying, I drove home.

———

"AND you still haven't received a prophecy," Judy said. It was nearly sunset, and the sun's last rays cast half her face in shadow, making her look like an oracle herself, the kind out of Greek myth.

I sighed. "Nothing. Which tells me that whatever looms in the future, I'm already doing what I should with regard to it. The oracle doesn't usually guide me unless a prophecy will steer me in a direction I'm not taking yet."

"Or you're not asking the right question," Viv said. "Hey, it's a possibility, don't give me that look!"

I transferred my scowl to my view of the road ahead. "It's a possibility. I just don't like thinking about it, because then I get frustrated. *I'm* the oracle, after all, and even though I talk like we're separate sometimes, ultimately if I don't get an answer, it's on me. Subconsciously or otherwise. And right now I feel like I'm losing a game of Twenty Questions with myself."

"You're the one who always says it's bad to put all your decisions on prophecies," Judy said. "The oracle isn't going to tell you what to have for lunch. Isn't it more likely that you know, deep down, that these next steps are up to you?"

"Well—" I paused, considering. "Actually, yes. In fact, I think I've been going about this the wrong way. The whole thing with the adepts and the Savants and the barrier is so outside my experience I've been looking to the oracle to not just guide me, but tell me what choices to make. And that's not how it works." I flicked on my turn signal and drove into the LaserPinz parking lot. "I guess I still have things to learn even after ten years."

There weren't many cars in the lot, which made me sad because it was a sign that the bowling alley was going downhill. It still looked as nice as it ever had, which wasn't terribly nice but wasn't seedy or rundown, but fewer people seemed interested in bowling and laser tag than when we'd started coming here years ago. The idea that LaserPinz might disappear sent a pang through my heart, set in its ways as it was.

We'd arrived a few minutes before eight, and the lights went down for Lanes After Dark as we were getting our shoes. This, at least, wasn't going away any time soon, since it was the bowling alley's most popular attraction, so popular they now did it twice a week. I bought sodas for all of us and carried the large cups carefully to the table near our lane. Viv was already entering our names—or, rather, her whimsical nicknames for us.

"-E-R-B-A-L-L," she recited aloud as she tapped out the last of them. "Okay, Tiny Doom, you're up first."

Judy mock-snarled at Viv, but grabbed her bowling ball and walked to the head of the lane. "I'm never letting you pick the names again."

"And yet you never stop me," Viv said airily. "Go on, prove me right."

Another group of bowlers took the spot to our right. I glanced once at them—three men and a woman, their features indistinct in the dim light and glowing neon—then cheered Judy as she took out half the pins in our lane.

"I'm still—" Judy said, then fell silent as one of our neighbors approached the ball return. Every pair of lanes shared a single return, and with seven of us, it was going to get crowded. Judy eyed the man briefly, then said, "I'm still nowhere near as good as Helena. I mean, 'StrikeZone.'"

I glared at Viv while I covered my mouth to hide a smile. "You used that one already."

"I know. I like it. It makes you sound like a supervillain." Viv smirked.

Judy retrieved her ball and managed a spare. On my turn, I had to wait for one of the men to find his ball among all the ones sitting on the ball return. I smiled politely at him, but he didn't smile back, just turned away and ran at his lane like he meant to assault it.

I shrugged and collected my ball. I wasn't so avid a player that I had my own bowling ball, but I was picky about weight and color, and I often chose this one when it was available. Tonight, it felt like a lucky choice, and I bowled an easy strike on my first frame. Viv groaned and stood slowly, as if her ball weighed her down.

"Time for 'Gutterball' to shine," she said.

"You're so pessimistic," I said. "We've been playing for years. You're not terrible, you just think yourself into defeat."

"Thanks so much, Sun Tzu," Viv said without turning around. Sure enough, her first ball curved and dropped into the gutter. So did the second. Viv threw up her hands and dropped heavily back into her seat. "Not letting me use bumpers is just cruel."

"You'll never learn if you depend on the bumpers," Judy and I chorused. Viv groaned.

"There's still nine frames to go," I added, encouragingly though I really did feel Viv sabotaged herself.

I watched our neighbors' lane while Judy warmed up. The four names were Player One, Player Two, Player Three, and Player Four, and since I knew there weren't default names in the system, the foursome had had to choose those names themselves. Weird, but bowling brought out the weird in people. Two of the men were heavyset, one was short and skinny, and the woman was taller than average and moved gracefully, like a ballet dancer. They all bowled in eerie silence, not even offering encouraging comments or grunts of dismay at missing a spare.

"You're up, Helena," Judy said.

I walked over to the ball return and found myself facing the woman. Again, I smiled, though I didn't expect friendliness in return.

The woman gazed at me, not smiling. For a moment, she looked familiar, but I couldn't place her. Then memory intervened, gave her dark glasses and a ponytail, and I sucked in a startled breath. The woman in the red Camry.

My hand jerked away from my ball. "You," I said.

"Me," the woman said. "Don't move."

"I—" I began. The woman's gaze flicked downward briefly, and I looked where she did. My heart gave a thump that shook my whole body at the sight of the small but deadly-looking gun in her hand.

"Don't scream," the woman said, "and you might get out of this alive."

CHAPTER 15

My pulse pounded in my ears in time to the rapid, frightened beat of my heart. Casually, I rested my hand on my bowling ball, hoping I didn't look as scared as I felt. "You're going to shoot me in public? I don't think so."

Now the woman smiled, a nasty, knowing expression that frightened me more. "What, because it will make a commotion and we'll be arrested? You're not that stupid, Ms. Campbell. You know we have the resources to cover anything up."

"Helena, what's the holdup?" Viv called out.

The woman gestured with the gun. "Tell her you have to go to the bathroom."

"She won't believe I wouldn't take my turn first," I said.

My enemy arched one eyebrow. Her brows were thin and flexible and it looked like someone snapping a whip. She tucked her gun into her waistband. "Go ahead. But don't go near them."

I picked up my ball and walked slowly to the head of the lane, rapidly running through possibilities. I took my time lining up my approach, then sent the ball down the lane so it veered to the left and took out only four pins. Viv and Judy made encouraging noises. Mindful of the woman's instructions, I walked back to the ball return to wait. One of the woman's companions was taking his turn, but the woman herself still stood near the ball return, smiling that nasty smile.

"You're slipping," Viv said. "What happened to that perfect game you were going to bowl?"

I shot a glance at the horrible woman, then turned back to my friends. "I guess it's not my night," I said. "Too bad there's no magic to make the ball go where you want. That would be miraculous."

Viv and Judy looked at the empty lane and the six pins clustered at the end. "Miraculous," Judy said. "But I guess that would be an inconsequential use of something powerful."

"Inconsequential was the word I was thinking of, yeah," I replied. My ball rattled up the track, and I hefted it and returned to our lane. My hands were still shaking, but I picked up the spare easily. "I need the bathroom," I said. "Back in a minute." I walked away, leaving my purse behind.

For a second or two, I considered running. My phone was in my pocket; all I needed to do was get far enough ahead of the woman to call Malcolm. But it was possible the woman might shoot someone else out of spite or to convince me she was serious, and I decided not to do anything rash. Instead, I crossed the darkened video arcade to the ladies' restroom and pushed the door open.

I waited inside for only a few seconds before the woman entered. Her gun was still in her waistband, but now that I could see her clearly, how athletic her build was and how she stood like someone used to fighting, I guessed she never depended on her weapon to do violence. Her smile grew when she saw me. "Smart girl," she said. "I might have guessed from how you lost me on the freeway that you were clever. Clever enough not to risk a bullet."

"What do you want?" I asked. I'd stopped shaking and my voice was steady.

"We're going for a little ride," the woman said. "There's someone who wants to talk to you."

"What, Mr. Castellan didn't want to wait on my schedule?" I replied, making an informed guess.

The woman didn't react. "You're going to leave this restroom and walk slowly to the exit. I'll be behind you. You'll get into my car like we're friends. And nobody has to get hurt."

I said nothing. Now that I was calmer, I realized she probably wouldn't have shot me, not if Castellan wanted to talk to me. I might have gotten away with defying her. But I had Judy and Viv to think of, two people this woman wouldn't have any reason to leave unharmed, and the chances of her shooting another person to convince me to go with her were high. I'd have to obey for now, and hope my precautionary measures were enough.

I left the restroom and nearly bumped into one of the woman's companions. He was the short, skinny one who wore his T-shirt untucked over baggy jeans. Aware now that he was an enemy, I checked his waistline and saw the distinctive bulge of a gun's grip. I looked past him, back at where the bowling lanes were just visible, and saw one other thug still where he'd been when I walked away and the second big man headed our way. I couldn't see Judy or Viv at all.

The woman walked past me, jerking her head to indicate I should follow. I did, and the skinny man took up a position behind me. A moment later, the other big guy joined him. I felt like I was being herded, which wasn't an unreasonable feeling given that I was sure the big man was armed as well.

Outside, the woman led me to, not the red Camry, but a late-model Nissan Pathfinder, dull red under the lights of the parking lot. The car chirped as she approached, and she opened the front passenger door and said, "Get in." I climbed in without hesitation and fastened my seatbelt. Part of me screamed at myself for cooperating with my kidnappers, but it was shouted down by my sensible self. I couldn't accomplish anything by fighting except getting hurt, and pretending to be afraid might benefit me, if they believed I was timid and meek. Already they hadn't thought to search me for my phone.

The woman and the men climbed in, the woman behind the wheel, the men in the back seat. The woman started the car and waited. I watched the LaserPinz front door until the third man exited, then turned my attention on the woman, hoping the rest of them wouldn't think to keep watching the front door. The third man climbed in, the woman put the car in gear, and we drove away, as clean a kidnapping as I'd ever feared.

I rested my hands in my lap and said, "Where are we going?"

The woman ignored me. I shrugged and leaned my head against the door frame. "Sit up straight," the woman said.

"Or you'll shoot me?" I replied in my most sarcastic voice. My back pocket buzzed, and I blessed whatever impulse had made me turn off the sound before leaving the house. The vibration was strong, but I couldn't hear the buzz over the sounds of the engine and the tires on the road.

"Don't tempt me," the woman said. "And don't think you're safe just because I'm driving. My friends are all armed, and there are lots of places we can shoot you that won't kill you outright. So if you'd like to see how it feels to lose a kneecap, go ahead and ignore my orders."

I sat up, slowly, just this side of insolence. "What's your name, then?" I asked. "So I'll know who to curse when you shoot me."

"You don't need to know," the woman said. "It's not like we're going out for coffee. Just sit there and be patient. It's a long drive."

"What, no music?"

The woman smiled, but said nothing. She also didn't turn on the radio.

I watched the road ahead. We were going north on the 5, which didn't surprise me. Castellan's operation, his house, even, were in Seattle or thereabouts. It *would* be a long ride.

We crossed the Columbia into Washington and sped through Vancouver without stopping. I sat erect with my hands folded in my lap and considered my predicament. Judy had reacted to my code words with the right response, so she knew I was in trouble and could probably guess it had something to do with the little group at the lane next to ours. She would contact Malcolm, who could track me using my phone —I felt grateful beyond belief that my kidnappers weren't as meticulous as they could have been. And the key fob to the land yacht was in the purse I'd left behind, so Judy and Viv weren't stranded. This kidnapping could have gone a lot worse for me.

The presence of all the guns at my back kept me from falling asleep from the monotony of the drive and the lulling sound of the car's engine. My phone buzzed twice more, then stayed silent, probably because Malcolm knew better than to try to call me where my kidnappers could hear. I amused myself by looking for mile markers and watching the road signs that said how many miles to Seattle, waiting for my captors to become complacent.

We drove for what felt like hours, passing sign after sign. The sign for Enumclaw made me tense again. I hadn't spoken to Cassie since visiting the slip, and I wasn't sure if Malcolm would think to tell her Castellan had kidnapped me. More to the point, I wasn't sure if he *should* contact her. We might be allies, sure, but if they hadn't defeated Castellan in the past, there was no reason to believe they'd be able to now.

I glanced sideways without turning my head, watching the woman out of the corner of my eye. She seemed intent on the road, completely unconcerned about me. I wished I could see the three men, but I didn't want to draw their attention by turning around, and the rearview mirror was angled the wrong way. It was possible they weren't watching me closely, since where could I go? But I was sure even if they were inattentive, they'd come alert if I moved.

I cast my eye on the oncoming sign. SEATTLE 45, it read. I had to take the chance that no one was looking at me, that I'd successfully fooled them into thinking I was harmless because I was trapped in the car at gunpoint. Harmless, maybe, at least as far as wielding a weapon went. I closed my eyes and let a question sink deep within me: *What happens at the end of this road?*

Images welled up like bubbles floating to the surface of a well, silent and vivid. I saw a white room with windowed walls looking out over a watery expanse, dark but streaked with silver where the light from the swollen half-moon touched it. I saw Castellan, dressed casually in jeans and a T-shirt, flickering through half a dozen poses, some where he wielded a gun, some barehanded. I saw Cassie and Gabriel, Malcolm and Viv and Judy, whirling past like ghosts. Memory echoed in my ears, Alastair saying something about choosing between humanity and its enemies. And knowledge sank into my bones: *You will lie, or you will die.* No clue as to what I had to lie about.

I came to myself, blinking, to discover the freeway was wider and the lights were brighter. Instead of forests, buildings rose up on both sides. Traffic surrounded us, light at this hour—it had to be coming up on midnight, though I couldn't see the clock on the car's display—but still heavier than it had been most of the journey. The woman drove faster than the cars around us, probably faster than the speed limit, which angered me. No doubt she had some way of avoiding the cops, or maybe she would kill anyone who dared pull her over. It was stupid of me to hate her for something I was only guessing at, but she'd done enough other things I figured my hatred was justified.

No one said anything to indicate they'd noticed my moment of extreme stillness. I didn't see any more signs but ones indicating street names of freeway exits, so I likely didn't have much more time. I thought briefly, then asked myself the question *What does Castellan want from me?*

Nothing happened. I remembered Castellan's weird ability and wished I could swear aloud. Finding a way around it was something I didn't have enough time for. I pushed my annoyance aside and thought *What use do the Savants have for me?*

The answer came more quickly than the previous one, and in less coherent images. I saw men and women with sharply etched faces who resembled Gabriel, saw dark forests I knew were not earthly, smelled rot and decay and the odor of a house long closed away. Faerie. The vision made no sense. Why the Savants thought I could give them access to Faerie, I couldn't begin to imagine. But I did not doubt the prophecy. At least the oracle was responding now.

In passing, I felt irritated that I hadn't seen anything to prevent my kidnapping, but I knew my gift too well to resent it for any perceived failing. Somehow all this would lead to something important. I hoped I had the strength and understanding to face it, whatever it was.

A few minutes later, the woman exited the freeway and turned west. We drove through nighttime streets, past houses dark except for porch lights here and there. The streets curved seemingly at random, and I didn't bother trying to remember our route. It wasn't as if I'd need to find my way back. However this played out, I was sure I wouldn't return this way.

Eventually the woman drove up a narrow, curved driveway lit by old-fashioned lampposts whose lights flickered as if they were real flames, though they were too white for that. The driveway ended at a small paved area in front of a house, barely big enough for a car to turn around. The woman parked and said, "Don't get out yet."

I continued to sit still while the goons got out of the back seat and the woman came around to my side of the car. She opened the door and bowed, mockingly. "Out."

I obeyed, tugging my shirt down in back to obscure the top of my phone. This time, I paid attention to my surroundings, hoping to see something I could use. My visions might be guiding me to encounter Castellan, but I wasn't going to give up on the possibility of escape.

The house was two stories tall, painted a navy blue that made its outline vague against the midnight sky. From where I stood, I now saw the driveway actually continued on past the house, probably to a garage around the corner, but there were no lights there and that side of the house was in shadow. Many unlit windows lined both stories, their glass catching the lamplight and making the house's frame even less distinct by contrast. Three steps led up to the front door, which was flanked by more windows, these tall and rectangular and filled with leaded glass.

"Seen enough?" The woman's mocking voice made me want to hit her. Her gun was in her hand once more and she waved its muzzle toward the house. "Inside. You're not getting the grand tour."

I followed the skinny man up the steps and waited for him to open the door. The leaded glass was clear, not colored, and each window bore a pattern like a long-stemmed rose in its center. I hadn't expected anything so pretty, and I couldn't help thinking that the house and I had gotten mixed up with the wrong people. Then the skinny man entered, and I had to follow him or risk being jabbed in the ribs with a handgun.

The hall beyond was unlit, the only light coming from the door behind me and another doorway well ahead. My footsteps echoed briefly, telling me this room was very large, and then I stepped onto carpeting that silenced the noise. Behind me, the others entered, and the woman said, "I didn't tell you to stop, Ms. Campbell."

"I can't see anything," I said irritably. "And it's not like I know where to go."

Lights bloomed all around the edges of the room, fat globes in brass sconces like a Victorian mansion's archaic gas lamps. I blinked away tears—I'd accidentally been staring right at one of the globes when it came on—and looked around. The room was even larger than I'd guessed, a full two stories high and thirty feet from where I stood to that other barely-seen door. Stairs to my left, wide and glossy with polish, rose to a landing, turned a right angle, and rose again to a balcony above.

The rug I stood on was patterned in turquoise and rose, and at the sight of it, I finally relaxed, because it was the same pattern as that of the carpet in the elevators at the Board's headquarters, though those were worn from time and thousands of footsteps and this one looked new. Both carpets were equally ugly, though the newness of this one made it even less pleasant to look at, and despite my situation I had to suppress a laugh. Michael Castellan might be dangerous, he might be an immediate threat, but irrationally I had trouble taking seriously anyone who thought this carpet was a good idea.

The cold muzzle of a gun poked me just above my waist, and my stupid mirth vanished. "Now that you can see," the woman said, her voice sarcastic, "you can keep walking. Through that door ahead." I couldn't see her gesture, if she gestured at all, but there really was only one open door, and there was no point playing games with her. Besides, she'd come awfully close to hitting my phone rather than my back, and even though I couldn't get at it now, it was an advantage I didn't want to give up.

So I walked at a normal pace to the doorway, through which a colder, whiter light glowed. My eyes insisted it was moonlight, even though I couldn't feel or smell the night breezes and I knew the door didn't open to the outside. When I entered, however, I realized I was only part right: the room was lit dimly not by electric lights, but by the moon shining through a wall of windows I'd seen in vision only half an hour before.

A man dressed in jeans and a red T-shirt stood in front of the windows with his back to us and his hands clasped loosely behind him. Beyond, a patio gleamed whitely in the moonlight, and past that a dark lawn extended down a short slope to the water's edge. Moonlight glittered on the broken waters of Puget Sound, constantly in motion and black where they weren't silver from the light. I gazed at the man, who did not look familiar, and uncertainty gripped me. I recalled my realization that I didn't know for sure the woman worked for Castellan, and suppose this was some stranger, an enemy I didn't know about? But— no, my vision had clearly showed me—

The man turned to face me. "Ms. Campbell," Michael Castellan said. "I'm glad you saw the wisdom in accepting my invitation. Please, have a seat."

I didn't move. "You have a funny way of delivering an invitation."

"Well, I did intend to wait for you to set the time for our next meeting." Castellan smiled, a friendly, non-threatening smile with no malice in it. "But matters have changed, and I no longer feel the need to wait on your schedule."

"Really?" I said, keeping my tone light though I'd started to feel afraid again. "Why is that?"

Castellan walked toward me, slowly, his hands still clasped behind his back. "Because," he said, "you are going to open a way into Faerie for me."

CHAPTER 16

"Am I?" I said, trying for a light but not insolent tone. I didn't know Castellan well enough to predict what he'd do if he became angry, or if he thought he needed to force me. "Why would I do that?"

"Because you care about humanity," Castellan said. "Whatever else —oh, let's sit, shall we? This whole standing thing, me looming over you, it sets the wrong tone. Please."

I didn't move. "You can tell your goons to stop pointing guns at me. If you're so interested in not setting the wrong tone."

Castellan's gaze focused on someone behind me. "Eris, that's enough. Ms. Campbell isn't going to fight us. And let's have some light in here, Trenton."

A moment later, the overhead lights came on. They were white-tinged daylight bulbs, not warm and welcoming, and while they brightened the room, they didn't change its essential moonlit appearance. With the lights on, the wall of windows became an imperfect mirror, reflecting most of the room and obscuring the outside view. I saw one of the big guys at the door, next to a light switch, and the woman, Eris, stood behind me, just sliding her gun into her waistband. The image wasn't clear enough for me to make out expressions, at least not when the person was far from the glass, but I didn't need to see her face to know she was smiling that horrible smug smile again.

White leather-upholstered sofas and chairs surrounded a glass-topped coffee table, as old-fashioned as the awful rug. Castellan took a seat with his back to the windows, and after a moment, I sat opposite him. The carpet was as white as the furniture, and I wished briefly that my shoes were muddy so I could track dirt all over its pristine whiteness. It was a stupid wish, but I felt cold and frightened inside despite the oracle's assurances—though it hadn't assured me I would get through this unharmed, so fear might be justified.

Castellan rested his elbow on the arm of the sofa and leaned his head against his hand. "Ms. Campbell—Helena, may I call you Helena?"

"I'd rather you didn't, Mr. Castellan." I leaned back and crossed my arms over my chest.

He smiled, a somewhat sad, regretful expression. "We're on the same side, you know."

"My allies don't need to force me to go somewhere at gunpoint." I was walking a fine line, but much as I didn't want to antagonize this man, I couldn't bear to cooperate with him like a coward.

Castellan shrugged. "You've been told enough lies about me that I was sure you wouldn't agree to come without a little incentive. They wouldn't have shot."

I said nothing, but I glanced at Eris's reflection in the glass. She stood close behind me, close enough that she could grab me if I tried to flee. Even that imperfect mirror told me she would have enjoyed shooting me.

"At any rate, I apologize," Castellan continued. "I'm afraid the situation is dire enough I had to act first and hope to gain your forgiveness afterward. But that's not important. What matters is I need your help."

"Again, why should I help you? Even if I excuse the kidnapping, I know who you are. And I know your Savants want to conquer Faerie."

"So?" Castellan sounded surprised. "You know nothing about Faerie—you only learned of its existence recently. Why should you care what happens to creatures who are determined to eradicate humanity?"

"Because genocide is wrong, no matter who you're exterminating," I shot back. "And you aren't altruistic. You want Faerie's magic so you can dominate this world."

"That's Cassandra Leighton talking." Castellan didn't sound angry, or scornful, or anything but calm, as if we'd been discussing something innocuous like gardening or the weather. "She and her people know nothing of my goals. And you have been brainwashed by her. Suppose I told you we have humanity's best interests at heart?"

"You'd have to prove that."

"I can, and I will." Castellan laced his fingers together and rested them on his knee. "Astraeus Resources seeks the same things your corporation does, Ms. Campbell, but—if you'll excuse me—on a much, much larger scale than you're capable of. Not only do we maintain charitable organizations, we fund research into clean energy, improved food production, better sanitation in impoverished regions—things that improve the quality of life everywhere."

"That's laudable. It doesn't excuse destroying someone else's world."

"Doesn't it?" Castellan leaned forward. "Then what *would* excuse that? Is it only when the enemy is monstrous aliens that suck the magic out of human beings that genocide is justified, Ms. Campbell? Is that the excuse you tell yourself?"

His words hit me like a brick to the face, shocking me so my entire body was numb for a moment. Castellan's expression was no longer neutral, but fierce, as if we were battling with weapons and not words.

I regained control of myself. "Who told you that?" I asked, stalling for time. Of all the things I'd imagined Castellan bringing to bear on me, my past was not one of them.

"Does it matter, if it's true? You destroyed an entire alien civilization for the sake of protecting humanity. How are we any different?"

I swallowed. "The invaders were mindless creatures, incapable of being reasoned with, and there was no other way to protect this world. Elves are intelligent beings—"

"Who also can't be reasoned with."

"It's been a thousand years since anyone's spoken to them. You can't know that."

"It's not a risk I'm willing to take." Castellan sat back. "My point is, you understand as no one else does how committed I am to guarding my fellow humans. I hoped to convince you that what I intend will benefit humanity."

I shook my head. "No," I whispered, then in a louder voice, "no. Mr. Castellan, I'm willing to give you the benefit of the doubt that your motives are pure. You're right, I know Cassie and Gabriel's side of the story, not yours. But I disagree with your conclusions. I won't help you—"

I was about to add *even if I could,* and a spontaneous prophecy filled me, warning me to say no more. I blinked and hoped that hadn't taken long enough that Castellan had noticed.

Castellan watched me, his expression neutral again. "I see," he said. Then he grabbed my hand, too swiftly for me to evade him. "You won't tell me how you opened a portal to Faerie?"

Again, I wondered madly where he'd learned all of this. "I won't," I said. "Though I wish you would tell me who told you this. About the portal, and the invaders."

He smiled. "Wondering who among your allies is the traitor?"

"It's a natural curiosity, don't you think?"

"I do. But most of what I know, I learned through investigation." His smile broadened. "And Ms. Stirlaugson was forthcoming about the rest. About the invaders, and the Long War. Ah, you look as if you believe she betrayed you. How is that secret information, any more than your knowledge of my group's activities is?"

I opened my mouth to protest, shut it again. He was right; those things didn't have to be secret. It was only that he'd turned my part in ending the Long War into a weapon aimed at my heart that I was resentful. "All right, maybe not," I said. "I'm used to not revealing anything about the magical world, but it's true, you're part of that world too, even if we didn't know anything about each other until recently. But that still leaves us at an impasse. I don't agree that destroying Faerie is necessary—and, fine, maybe that makes me a hypocrite. It's still how I feel. And I plan to act accordingly."

"I see." Castellan released me and sat back. "Then you're right. It's an impasse. And I'd prefer—"

Behind me, Eris raised a hand to her ear as if touching an earbud. I hadn't noticed one, but I'd been distracted during most of our interactions. Then she nodded. "Sir, the perimeter guard caught someone."

My heart sank. I knew Malcolm wouldn't let himself be seen by whoever was guarding this place, and his people were equally sneaky. But they weren't the only ones who might have followed me. I closed my eyes briefly and sent up a fervent prayer that Viv and Judy hadn't been stupid.

Castellan glanced at me. "A rescuer? How noble. Eris, have the intruder brought here."

Eris nodded and turned away, speaking in a low voice words I couldn't understand. The big guy near the door, Trenton, left the room without a word. My heart hammered painfully against my ribs. Castellan clearly believed I had the capacity to bypass the barrier, and I didn't intend to reveal the truth. As long as he remained ignorant, I could play for time until Malcolm showed up. But if Viv was here, and Castellan discovered she was actually the one with the power, I was certain he would use me to manipulate her.

"I hope you weren't counting on a rescue," Castellan was saying, and I brought my attention back to him. "My people are very good. But I'm glad you aren't the helpless heroine you're pretending to be. Someone who can destroy an entire species shouldn't cower before a merely human threat."

"You said you didn't intend to hurt me. *Are* you a threat?"

"It was a figure of speech." He waved a hand casually in the air. "You must have tremendous magical power to have managed it. Ms. Stirlaugson wouldn't tell me any details about you, but I could fill in the gaps. No wonder you were able to bypass the barrier."

That explained a lot about his misconceptions. "I'm surprised you aren't afraid of me, knowing how powerful I am," I said.

"You don't strike me as a violent person," Castellan said. "If you were, you'd have taken over the world by now. No, for whatever reason, you choose to hide your gift. I wish you'd consider joining me. You could do so much more than these small donations."

"Not likely." I clasped my hands to still their shaking. Castellan's calm assurance frightened me. It felt as if he knew secrets he wasn't telling me—well, that was probably true, but I was sure he was withholding information until the moment revealing it would hurt me or the Wardens most.

Footsteps sounded outside, and I turned, not caring if it made me look vulnerable. Trenton entered, followed by Judy and Viv and then the other big guy. My friends didn't seem hurt, and they weren't restrained, but Judy looked angry and Viv was biting her lip the way she did when she was uncertain. Both of them stared at me as if checking to see if *I* was okay.

"Two of them! They don't look like much of a threat." Castellan stood. "Who are you?"

"My friends," I said, quickly enough to override Viv and Judy's replies. "They were with me when you kidnapped me."

"We shouldn't have gotten so close," Judy said. "I'm sorry, Helena."

"It's all right," I said. "Mr. Castellan, please, let them go. They don't have anything to do with this."

"Oh. So they don't know who you are?" Castellan tilted his head curiously. "I suppose you don't want to enlighten them?"

My relief that Castellan's information gathering hadn't included my best friends soured when Viv said, "We're Wardens. Don't think you can play us off against each other."

"I see." Castellan resumed his seat. "And what are your positions in the organization?"

Judy and Viv said nothing.

"Interesting," Castellan said. "You realize I don't actually care. It's Ms. Campbell whose power matters to my plans. So unless one of you knows how to open the barrier to Faerie..."

Viv's eyes widened, and her mouth fell open. I squeezed my eyes shut and silently cursed. She had the worst poker face I'd ever seen.

Castellan sat upright. "You do," he said. "I wasn't serious, but it looks like I found a secret." He stood again and walked slowly toward Viv, looking like a predator approaching a creature that might be edible. "What do you know about the barrier?"

"Like I'm going to tell you," Viv said.

Judy elbowed her in the side, a clear command for Viv to shut up. Castellan continued to approach until he was just inches from Viv. "You know something, clearly. I wonder—"

"She's lying," I said. "She's pretending she knows something so you'll leave me alone."

Castellan looked back at me. "You know, I don't think that's true," he mused. "She was honestly surprised just now, and she doesn't act like someone who conceals her feelings. I think...I think maybe I have things the wrong way around."

"Really?" I said. "You think some random Warden, someone not even important enough to show up in your investigation, can do more than I can?" My memory of the oracle's insistence that I lie inspired me. "How do you think I reached Faerie, then?"

But Castellan was watching Viv, who twitched visibly every time I lied. "You didn't," he said. "She did."

"No—"

"That's enough out of you. I respect your power, even if it's not what I need, but I despise liars." He grabbed Viv's chin and held her so she looked right into his eyes. "How did you do it?"

Viv's lips pinched tight together, but I could see fear in the way her eyes moved, as if she was frantically looking for an exit.

Castellan squeezed her face harder. "I will learn the truth eventually," he said. "You can make this easy, or you can regret making it hard."

Viv shook her head as best she could against his grip. "I won't."

Castellan released her and stepped away. "Final chance, Ms. Campbell. It's humanity or its enemies. You have to choose."

I glared at him. "You're the only enemy of humanity here. We won't help you."

Castellan's eyes narrowed. "Eris," he said. "Shoot the other one."

He said it so dispassionately I didn't understand his words until Eris drew her gun. Then I lurched up from my seat, throwing myself at Eris. I hadn't taken two steps before the gunshot split the air like thunder striking indoors. Judy screamed and collapsed. I dove at Eris as Viv dropped to Judy's side. Instantly, Eris trained her gun on me, and I froze. "Sounds like we don't need you anymore," she said.

"Don't shoot her, Eris, I've made my point," Castellan said.

I turned on him, fists clenched. "You bastard," I said, grinding out the words so I wouldn't launch myself at his face. "You didn't need to do that."

"Of course I did," Castellan said. "Your friend here needed the right incentive. Now she knows I'm serious about gaining her knowledge."

I fell to my knees beside Judy, who was whiter than usual and whose face was scrunched in pain. She clutched her side, where a dark red stain spread beneath her fingers. Viv removed her multicolored silk scarf from around her neck and tried to move Judy's fingers to press the cloth against the wound. I helped Viv pry Judy's fingers loose from her side, whispering, "It will be all right. Malcolm will be here soon."

Judy nodded, the faintest motion of her head. "...damned posturing Savant..." she murmured.

I sat back on my heels. "Now what? You've proved you're a lying bastard who doesn't actually believe the nonsense he spouts about protecting humanity. You going to shoot me, too?"

Castellan regarded me silently for a moment, his expression unreadable. Finally, he said, "I'm even more curious about your power than before. No, I think you'll come with us. Eris, Tommy, bring them both."

"Both?" Viv said. Her face was streaked with tears, but her voice was strong.

"Leave the wounded one. Whoever is following Ms. Campbell can deal with her."

"Don't you *dare*," I said, rising to my feet and taking three rapid steps to face him. "If she dies—"

"Oh, please, spare me your dramatics," Castellan said. "Eris is an excellent shot. The woman won't die if your Campbell Security people are quick, and my information says they're competent, for such a small organization." He smiled. "What, you thought I didn't know? Half the point of abducting you was to involve those who might otherwise interfere with my work in a distraction. Now. Give me your phone."

I glared at him, but despair had flooded through me, and it made defiance seem both pointless and wearying. I pulled my phone out of my back pocket and slapped it into his palm, hard enough to sting, I hoped.

Castellan smiled more broadly, as if I'd given him a wonderful present. He walked to the wall of windows and opened a glass door that fitted into the frame so perfectly I hadn't seen it. Then he stood in the open doorway and flung my phone away like tossing a frisbee. "That will keep them focused on this place. That, and how open I was about my address. Obviously, this isn't my real house."

That made me feel even worse. Castellan had played us the whole time. I felt so stupid at how casually I'd assumed he didn't have any idea what our investigation had revealed.

My despair must have shown on my face, because Castellan laughed —not a mocking sound, but the laugh of someone genuinely amused and hoping others would share in the joke. "I thought you Wardens knew more than you apparently did. Well, that will teach me to overestimate my opponents. Eris, bring the pink-haired one—so dramatic a statement, pink hair. I'd call it feisty, but you certainly crumbled fast, didn't you?"

He took my arm and marched me to the door leading to the enormous entry hall. I only fought him briefly. It didn't take despair to tell me fighting was pointless. I heard Viv shout, and looked back to see her fighting Eris while trying to keep her hand pressed against Judy's side. Eris cracked the butt of her pistol across Viv's face, snapping her head back.

"Stop!" I shouted. "Viv, don't!"

"She's going to die if we leave her here," Viv gasped. Eris wrenched her arm behind her back and hauled her up.

"It's not a bad wound," Castellan said. "And you should worry more about yourself than your friend. Let's go."

I stared back at Judy, lying curled in a pool of blood on the white carpet, and felt sick. If Malcolm didn't hurry...but there was nothing more I could do for Judy now.

Outside, a dozen goons waited, all of them armed, and there were three other SUVs besides the red Nissan. This time, Michael opened the door of the Pathfinder for me. I climbed in, frantically going over options. He had the keys, so I couldn't make a break for it. There were too many goons for me to run away. And running away would mean leaving Viv, who looked too shaken to react. That was good, because unlike me, Viv knew how to fight, and we'd already seen that fighting these people would get her hurt or maybe even killed, never mind what Castellan said about needing her.

Eris shoved Viv into the back seat and climbed in after her. Castellan got behind the wheel, and I heard the faint but terrible sound of the door locks engaging. "Where are we going?" I said, wishing I didn't sound so weak.

Castellan started the car. Behind us, men and a few women piled into the other vehicles. "We're going to save the human race," he said. "And you're going to make it possible."

I didn't know which of us he'd addressed, but it didn't matter. As far as Castellan was concerned, both of us would help him, or both of us would die.

CHAPTER 17

We drove back the way Eris had brought us, back to the freeway. This time, I leaned to the side, pressing my face against the glass. Castellan didn't order me to sit up. He obviously didn't think anything I might do was a threat. Well, that felt true. I remembered my last sight of Judy and squeezed my eyes shut against tears. Crying wouldn't help any of us. But the oracle might.

I calmed myself, made myself stop thinking of Judy and the possibility that Castellan was right and he'd sidetracked our potential rescuers. I had to assume Viv and I were on our own, and I was not going to wait around like a helpless maiden for a rescue. I glanced swiftly at Castellan, whose attention was on the road ahead, then closed my eyes. With luck, he would think I was deep in despair. He hadn't struck me as the type to gloat, so I was probably safe from him striking up conversation. Right now, our only advantage was that he didn't know about the oracle.

Breathing slowly and not too deeply, I considered my options. I settled on *How can we escape?* and let the question settle deep into my bones. Immediately the image of a wooded clearing appeared behind my eyelids, more brightly lit than the moon could manage. I didn't try to find the source of the lights. My attention was drawn to a glow hanging in midair, golden and sparkling and familiar. No door frame surrounded it, but my visions rarely showed every detail, just the ones that mattered.

As I watched, the golden barrier parted like a curtain being drawn back, revealing blackness so complete it sucked at my eyeballs even though it wasn't physically there. Three breaths later, the curtain descended, and I came swimming up to full awareness.

The car was still silent except for the sound of the tires on the road. I risked a glance at Castellan, but he didn't look as if he was waiting for an answer to a question I hadn't heard. That was good, because my heart was pounding and I was sure I'd sound like an out-of-breath runner if I tried to speak. The prophecy had been unambiguous for once. Escape meant opening the barrier.

Despite my many years' experience with the oracular gift and its accuracy, my mind threw up all sorts of objections. Opening the barrier was what we did *not* want to do. It would help the Savants conquer Faerie and it would lead to the elves invading our world. What was more, I had no idea how to do it. Viv's scrying had connected our world and Faerie briefly, bypassing the barrier—the barrier itself hadn't been affected.

The more I thought about it, the more I understood the prophecy's instructions, though. If Viv opened a portal, it would let humans pass, but the barrier would still prevent the elves from leaving. And that was exactly what Castellan wanted. So the only answer was to give elves and humans equal access...except that was likely to destroy two worlds, and I fought the idea even though it had been the oracle's and not mine.

I opened my eyes to discover we'd left the freeway behind for a smaller, two-lane highway similar to the one that paralleled the Washougal River. Trees grew close to the road, too close for my comfort, though the closeness was probably an illusion that rose from how dark it was. The moonlight that had shone on the water outside Castellan's house didn't reach beneath the trees' branches. We drove in a moving pool of light made by the car's headlights that reached just far enough ahead to keep me from feeling we might miss a sharp turn and drive headlong off the road.

I swiveled in my seat to look behind us, not at Viv and Eris but through the back window. The three other cars were still there, or at least I assumed all three were, because I could only see the one right behind us and, past it, the lights of another. Hope tried to rise within me, and I suppressed it. Castellan might only have a dozen goons, but I had no idea how many people Malcolm might bring, and they might still be outnumbered.

I stopped looking out the rear window, and my eyes met Viv's. She no longer looked uncertain, but angry. A vivid purple-black welt high on her cheekbone looked even more vicious against her pale skin. She jerked her head in Eris's direction, the smallest motion. I turned to Eris, who was watching me. I wanted to punch that smug smile off her face. "Plotting an escape?" Eris said.

"Not much point to that, is there?" I said, trying to sound defiant in a way that would make me seem even less of a threat. I had no idea how we might escape if the oracle's solution wasn't possible, but if they underestimated me, so much the better.

"Don't think I'm going to relax just because you're pathetic," Eris said, sneering. I ignored her and turned back around.

"Eris, that's unnecessary. Ms. Campbell is cooperating. So is her friend—I'm sorry, we weren't introduced. I'm Michael Castellan."

Viv said nothing. Eris jabbed her in the side with her pistol, making Viv squeak. "It's all right," I said. "It's not like our names are state secrets."

"Viv," Viv said, sounding resentful.

"Well, Viv, I'm glad you were willing to see sense." Castellan sounded as cheerful as if we were all good friends. Now he was the one I wanted to punch.

I settled back against the window and closed my eyes. Time to try again. *Where is Malcolm?*

Again, I felt the swooping sensation of a prophecy enfolding me. This time, I saw the landscape from above, as if I were a bird flying in great circles. Forests lay beneath me, as far as my vision reached, with no houses or roads to break the unrelieved foliage. My mind's eye drew back, and the forest turned into a drawing of a forest—no, a map, but not a modern map, something old drawn on yellowing parchment. Small circles, three of them, were drawn on the forest seemingly at random, one red, one white, and one yellow. My eye was attracted to the white circle, and I knew instinctively this was Malcolm. Then the vision faded.

Frustrated, I let out a deep breath, and immediately regretted it when Castellan said, "Something wrong, Ms. Campbell?"

"Just wishing I'd never met you," I lied.

Castellan laughed. "You don't think we would have encountered each other eventually? My group and yours, I mean?"

"I don't know. But you're dragging me and my friend into your plot. Why shouldn't I resent that?"

"I suppose that's reasonable." Castellan focused on his rearview mirror. "Do you agree, Viv?"

"Of course," Viv said. "And if Judy dies, you'd better believe we'll come after you."

"I told you, she'll be fine. Well, obviously not *fine*, not with that hole in her side, but she'll survive it." Castellan looked at me. "So, how did you do it? How did you destroy an entire alien species?"

I hated the way he said that, as if the invaders hadn't been bent on human destruction and I'd made a selfish choice. "Magic."

That made him laugh harder. "All right, I deserved that," he finally said. "You don't want to tell me? Afraid I might come up with a use for you, after all?"

That chilled me, the thought that to him I was nothing more than a tool. I didn't want to give him any hints as to how that tool could be used, even though I didn't know what he could make of that knowledge. I already knew better than to underestimate Michael Castellan. "It's complicated. I can't explain how it happened."

"Don't withhold information, Ms. Campbell. Eris could still shoot you."

"More threats. You still want to pretend you're not my enemy?" I glared at him.

"I don't care anymore what you think of me. You don't understand the value of my work." Castellan shook his head, slowly, as if despairing over an ignorant child's tantrum. "I *will* protect Tempus from Faerie, and I'll do whatever it takes to make that happen. If you stand in my way—"

"I get it. Don't bother." I sighed. "Look, it really was too complicated to explain. The truth is, I don't understand myself everything that happened when I destroyed the invaders' reality. Sometimes, looking back, I wonder if I even had any control over that destruction." Lying to Castellan felt good, like striking back in the only way left to me.

"I see," Castellan said. I waited for more questions, but he fell silent, so I returned to looking out the window at the trees rushing past.

I reviewed what the oracle knew. Escape by removing the barrier. Malcolm was somewhere in the forest—this forest, I hoped—but knowing his location wouldn't help me, or that vision would have been clearer. What else could I ask? Well, as long as I was desperate, I could ask a desperate question: *How do I stop the Savants from destroying Faerie and taking its magic?*

The swooping feeling dizzied me even more than before, and my hand closed convulsively on the door handle, though it couldn't steady me. Colors swirled around and through me, and I was reminded of the invaders' reality, how my mind had perceived it as filled with colors that felt deeply unnatural and wrong. Except I didn't have that feeling now; instead, I felt poised on the brink of a hill, atop the steepest, highest roller coaster ever built, waiting for the plunge.

Then it came. I fell, and instead of fear I felt exhilarated, like I was flying instead of falling. Images flashed past so rapidly I barely recognized any of them. I saw Night-Noon, or a cat that looked just like her; saw the trees of Faerie with their tiny, odd flowers; saw buildings whose shapes were subtly alien; saw masses of people, tall and lithe with sculpted faces. Then the barrier appeared again, and this time it was ragged, like a shredded curtain, and the space in its center was even blacker than before. That vanished, and now I heard voices speaking in a language I didn't understand, a language that didn't sound like any foreign language I'd heard before.

"Helena," Viv said, sounding alarmed.

I jerked alert. "What?"

"I asked about your family," Castellan said. "Were you asleep?" He sounded skeptical, like he knew I couldn't have been asleep but couldn't think of any other reason why I'd ignore his question.

"I'm not telling you about my family," I snapped, "so don't ask. Besides, you've already investigated me, so you know all the answers already." I hoped my hostility would conceal my fear. Castellan had no reason to suspect I was an oracle just because I'd been in a trance, or whatever that had looked like. Damn him for interrupting that vision before I understood it.

"For a small organization, your Wardens are remarkably thorough," Castellan said, sounding impressed. "Nothing we did penetrated the illusions and misdirections you set up. All we were able to find were hints, here and there—you have children, I'm sure—"

I turned on him, snarling. "Don't. You think you're clever, taunting me with how special and amazing your organization is, but if you make this personal, I will find a way to destroy you."

Castellan's eyebrows raised. "So fierce! I suppose you think we should have some kind of gentlemen's agreement, no involving our personal lives? That sort of thing is so nineteenth century, pistols at dawn and so forth."

"I don't care what you call it. And I'm not interested in making an agreement with you. I'm telling you how it's going to be."

Castellan pursed his lips in thought. "I can let you have the illusion that you have any degree of control, I suppose. When Faerie lies open to us, you won't matter anymore."

I rested my forehead against the glass, which was cold and felt a little sticky, probably because my anger had me sweating. If he made my children pawns in this horrible nightmare, I would stop him. I'd killed once, to protect myself and avenge Malcolm, and the memory still made me ill on occasion, when it caught me off-guard, but I knew what I was capable of, and Castellan didn't. Yet.

The car slowed, and then Castellan turned right onto a rutted dirt road not much wider than a game trail. Viv gasped, and I glanced back to see her eyes widen as she looked past me out the windscreen. Then her eyes met mine and narrowed in warning. She said, "You drove us off the road! This car can't possibly make its way through *all those trees*."

I immediately turned around and made myself grip the door handle with one hand and the front edge of my seat with the other, pretending to be scared. I'd forgotten my other advantage, the ability to see through illusions, and Viv's warning came just in time not to give away that I could see the actual road.

"It's an illusion," Castellan said. "We'll be past it soon." He didn't sound suspicious at all, but I didn't relax my grip or the stiffness of my body until he said, "There, see? The illusion doesn't have to last long, just enough to distract any random hikers."

To me, the road looked just as it always had, a narrow path with matted grass growing down its center so it looked like two strips of rutted, dried mud. The Pathfinder bounced along the road, and now I had to hold on to keep myself from being tossed out of my seat despite my seatbelt. The jolting was severe enough to keep us all silent, and I closed my eyes and decided to try once more. *How do I stop the Savants from destroying—*

The car slowed to a stop, and my eyes flew open. I sat up, slowly, unable to believe what I saw. We'd come to a halt in a clearing big enough to be a football field, surely too big to be natural in a forest this size. Many other vehicles were parked nearby, and "vehicle" was the right word, because with the exception of a few full-size pickup trucks, all of them were Army surplus Humvees or Jeeps. Tall lights on stands circled the clearing, shedding the kind of bright light I associated with stadiums or airport runways. Olive-green and khaki tents, more military-grade supplies, occupied the far end of the clearing, some larger than others. My assessment of the Savants' operation changed instantly. This wasn't a corporation, it was a paramilitary organization.

Castellan turned the engine off and said, "Let me show you around."

"What, like a tour?" I said.

"If you like," Castellan said. "I want you to understand what we're capable of. I'm sure it won't convince you that I'm right, but maybe it will ease your mind to know we can defend humanity against the elves." He got out of the car without waiting for Viv or me. I didn't think there was any point in defying him. It wasn't even fear that he or Eris would shoot us; there wasn't anywhere else to go.

I followed Castellan as the other SUVs in our convoy pulled up and their passengers emerged. A quick glance told me what I hadn't seen in the relative darkness in front of Castellan's house—all of his goons were dressed plainly in dark clothes, not quite fatigues but definitely not ordinary jeans and T-shirts. Castellan in his casual attire looked out of place next to them.

Viv moved to walk close beside me. She opened her mouth, and I said, "Don't say anything. He'll hear us."

"So wise, Ms. Campbell," Castellan said without turning around. He gestured at the clearing. "We're prepared for an initial incursion. Nothing big, a few dozen armored assault vehicles and about a hundred and fifty men—speaking generally, of course, since we don't discriminate on the basis of sex."

"How forward-thinking of you," I said.

"Your hostility is growing tiresome," Castellan said, but he didn't sound angry, more like he was reading lines from some supervillain's script. "We've developed weapons my researchers are convinced will work against elves. You know the legend about cold iron? Since we couldn't capture Gabriel Roarke for testing, we're not sure how much validity it has, but most things will be killed by the application of enough force."

More men and a few women in those paramilitary clothes walked past us, not apparently in a hurry. They didn't acknowledge us, didn't even acknowledge Castellan, and I was going to comment on that when Viv said, "What's that?" in such an alarmed voice I looked at her rather than where she was pointing. She didn't seem to notice me, but I felt her hand grab mine and pass me something hard and rectangular. I swiftly shoved the phone into my back pocket and tugged my shirt over it.

Eris and Castellan weren't watching us; they were looking at the missile mounted on the back of one of the larger vehicles. "A precaution," Castellan said. "We don't expect to use it, but it's sensible to prepare for the worst, right?" He resumed walking, and Viv and I followed. I was acutely conscious of Eris walking behind me, within sight of the phone I now carried if I hadn't been careful enough. Why Viv had risked revealing that we still had something Campbell Security could track, I didn't know. Possibly she'd thought that Castellan's attention would be more on her than on me now, and no one would think to search me for a second phone. In any case, the pressure of the phone on my backside made me feel more secure than I had in hours.

Castellan swept through the camp without paying attention to the activity around him. I didn't know anything about the military to judge what everyone was doing, but I was sure I saw much fewer than a hundred and fifty "soldiers." I wished I had Malcolm's eye, to judge how dangerous the situation was. Then I made myself stop thinking of him. He was nearby, somewhere, but without knowing where or how close he was, I had to act as if he might not get here in time. Not that I knew what "in time" meant, either.

The far end of the clearing looked like a solid wall of trees, their leaves picked out starkly by the white lights. It wasn't until we were within ten feet of it that I realized there was a gap. The gap was even narrower than the rutted path that had led here and showed signs of heavy foot traffic, grinding down any grass or plants that might once have grown there. Trees leaned in on both sides, their smaller branches snapped off as if whoever had used the path had grown impatient with how the leaves brushed against them. Beneath the trees, it was much darker, and soon we'd left the lights behind and I was feeling my way, waiting for my eyes to adjust.

Castellan walked with the same assurance with which he'd crossed the clearing, as if his vision wasn't impaired. I stumbled once and caught myself by grabbing one of those broken branches, which bent beneath my weight and almost made me fall again. Castellan didn't stop. Eris, behind me, nudged my back with something cold and hard. I managed not to turn on her.

The path made a couple of S curves, rising slightly, and then came out in another clearing equally brightly lit. My mouth fell open. Vaguely, I was aware of more paramilitary types handling large weapons or fussing with portable electronics. Eris nudged me again, but I ignored her. All my attention was on the structure at the center of the clearing.

It was made of brushed steel beams welded together at the corners to make a doorway easily thirty feet high and half that wide. Tiny lights coursed like traces of liquid fire up and down the uprights, pale blue and green and yellow the color of starlight. My mind tried to turn it into something normal, a modern art sculpture wrapped in Christmas lights or a prop on a Hollywood set, anything to help me comprehend it. It was absurd and at the same time it was the most real thing I'd ever seen.

"Our doorway to Faerie," Castellan said. "Magnificent, isn't it?"

CHAPTER 18

"Amazing," I breathed.

"There aren't many slips under our control," Castellan said, sounding smug. "Not because we lack the resources, but because we have requirements that aren't easily met. They have to be close to our centers of power, for one, and isolated enough to move materiel to."

"You can't use illusions?" Viv asked.

She'd sounded scornful, but Castellan ignored her tone of voice and answered straightforwardly. "I'm sure Cassandra Leighton has already claimed we can't use magic as easily as her group does. But the truth is, using magic when you don't have to is foolishness. We use our magical resources sparingly. There's no point making an illusion to conceal a convoy of military vehicles when you can move openly instead."

"Makes sense," I said, but my attention was still on the doorway. It wasn't active the way Gabriel's doorway had become through Cassie and Milo's magic, just looked like a doorway from one side of the clearing to another. As I watched, one of the Savants walked through it, her attention on the tablet she held, without seeming to realize where she was.

I recalled Gabriel's doorway, the simple tree trunks lashed together with hairy rope, compared that memory to what I saw now, and felt an unexpected pang. I'd wanted to believe anything the Savants created was evil, but their doorway gave off a sense of permanence that felt reassuring, not at all sinister. I didn't know what to make of that.

"So, Viv," Castellan said, in a cheerful voice. "What do you need?"

Viv glared at him.

Eris raised her gun and aimed, not at Viv, but at me. "Better reconsider," she said.

I ignored Eris, though I wanted to point out that using a weapon to constantly demand compliance just meant that threat lost potency over time. "I don't think we have a choice," I said.

Viv rolled her eyes. "The portal has to be active first."

"Of course," Castellan said. "Stand over there—though you're not elves, so it doesn't really matter where you stand." He waved in the direction of the gap in the forest we'd entered by. Viv and I walked to where we could still see the doorway clearly. Eris, to my relief, didn't follow. There were a few paramilitary goons near enough to hear us talk, but none of them looked interested in us. Castellan caught my eye and smiled, a smug expression that told me he knew he'd given us a chance to plot and didn't think we were a threat.

Even so, Viv said, "Now what?" out of the side of her mouth, not facing me as if we could have a private conversation that way.

"You don't have your gear," I said, quietly. Viv's caution was rubbing off on me. "Is it even possible?"

"I can think of a way. But should I? I don't want to help these bastards." Viv's hands were clenched, and while I couldn't see her face clearly because her flip was in the way, I'd seen her stubborn expression often enough to imagine it now.

"I don't know." I lowered my voice even more. "The oracle says the way we escape is through destroying the barrier."

"The barrier? Not making a path through the portal?"

I nudged Viv to remind her to keep her voice down. "No. Actually getting rid of the barrier. If it wasn't the oracle, I wouldn't believe it."

"I suppose that means equal opportunity invasion, not one world being trapped while it's invaded by the other."

"That was my thought." I surveyed the clearing. People were moving more rapidly, running from one side of the clearing to the other. Most of them carried metal boxes, but a few held devices I didn't recognize, strange glass tubes connected to rubber squares or long ribbed hoses that ran through what looked like pressurized metal containers, like oxygen tanks only crescent shaped instead of oblong.

Every so often, someone hurried to the doorway and deposited a load there. Five men knelt or crouched at the base of the left-hand upright of the door, apparently assembling... something. Their bodies obscured whatever they were working on, but I caught glimpses of something the same metallic color as the doorway, along with those mysterious devices. One long ribbed hose, fat enough I didn't think I could wrap my hand around it, coiled up the length of the upright and attached to an extrusion near the top. I couldn't tell if it was an opening, like a vent, or a hook or something, but the hose looked like it was plugged into the doorway.

"That's not much of a solution, though," Viv murmured. "Since neither of us knows how to do that."

"I was hoping for inspiration when I see the barrier again." I was hoping for more than inspiration. Malcolm and his people bursting into the clearing, maybe, or the Savants being unable to open a portal. But those were unlikely events, and except for Viv's presence, I was back to where I'd been when Eris kidnapped me—on my own.

"I can keep their attention on me, if that helps." Viv pushed her flip back from her face, tucking it behind her ear. "You know they'll kill us once we've done what they ask."

"I know."

"That was discouraging. Sorry."

"No. I don't plan on letting them do it." Though, again, the odds were not in my favor.

Castellan approached the men near the doorway. I saw his lips move, though he was too far away for me to hear, and one of the men replied. The man wore a white knit cap that covered all his hair, much too warm for this weather, and ordinary vinyl gloves like I wore when I washed dishes. Those and the hat made him look like a cafeteria lady. Castellan said something else, nodded, and walked in our direction.

"Almost ready," he said, still in that horrible cheerful voice I hated.

"I take it you've seen a portal activated before. Do your adept friends do it differently?"

Viv and I remained silent. I figured giving Castellan any information, even information I didn't know how he could use, would be a mistake.

Castellan chuckled. "So wise of you. That's all right, I don't actually care. It's not as if my people can do this any other way. And our way is more efficient." He faced the doorway, turning his back on me. "Watch. They'll start soon."

I kept my eyes, not on the space within the doorway, but on the men still crouched beside it. They'd coiled another, skinnier hose around the base, but this one's end was loose and lay disregarded on the ground a few feet from the men. Then, one by one, they stood and backed away until only the man with the cafeteria lady gloves still knelt by the contraption. I craned to see past him. Lights blinked, two green, one amber, across the top of the thing, which was knee-high and covered in crinkled aluminum foil. The material was probably something more scientific and considerably more expensive than aluminum foil, but the resemblance was great enough I couldn't help seeing the machine as a cheap prop for a '50s science fiction television show.

The man stood, staring down at the machine. He held something long and black, flipping it over his fingers like a baton. From a distance, it looked like a remote control. Then he tossed it from his left hand to his right, turned his back on the doorway, and walked briskly across the clearing to join Castellan. His careless movements made me nervous. They were so different from how everyone else had behaved, so unafraid where the others had looked almost spooked by the metal frame, that they frightened me, as if the doorway was a dangerous animal and he alone knew the secret of taming it.

"Almost ready," the man said when he neared us. "That secondary connection is still wonky. My guys haven't figured out what's wrong. I want to take the system offline and replace it when there's time."

"Soon, it won't matter," Castellan said. "Stuart, this is Viv. She's going to bypass the barrier for us."

Stuart whistled, long and low. "You convinced an adept to work with us?"

"Better. Viv is one of the Wardens. Her magic isn't like ours." Castellan didn't introduce me, which was fine as far as I was concerned. Even if I suspected he didn't do it because in his mind, I was already disposed of.

"Hey, great!" Stuart grabbed Viv's hand and shook it enthusiastically. "This is going to make history."

Viv snatched her hand away and glared at Stuart, but he'd already turned to face the doorway. "The faulty secondary connection means it takes time to build up the magical concentration, but it should be ready...right about now."

I didn't see any change in the machine at first, but then I realized the amber light had turned green. Stuart pointed his remote control at the machine and pressed and held two buttons. A deep rumble filled the clearing, bringing everyone to a halt. The sound vibrated through me, and I clenched my teeth to stop them clicking against each other. My skin tingled unpleasantly, even when I rubbed my arms. The rumbling grew and grew until my bones ached and I had to brace myself so I wouldn't fall over.

Then the noise faded, and the clearing was still. Nobody moved. The doorway hadn't changed—except it had. The lights running over its surface were brighter now and painful to look at directly. I turned my head so I could watch them out of the corner of my eye. They flowed like water, but in angular lines, and with that, I realized why it looked so comforting: the lines of light had the exact shape and movement of the gray and blue Etch-a-Sketch traceries of the Athenaeum access points. They even made right-hand turns. And there were more lights drawing lines now, so the surface of the doorway looked like the circuit board Alastair had built at computer camp last year.

Stuart lowered the remote and pressed three more buttons in a row. The light intensified so I couldn't look at it from any direction. Then it flashed, brightly enough I was blinded for a moment. Viv exclaimed in surprise and pain. I blinked away afterimages and wiped tears from my eyes.

And there it was. The barrier shifted and glowed within the door frame, rippling like water just as I remembered. I thought the golden glitter was less vibrant than before, but I couldn't be sure, and I didn't know if it mattered. As far as I could tell, it was the same.

"Excellent," Castellan said. "And dispose of whoever is responsible for failing to identify the flaw in the device. We don't need incompetents."

Stuart gaped. "I...okay, sure. No problem." He walked away a lot faster than he'd approached, almost running. I felt sick. I had no doubt that whatever disposal Castellan had in mind would be far more permanent than firing someone.

Castellan turned to Viv, rubbing his hands together like a supervillain anticipating victory. "Now what?"

"I don't have my tools, so—" Viv began.

Castellan's smile vanished. "I hope you're not playing me, Viv. That would be a mistake."

Viv rolled her eyes again. "No, I'm explaining that I'll need to make do with what's here. Some of those glass tubes, for starters, and a pair of sunglasses, and—look, it's faster if I show you." She walked toward one of the many stacks of supply crates placed here and there throughout the clearing, well away from the doorway. After a pause, Castellan followed her, leaving me alone.

I waited a moment to see if anyone, and by anyone I meant Eris, was going to interfere with my free movement. Then I strolled to the doorway and stopped inches from the barrier. No one yelled at me to get away from it. I brushed my fingers against the golden surface and felt nothing, not even an increased warmth or the movement of millions of particles shifting. I couldn't help wondering what would happen to an elf touching the barrier, whether the elf would explode, or unravel, or disintegrate. It was a gruesome line of thought, but after a few seconds, I realized it hadn't been entirely mine. The effect the barrier had on elves was key to knowing how to destroy it.

I closed my eyes and asked, *How do I destroy the barrier?*

The dizzying sensation of a prophecy swept over me, and I drew in a centering breath and watched the images unfold, overlaid on what I remembered of reality. As if I had my eyes open, I saw the doorway and the barrier, but golden chains made of billions of tiny letters coiled and stretched across my vision, familiar even though it had been ten years since I'd seen them. The magic of the oracle, extending from our reality to the invaders' and back again.

I watched, so fascinated I forgot I was looking for an answer. The chains unrolled and tautened, appearing to connect to all three sides of the doorway, though when I tried to understand how they hooked on, the images faded. Only when I stopped trying to understand did the image become solid again. The chains crisscrossed each other and quivered with pent-up energy, their surfaces constantly moving as the letters formed words and broke apart to form new ones.

Then the quivering intensified, shaking the links so they visibly shivered under tension. I held my breath, waiting for what I was sure would be something extraordinary. Before I could become dizzy from lack of air, one link near the center of the web dissolved, bubbling and hissing like something disintegrated by acid, and then another, and another, until the chains were gone. Except the tiny letters weren't destroyed; they flew away laughing in a great spiral of dust or water. I felt an unexpected relief, as if I'd accomplished something beautiful and good.

My eyes blinked open, and I glanced around to see if I'd been noticed in my reverie. Still no one paid any attention to me. Viv had two goons trailing her, their arms full of miscellaneous glass objects, with Castellan by her side. I still had some time.

It was an answer, but not an answer I knew how to use. Previously, before I'd permanently become the oracle, I had occasionally taken on the oracle's consciousness to direct its actions—become its hands, in effect. And I'd been able to create and manipulate those chains. But there was no oracle anymore, not the way there once had been, and I had no idea how to manifest any of the oracle's former power now. I didn't even know if that power still existed somewhere.

I tilted my head back to look at the top of the doorway. The liquid lights were gone, leaving the matte-silver metal as dully brilliant as a nickel worn down by years of handling. As with the adepts' doorway, the barrier looked like cloth of gold where it touched the lintel. The top of the door was too far away for me to reach it, so I tried touching the barrier where it connected to the upright nearest me. Still nothing. Frustrated, I retreated to where I'd stood before.

My back pocket buzzed. I almost clapped a hand over it before remembering that might draw attention, though in truth I didn't think anyone was watching me. I took a careful step backward, waited, then another. I didn't see Eris anywhere, which made me nervous, but Viv and Castellan were on the far side of the clearing, and I might never get a better chance.

I backed up again until I was pressed against one of the trees ringing the clearing. Slowly, I edged around it, continuing to step backward until I was surrounded by trees that obscured my view of the clearing. No one shouted for me to stop; no bullets zinged past my head. I took a few more steps deeper into the forest and then stopped, torn by indecision. I didn't want to abandon Viv. On the other hand, if I escaped, that might mean finding Malcolm and rescuing Viv. Castellan still needed her, so he wouldn't kill her when he discovered I was gone.

It was almost pitch black beneath the trees, and when I tried to run, all I did was trip and nearly brain myself on a low-hanging branch I hadn't seen. I snatched Viv's phone out of my pocket and started to turn on the flashlight, but remembered in time that light would draw pursuers to me. So instead I swiped past Viv's lock screen—she'd used the same combination for years—and with remarkably steady hands called Malcolm.

Nobody answered for what felt like an eternity. Finally, the call went to voicemail. I hung up without leaving a message. Even if Malcolm had somehow guessed it wasn't Viv who'd called, if he was out in the forest somewhere, he wouldn't answer and risk giving his position away. Knowing this didn't make me feel better.

The phone buzzed with an incoming text. <Viv. Where are you?>

I felt so relieved my hands shook. I calmed myself and texted back <It's Helena. Castellan kidnapped us, he shot Judy, she's at his house except it's not actually his house>

<I know. We're close to you. I can see lights in the forest>

Puzzled, I texted, <Didn't you trace my phone? Castellan threw it away>

<We had a different kind of guidance. Don't worry. Stay where you are>

At that moment, I heard the rustling of someone approaching. "So clever," Eris said. "I'll admit you fooled me for a minute there."

I reflexively hit the power off button and hid the phone behind my back, though I guessed she'd seen it. Her dark figure approached me, her gun pointed steadily at my head. "Like that was hard," I said, unable to resist taunting her even though my heart was in my throat. We were alone and unobserved, and there was no one to stop Eris killing me. I didn't even dare reach for a prophecy to give me a way out.

Eris was close enough I could see her smile. "It's like you're asking me to shoot you," she said, taking more careful aim at my chest.

To my right, I heard more noises of someone approaching. It wasn't from the direction of the clearing, but hope filled me at the thought that maybe Eris wouldn't shoot if she had witnesses who might tell Castellan she'd killed me. Then I remembered Castellan didn't need me anymore, and hope vanished.

Eris didn't act as if she cared that someone was coming. In desperation, I said, "Who's that? Mr. Castellan doesn't want me dead, does he?"

Eris's brow furrowed. "You're pathetic," she said. "Trying to make me think someone else is here. It's just us."

As she spoke those three words, someone in black fatigues and a black balaclava emerged from the darkness. He walked rapidly, not trying to remain silent, but Eris didn't turn, just as if she didn't see or hear him. My mouth fell open.

Eris said, "I'd say goodbye, but you're not worth my time." And the fatigue-clad man grabbed her from behind in a choke hold so perfect Eris made no sound. His other hand secured her gun, forcing it out of her hand to fall on the ground. I snatched it up, fearing Eris getting free even though it was obvious she wasn't going anywhere.

The man lowered the unconscious Eris to the ground, not being very gentle. "Helena," he said, and I recognized Mike Conti's voice. I drew a shuddering breath and held out the gun. Mike took it and put it away somewhere I couldn't see because I'd heard more footsteps rustling the undergrowth and was looking for Mike's companions. Then a figure I would recognize anywhere, no matter how his face was concealed, strode toward me, and I rushed to throw my arms around him.

Malcolm and I held each other for a few seconds, and then Malcolm said, "Is Viv with them?"

"Mr. Castellan is forcing her to open a portal to Faerie. She's stalling, but she can't do that for long. Malcolm, are we outnumbered?"

"Yes, and no," Malcolm murmured. "Mike's illusions give us an advantage, as do the prophecies Alastair and Duncan provided us—"

"Alastair and Duncan?"

Malcolm smiled. "They asked to help. Even Duncan, who said I should tell you 'it fights when you fight it' and wouldn't explain further. I hope that has meaning to you."

"I...maybe." I shoved Viv's phone back into my pocket. "Tell me what to do."

"Stay here for now. We'll see if we can extract Viv." Malcolm's mouth was set in a grim line. "We are still outnumbered, and the best outcome would be to leave this place without getting into a fight that would certainly cost lives. If things go bad..." He sighed. "I would like to tell you to run, but I doubt you know where to run to. You may have to depend on the oracle to get yourself safely away."

I nodded and kissed him. "Good luck."

I wasn't completely obedient; I followed Malcolm, Mike, and the rest of their people to where I could see the clearing, or at least what was visible of it through the trees. Then I watched, my fingernails cutting into my palms as I clenched my fists, as the Wardens walked out from beneath the trees and into the clearing without trying to hide. I knew Mike's illusions were powerful, but being able to see through them made me more anxious, as if my perception weakened them.

I was about to seek another prophecy when I again heard rustling footsteps behind me. "Are there more of you?" I asked, turning around. "We can't be that outnumbered—"

It was Cassie Leighton.

Stunned, all I could do was stare. Cassie arrived at my side slightly out of breath, as if she'd been running, though I didn't know how anyone could manage that in the terrible darkness beneath the branches. She smiled slightly and said, "I hope we're not too late."

My gaze moved past her to take in Gabriel and Milo, coming up behind her, and then pale Emily who made Felicia next to her seem virtually invisible. "How did you find this place?"

"You're not the only one who sees the future," Gabriel said.

"Though what Emily does with her tarot cards isn't exactly seeing the future—but that's not important. Is Castellan here somewhere?"

"He is. He's got Viv. She knows how to open the way to Faerie and bypass the barrier, and he's going to—"

"What?" Cassie said in a forceful whisper that nevertheless had Milo and Felicia trying to shush her. "When did she figure that out? Were you planning to tell us?"

I was too overwhelmed to feel guilty. "Malcolm and the Wardens are going to rescue her—they're all under illusions far more powerful—"

Someone in the clearing shouted, the words incoherent but the emotion clearly a warning. Then the staccato rattle of gunfire blasted through the still night, and more shouts joined the first. "Never mind," I said, and ran for the clearing.

CHAPTER 19

I grabbed hold of a tree trunk to stop myself stumbling into the open. The clearing was alive with movement, people running, people shooting. Everything was so hectic I couldn't make out which of the figures were Wardens and which Savants despite the brilliance of the lights. In the middle of it all, the doorway stood like the gate to an ancient temple, the barrier glowing—

I felt sick. The golden glow had vanished, and now the barrier was a deep blue, still sparkling, but looking less gaudy and more sinister. "She did it. We're too late," I said.

"What now?" Cassie said from beside me.

"I don't know," I replied. I scanned the clearing, looking for friends or at least allies. Through the crowd, I saw Viv, and I took a step toward her. Then I realized she was backing away from Castellan and the gun he aimed at her. Without another thought, I ran, dodging fighting figures and hoping I wasn't already too late. I didn't know what I could do to stop Castellan, but I couldn't stand by and watch him shoot Viv.

I darted past a couple of men wrestling hand to hand and was within ten feet of Viv when Castellan's gun exploded. Not an explosion with sound and light; the weapon fell apart into all its component pieces that shot in every direction.

Castellan swore loudly and looked around, searching for whatever had done it, and Viv launched herself at him with a perfect kick to his stomach. Castellan stumbled back, and Viv followed him, aiming more kicks at his leg and knee. His leg shot out from under him. Castellan went down, and Viv landed one final kick to his left temple that snapped his head back. He collapsed in an awkward heap.

Viv hurried to my side. "What happened to his gun?"

"That was me," Felicia said. "I took it back to a much earlier time, before it was assembled. Connections and correspondences." She was breathing heavily as if she'd finished a marathon, but she didn't look exhausted.

A bullet pinged off the side of the doorway, making all of us drop into a crouch. I counted: me, Viv, Felicia, and Emily. "Where did the others go?"

"They're going to disable as much of the machinery as they can," Emily said. She didn't look as if age had slowed her down. "We need to shut down the portal in case they're not successful."

"It can't be shut down," Viv said.

I stared at her. "What?"

Viv's fair skin flushed a dull red. "The only way I could open it with the makeshift equipment here was to set up a...you know, the details don't matter. Basically the portal feeds in on itself, like a permanent influx of power. And it can't be stopped. I'm sorry, Helena, but he was going to kill me—"

"It's all right," I said, putting a hand on hers. "The Wardens will stop the Savants, and it won't matter whether the portal is permanent or not."

"Except it will still be here, and Castellan has resources you can't imagine," Felicia said. "Resources, and subordinates who will carry out his plan even if he's dead. And I'm not so sure your Wardens will win." She glanced at Castellan's unconscious body. "I can't kill him."

Viv and I exchanged glances. I knew I couldn't kill a helpless man, and I was sure Viv couldn't either. But if Felicia was right, his death wouldn't make a difference. Relief warred with guilt and shame inside me.

The sound of tortured metal screaming as it was twisted out of recognition drew my attention from Castellan. One of the vehicles, a miniature tank, had started to move forward, but the long muzzle of its gun was twisting upward as if some invisible hand had grabbed it and pulled. It hadn't stopped the tank moving, and I couldn't understand why the driver hadn't stopped. Then I realized it was headed straight for us—or, more likely, for the doorway.

"We have to move," I said. I took a few steps, hesitated, then returned to drag Castellan's inert form to the side where the tank wouldn't crush him.

After a second, Viv joined me. "This is stupid," she said. "We ought to let him get run over."

"I can't," I said, and released him. Now he lay next to the aluminum foil device, which looked even more ridiculous up close. All its lights were blinking amber, which probably meant something. I didn't care.

Then I saw Malcolm on the far side of the clearing, shouting and waving his arm in a circle over his head. More Wardens joined him, and together they rushed the tank. I hoped at least one of them was a stone magus, someone who could use telekinesis to knock the tank over. Instead, armor plating started peeling off the tank as if it had some horrible skin disease. Malcolm appeared at the top of the turret. With one hand, he tore the hatch off and flung it away. With the other, he pointed his gun inside the turret and shouted something.

"Helena, get down!" Viv exclaimed. I cried out as she tackled me and brought me to the ground. "You were standing in the open like an idiot," she panted into my ear.

"I forgot," I said. I didn't stand, but surveyed as much of the clearing as I could see from where I lay prone. The fighting was worse than before, and as I watched, a Warden jerked and fell, shot in the chest by a paramilitary Savant goon. There were so many of the Savants I felt sick. Malcolm wasn't visible at the top of the tank anymore, but the vehicle had stopped, which was something.

Then an engine roared, higher and faster than the tank's low growl, and it was joined by a second and then a third. Two Jeeps sped past the stalled tank, followed by a slower Humvee. The Jeeps were through the portal in the time it took me to realize what they intended. I pushed myself to my feet and stumbled toward the doorway with no idea what I meant to do. The Humvee passed me as I was within feet of the doorway. It drove through the billowing midnight curtain and vanished as thoroughly as the Jeeps had.

"That's it," Felicia said. "It's over."

I drew in a deep breath and let it out slowly. "No," I said, "it's not."

I walked the final few paces to the doorway and rested my hand on one of the gleaming steel uprights. We could destroy the portal if we could destroy the frame, or so the adepts had said. This did not look like something anyone could casually take apart. Which left me with the oracle's prophecy: destroy the barrier to defeat the Savants.

I breathed in deeply again, centering myself, and focused on the barrier. Now that it wasn't a brilliant gold, its appearance soothed me. I had a flash of memory of a creature just this color, midnight blue and looking soft as velvet, but I pushed the memory aside. Instead, I remembered what I'd seen in vision just minutes before, the golden chains of the oracle's power crisscrossing the portal like a web. I couldn't summon those chains again, but maybe there was something else I could do.

The clamor of battle fell away from my awareness, leaving me alone with the barrier. I continued to center myself and observed it, drawing it deep inside me. Now it resembled the glitter goop I'd bought the kids on a whim, endlessly malleable and shimmering as it moved. The goop had been a mistake, because it got everywhere, but this would never overflow its bounds—I was certain that was part of its structure. Filling the doorway...

...except it wasn't just here, was it? It existed all through our reality like a net encircling us, visible when we made it so, but still there even when it was invisible. Like a mesh of chains.

Excitement welled up inside me. I stepped closer until I was in the middle of the barrier and closed my eyes. And this time, I perceived something. It was more of a feeling than anything concrete, but that feeling was of connection, of billions of motes that clung to each other until they released their hold to join with another. If I hadn't had the experience with the oracle's power, I was sure I wouldn't have been able to see any of it, if "see" was even the right word. It felt like a mesh, but not of chains, more like tiny magnets clinging and releasing a thousand times a second so it was the most flexible substance I could imagine. If it was thinner than it had been in the past, as Viv had said, it didn't give any sign of that.

Slowly, feeling like I was approaching a skittish dog, I pictured myself touching the mesh. To my surprise, I felt something warm and pliant like wax not yet at the melting point. Where I touched it, the mesh contracted around my fingers, holding them. I realized it was examining me as closely as I was examining it. I held still. The mesh rolled on over my body, and I had to remind myself that none of this was real so I didn't panic at being engulfed. Then I nearly did panic at the thought that I might be wrong, and this was the most real thing that had ever happened to me.

The mesh became suddenly rigid, as if it sensed my fear. Instinctively, I grabbed it, and it retreated entirely, chilling my skin with the speed of its flight. I opened my eyes. The barrier looked just as it had before, not as if I'd damaged it.

Frustrated, I turned to speak to Viv and saw another Humvee barreling down on me. I shrieked and leaped away from its path just in time. My hair flew about my face with the wind of its passing. My heart racing, I put a hand on the door to keep myself upright and assessed my surroundings. Emily and Felicia were gone. Cassie crouched over the aluminum foil device, prodding at it as if she was afraid it might explode if she touched the wrong thing. Castellan still lay unconscious nearby.

Viv knelt beside the doorway, well to one side. She looked up at me. "We're losing," she said. "I've tried to close the portal, but it's not working. I think we have to get out of here."

"We can't," I protested. "Malcolm won't give up."

"Helena—"

"Just—watch over me, all right? I have an idea." I didn't have an idea so much as an inkling, but I didn't want Viv to fall deeper into despair. I put just my hand inside the barrier and closed my eyes, hoping my awareness of the mysterious mesh wasn't a one-time event.

But it was still there. This time, I didn't wait for it to react; I grabbed hold of it and twisted, hoping to free some of those billions of connections. If I could make a hole—

Power shot through my arm to my chest and struck my heart. I gasped and fell backward, releasing my hold, and pounded on my chest, though I didn't know if my heart had stopped and CPR probably didn't work that way. In the next moment, sanity reasserted itself, and I realized I'd just had a nasty shock. I lay on my back on the grass of the slip and breathed in deeply, ignoring Viv's demands for an explanation.

"I'm fine," I finally said. "And I should have known better." Duncan's warning "it fights when you fight it" came to mind, and I wished I'd remembered it sooner. Well, that was one piece of information I had. I couldn't force the barrier to fall apart.

But that wasn't all I knew, was it? I'd forgotten, temporarily, the prophecy that said what the barrier did to elves was key to destroying it. I sat up. "Cassie," I shouted, "tell me again what the barrier does to elves who touch it."

Cassie's head jerked up as if I'd startled her. "What?" She scuttled across the space between us to kneel beside me.

"What does the barrier do to kill an elf?"

Cassie glanced at the barrier, which remained beautiful and apparently innocuous. "It attaches to their magic and unravels it. With elves being creatures of magic, that leads to unraveling their bodies. That's the theory, anyway. We've never seen it happen because all the elves who might have been killed by it were on the Faerie side."

"Okay. Thanks." I got to my feet, more slowly now, and leaned heavily on the upright until I regained my balance.

"Thanks? Why does it matter what the barrier does?" Cassie asked.

"I'm not sure yet." I looked around the clearing once more. Another tank, this one undamaged, was rolling in its ponderous way toward us. I didn't like feeling grateful that Wardens were keeping the Savants' attention away from me. I wished I could kick Michael Castellan in the head myself. But there was no point thinking like that. Once more, I sank into the awareness of the barrier.

It didn't react at all, which heartened me; I'd been afraid maybe my attack had put it on edge. Once more I reached out to it, and the warm, pliable sensation caressed my fingers. I didn't fight as the barrier's links poured up my arm and over my body. That might or might not be real, but the sensation of heat was real enough, quickly going from a pleasant warmth to the discomfort of full sunlight on the hottest July day imaginable. I made myself relax. I would not give in to fear.

Instead, I turned my attention to the shifting, shimmering links. I didn't see anything at first, just felt that sensation of millions, maybe billions of connections being made and broken and made again. Gradually, shapes came into focus, either because my understanding had grown or because my imagination had caught up. I saw tiny cubes no more than a few millimeters on a side, silver and gold and pewter and copper, that sparked when they came in contact with one another and then separated to make another connection. I felt the sparking was the cause of the heat, though I couldn't say why.

And the heat was becoming unbearable. I didn't think I had more than a minute left before I would have to return to consciousness and leave the barrier behind. I focused my attention on the place where the mesh covered my hand. Then I gently spread my fingers, hoping I'd guessed right.

The mesh spread apart, and gaps appeared in the mesh, but no lightning speared my chest. I willed the mesh to see what I saw, hoping I was right about that, too, that the barrier had a rudimentary intelligence. "You're made to unravel," I whispered, or thought, or willed. "It's your job to unravel. Those sparks are what happens when you cling together. Look. It's possible." I opened my other hand and wiggled my fingers as the mesh there split apart.

I was breathing heavily, inhaling heat-laden air that scorched my lungs, but I wasn't going to give up until I knew it was impossible. "You served this world for a thousand years," I said. "It's time for you to be free. Let go."

The gaps flexed and began to close. I exclaimed, and the mesh constricted around me, becoming rigid and hard. With my last breath, I made myself relax and shouted, "Don't be afraid!"

I stumbled backward and inhaled cool night air. Sounds gradually returned to my world like a speaker being turned up. Viv had a hand on my arm and was shouting in my ear, words that didn't make sense at first, but after a moment fell into place: "—have to go now, Helena!"

I didn't resist as she dragged me away from the doorway, but I let her guide my footsteps as I stared back at the barrier. It looked just the same as always, and I wanted to cry at how close I'd been.

Then light sparkled across the midnight blue surface like a handful of glitter under an incandescent bulb. I stopped and pulled free of Viv's hand. "Look," I said. "Look at that!"

The barrier hadn't stopped rippling, but instead of moving in all directions, now it flowed only up. And as it reached the lintel, it poured over the steel beam, over and up into the night sky. I watched in astonishment as the barrier dissolved, the thick blue substance vanishing, leaving only motes of blue light that caught the wind and flew away. In less than a minute, the barrier was gone.

I realized the clearing was silent now and took a look around. Everyone, Warden and Savants, stood watching the doorway, which looked empty now, as if it led only to the rest of the clearing. Then something like a thin, transparent film within it caught the white light from one of the Savants' enormous reflectors, and for just a second, I saw something else in the frame—an alien forest with flowering trees, dark and foreboding.

Someone grabbed me from behind, and a knife pricked my side. "That is *enough*," Castellan shouted, making me flinch at the loudness. Then I froze, because the knife pressed more firmly against my kidney. "Put your weapons down. Don't think I won't kill her."

Someone emerged from behind the damaged tank, his gun pointed at Castellan. "She's a Warden," Malcolm said, his voice low and emotionless. "She knows the risks. We don't sacrifice the many for the one."

I held very still. I knew Malcolm was bluffing, and the smart move was for me to keep from getting in the way of whatever he meant to do to Castellan. Knowing that didn't stop me from feeling sick and afraid. The last time I'd been a hostage, Malcolm had shot through me to stop the man, knowing my injury wouldn't be fatal. I really didn't want to go through that again.

"You'll sacrifice for this one, though." Castellan's voice rasped like he'd been gargling with stones. "She brought down the barrier. I doubt there's more than one of you Wardens capable of that. Which means you won't want her dead."

Malcolm stopped about twenty feet from us, though he didn't lower his gun. "What do you want, Castellan?"

"I've already got it," Castellan said. "My men are in Faerie right now, securing a position. You've done some damage, true, but I still have enough weapons and vehicles to begin my invasion. All you have to do is walk away."

"Not going to happen," Malcolm said.

"Oh, for God's sake, why not?" Castellan shouted. He sounded like he'd just reached the end of his rope and wasn't going to hold on much longer. "Why do you care about a world full of creatures who only want humans dead? I'm doing you a *favor*, you musclebound idiot. Back away, leave this place, and—"

"Shut up," Viv said. Her voice wasn't very loud, but it cut across his words like a knife. "Look. Look at that. Something's coming through."

The knife at my side shifted as Castellan's hand relaxed, though not enough for me to consider breaking free. "You see? My people are reporting back already."

The otherworldly shimmering film across the doorway rippled, but not like the barrier had; this was more like heat haze, the far side of the clearing disappearing to reveal the Faerie forest and then reappearing, over and over again. And something was clearly coming through. Whatever it was moved slowly, tentatively, like someone unsure of his welcome. I was convinced this wasn't Castellan's men.

Then the figure emerged fully from the doorway. He was tall and thin, almost too thin, with a face like a hatchet made of bone. Lank hair hung around his face, colorless in the bright lights. His leather coat and pants were covered with bronze-colored plates, like some kind of armor, and he wore knee boots that were much shinier and newer-looking than the rest of his clothing. He looked like an extra from a fantasy movie, except no extra would have such elaborate, terrifyingly realistic clothing.

He paused just outside the doorway. Slowly, he surveyed the silent clearing. Then he raised his arm, and I saw what his body had concealed: a long, wickedly curved bronze sword whose blade ran red with blood.

CHAPTER 20

Castellan's knife fell away from my side, and his hand on my shoulder relaxed. Instantly, I elbowed him in the stomach and wrenched away from his loose grip. Castellan let out a gasp, and his fingers closed on loose strands of my hair, sending a sharp twinge through my scalp, but I was already running for Malcolm. It occurred to me that I might be blocking his shot at Castellan, and I swerved, but Malcolm didn't shoot. I raced past him and stumbled to a halt.

The clearing remained perfectly still. Everyone was still staring at the elf with the bloody sword. He, in turn, scanned the clearing from left to right in a slow, deliberate turn of his head. His expression was totally unreadable, and while I didn't know if that was because he was alien, or because he had amazing self-control, I was certain he felt no fear despite being outnumbered. His eyes were large and dark, with irises so large the whites were practically invisible, and against his chalk-pale skin they looked like holes in his head. But his regard when it passed over me without hesitating sent a chill through me.

A voice called out in a language I didn't recognize. I risked looking away from the elf and saw Gabriel approaching. He was unarmed, and he moved slowly, like the elf was a skittish dog who might be rabid. He spoke again. The words weren't just unfamiliar, they sounded like nothing human. But it was clearly a language and not nonsense syllables.

The elf's pale brows, almost invisible against his skin, furrowed the tiniest bit. Then he spoke. His voice was beautiful as he was not, musical and flowing, and it took me a moment to realize his words didn't sound anything like Gabriel's, at least as far as I could distinguish.

Gabriel's expression didn't change, but he stopped moving and lowered his hands. "We don't speak the same language," he said.

"A different country, or a different society?" Cassie asked. She'd followed Gabriel, but stayed well out of his way.

"It's been a thousand years. Languages change in that time." Gabriel spoke again in that strange language, but this time his words were clearer, and he paused slightly between each one.

The elf tilted his head. Then he laughed. Unlike his speaking voice, his laugh was harsh and menacing. He took a step forward, bringing his sword into a different position. I'd seen Malcolm train with knives often enough to recognize it as the precursor to an attack.

Apparently, Castellan drew the same conclusion. "Shoot him!" he shouted.

I gasped and stepped forward like an idiot. I didn't know why my instincts were to protect the elf, who had no doubt killed Castellan's advance troops and would certainly not stop there. But it didn't matter. The goons opened fire, fifty or more of them shooting at the tall, horribly thin figure in the doorway.

Then I screamed, because Viv, who had been closer to the door than I was, fell to the ground and didn't move. I tried to rush forward, but Malcolm grabbed me and shouted, "She's fine! She just dropped to get out of the line of fire! Look!"

I looked, and saw Viv press her face into the ground and cover her head with her arms. My fear for her lessened slightly, but she was still closer to the rain of bullets than I liked.

The elf jerked spasmodically as the bullets struck, as if he was doing some crazy alternative dance. Most of the bullets bounced off the metal plates, not even leaving dents. But there were still many that found their mark. At first, the elf staggered. Then he took another step. His movements smoothed out, and then he was running at the first rank of goons, his sword raised high.

The goons, to their credit, didn't flee from the maniac bearing down on them. Two of them shot him point blank, one in the chest, one in the face. Both bullets pinged off his flesh as if they'd struck the metal plates instead.

The elf snarled and brought his sword down in a shining arc. It cleaved through the neck of the first goon and kept going, cutting off the second goon's arm and stopping midway through his chest. Blood spurted, covering the elf. He licked a smear of blood off his upper lip, and smiled.

Now the goons ran.

All this happened in a matter of seconds. I hadn't finished gaping when Malcolm dragged me behind the destroyed tank. "Stay here," he said.

"Malcolm, you're not going to attack him?" Fear hit me again, this time fear for my husband, who was a skilled fighter but whose gun wasn't any different from those goons'.

"We can't let him get away. Imagine what he could do to a civilian population." Malcolm holstered his gun and drew his steel knives from their sheaths at his thighs. "It will be fine. There's just one of him, right?"

I looked past him at the doorway. "Um," I said, "I don't think that's true."

The film across the doorway was rippling again, and someone was emerging. This time, it was a woman, as tall and pale as the male elf, but with long dark hair tangled like she'd been running through the forest. She, too, wielded a curved blade, streaked with blood. Malcolm swore under his breath. "There's no alternative," he said, and ran at the newcomer.

I watched, my heart in my throat, as Malcolm engaged the woman in battle. They were the same height, but next to the elf woman, Malcolm looked solid and real, not as if he might break in half given the right blow. The woman parried his first attack and swung, forcing Malcolm a step back. I was terrifyingly aware that Malcolm hadn't had a real fight in nearly ten years, and that daily training with blade and gun wasn't the same as fighting for your life.

But Malcolm didn't seem to feel the lack. His blades flashed silver in the bright lights, moving faster than I could follow. And the elf woman was forced back. Her expression was furious, as if Malcolm's attack was a personal insult as well as a physical threat, and time after time her blade skittered to the side where it should have impaled Malcolm. It took me a few seconds to realize the problem. Malcolm and the elf were closely matched—so closely it was going to take a mistake on one or the other's part to end the battle, because their skills were effectively the same.

Nearby movement drew my eye, and I realized Viv had gotten to her knees now that the gunfire had slowed—not stopped; there were still a few goons who hadn't realized bullets were futile—and was crawling rapidly in my direction. I ran to her side and helped her stand, and then we scurried, crouched over, to the dubious safety of the tank. It barely looked like a tank anymore, with the gun twisted at right angles to the turret and most of the armor plating gone, but it was still taller than us, and I felt sheltered by it.

We clung to each other for a moment. "I don't know where Jeremiah is," Viv said. "If bullets don't work—what was it about cold iron he said? A wooden staff is about as far from cold iron as it gets, even if cold iron is just poetical for steel."

"He'll be fine," I said. "He knows the limitations of his staff. He's probably helping organize the fighters."

Viv nodded. "And—oh, there's another one!" She was crying now as a third elf emerged from the portal. "This is my fault!"

"It is not. It's my fault for breaking the barrier, remember?" I thought I'd feel more guilty about that, but strangely, I felt nothing but calm when I considered what I'd done. "And maybe it looks bad right now, but I'm certain the oracle knew the truth."

The third elf was also male, and even thinner and taller and paler than the first two. His skin was taut across the sharp bones of his face, like a flesh mask, and his eyes were pale blue rather than dark, pale enough that they were only a few shades darker than his skin. Instead of a sword, he wielded two long daggers, longer than Malcolm's knives.

With that, I remembered my husband was fighting for his life. He had moved out of sight, and without thinking of my own safety, I hurried forward to see around the nose of the tank. Malcolm and his opponent were still fighting fiercely, but neither of them were unmarked; blood covered Malcolm's cheek, and the elf's left arm dangled uselessly at her side. But Malcolm was gradually being forced back, and soon he would be backed against the trees, and then—

I resisted the urge to run screaming at them, waving my hands as a distraction. Malcolm didn't need my help, and the best thing I could do for him was to stay away.

"Helena!" Viv shouted.

I turned, startled, and then screamed and ducked as something large and dark and shapeless hurtled right at my head. It whooshed past, ruffling my hair and my shirt, and as I turned to see it go, I realized it was a sheet of the tank's armor, flung at the third elf so it spun like a sawblade. It took the elf square in the chest, knocking him on his back to lie across the portal entrance. I wasn't sure his body was a permanent deterrent for any other elves wanting to come through, but the plate was embedded deeply in the elf's chest, he wasn't moving, and I wanted so badly for it to mean victory was possible.

Someone crouched beside me. "Helena, I'm sorry," Jeremiah said. "I didn't see you there. You're not hurt?"

I shook my head. "I didn't know you were that good at telekinesis."

Jeremiah smiled. "I'm not, but leverage and angular momentum make up for a lot. Now, get down and stay down." He patted my shoulder and ran toward his fallen foe.

Then Viv was beside me, helping me to stand. "I have an idea," Viv said. "You'll think it's crazy—"

"We're fighting mythical creatures that look like the undead," I said. "It can't be a crazier idea than that."

"Then we need to get to one of these Humvees," Viv said.

There were still two of them parked near the edge of the clearing. Viv climbed up into the driver's seat and laid a hand on the dashboard. The vehicle hiccuped twice and then roared into life.

"Nice," I said. "Guess I didn't have to worry about leaving you my car keys."

"No, because that trick wrecks the ignition, and you'd have bitched about me ruining your land yacht for weeks," Viv replied with a grin. "You drive. You've got the experience."

The interior of the cab was stripped down and spare, but it had all the important parts and, to my relief, an automatic transmission. Malcolm had insisted I learn to drive stick, and I was competent, but I didn't practice often. I put the beast in gear and ambled forward, searching for prey.

Another elf had come through the portal in the time it had taken us to commandeer the Humvee. She crouched over the fallen elf with the tank armor embedded in his chest. Her sword—two swords, I saw as we approached—were sheathed at her back. I couldn't figure out how she could draw them without dislocating her shoulders, and then I decided I didn't care. Gunning the engine, I drove straight at her.

She had time to rise and face the Humvee, her expression curious, before I rammed her, knocking her back through the portal. I kept going without thinking of more than keeping her down, and it wasn't until Viv screamed at me to stop that I realized I'd passed through the portal myself.

No light came through the portal behind us, and the world we'd entered was night-dark. I remembered the Humvee had headlights and searched the console by feel, starting the windshield wipers by accident, until I found the headlights and turned them on. Then Viv and I screamed, because the lights illuminated another elven form, pasty white with tangled black hair falling over its face so it looked like that girl from *The Ring*. The elf raised a sword to point directly at us, and I screamed again and put the Humvee in reverse.

I wasn't cautious, and the vehicle slammed into the steel upright of the doorway, which spun the Humvee so it slanted across the portal. The vehicle wasn't big enough to fill the entire fifteen-foot space, but it blocked a good part of the entrance. I spun the steering wheel and hit the gas, straightening us out enough that I could reverse cleanly through the portal. Not so cleanly, unfortunately; the side of the Humvee scraped across the portal with a shrill *skree* that set my teeth on edge. The headlights illuminated the elf pursuing us, but he wasn't moving fast.

I continued to reverse until I came up against Wardens fighting, not the elves, but Savant goons. The sight angered me. Those elves were vicious and almost unkillable, so why did we have to waste time fighting Savants?

I faced forward again and saw the elf following us. He still moved slowly, like he was uncertain of what I was—or, more likely, had never seen an armored military vehicle before. I gunned the engine. Viv grabbed my arm. "He's not like the others," she said.

I looked more closely. The elf was bigger than his companions, not taller, but broader in the shoulders and more heavily muscled. That still made him no bulkier than Malcolm, but compared to the other elves, he was Mr. Universe. And the way he moved...he wasn't just watching me in the Humvee, he was surveying the clearing and everyone in it, like he was assessing the best plan of attack. His cold deliberation made me sick. "Hold onto something," I told Viv, and accelerated toward the elf.

The elf watched us speed toward him. Unlike the female elf, his expression was remote, closed-off like we were a bug to be swatted. He raised a hand palm-first—and the Humvee stopped as suddenly as if it had hit a concrete barrier, flinging us forward. I smacked my head on the console and saw flashing lights for a second. When I recovered, I heard hissing, and realized the entire front of the vehicle had compressed like an accordion.

I wrenched at the door and discovered the crumpling had extended along the side, deforming the door frame enough that I couldn't open the door. Viv, beside me, was swearing at hers. "Where did he go?" she exclaimed.

"I don't—" I began, and froze. The elf was right outside my door, watching me with those dead eyes. I screamed and flung myself backward, over the gear shift to land on Viv.

The elf didn't move. He continued to watch me with his large, dark eyes. Then he walked away.

Breathing heavily, I sat up and watched him cross the clearing. I couldn't see much from inside the Humvee, but the first elf continued his slaughter of humans over to my left, and that was where the scary elf went. Viv and I fought her door, but it was jammed beyond our strength to move, and all I could do was watch as the two elves joined in fighting whoever those men and women were. At this distance, I couldn't easily tell if they were Savants or Wardens, and I didn't care.

But the scary elf didn't draw his sword. He stood a short distance away, watching the first elf fight. Then, in a movement so swift I almost didn't register it, he grabbed the elf in a complicated lock and broke his neck as easily as snapping a pencil. He dropped the body carelessly, like throwing clothes on the floor, and once more surveyed the clearing. None of the surviving humans shot at him, though he wore no armor as the others had. After a moment, he turned and sauntered back to the portal, passing through it without looking back.

I realized I was clutching Viv's hand and released her. "Did you see that?"

"I didn't think it was possible to get any more scared," Viv said. "We have to get out of this thing. I wish I was a stone magus."

We pushed and strained against the passenger side door, which was less crumpled than the other, to no effect. Then it occurred to me that the rear doors might not have been affected. We crawled over the seats and found out this was true. Silently agreeing never to mention our stupidity, Viv and I climbed out of the damaged Humvee to hear— silence. No more gunfire, no shouts, no screams of dying men. Just the murmur of low voices in the distance.

I found Malcolm standing beside the fallen elf woman, whose throat was a mass of blood. Malcolm didn't look injured, but when I ran to him, his embrace was stiff, like his arm hurt. "I took very little damage," he assured me, "but that is because if I had taken a more serious wound, it would have been fatal. I have never fought an opponent that skilled before."

I buried my face in his shoulder briefly. "Did you see that elf kill his friend?"

Malcolm tensed. "What do you mean?"

I explained about the scary elf, how he'd stopped the Humvee with a gesture and stared at us like we were insects not worth squashing before killing the other elf and going back into Faerie. "Are they all dead? I mean, the others?"

"We managed to kill them all, but not without heavy losses," Malcolm said. "The Savants fled rather than engage with the enemy, though I believe that was wisdom rather than cowardice, as they didn't have magic and also lacked the right kind of bullets."

"But Mr. Castellan said his people had created weapons they believed would work on elves. He claimed they were cold iron."

Malcolm shrugged and winced as his damaged arm moved. "I saw some of those weapons. The Savants overthought the problem. Their weapons were a strange metal alloy I think we'll want someone to analyze, but they weren't solid steel, and that was the Savants' downfall."

"Then Jeremiah was right about cold iron."

"Jeremiah wishes he'd been wrong," Jeremiah said, limping to join us. Viv exclaimed over his condition, which was gory, but too gory for the blood to all be his. "Steel affected them where regular bullets didn't. Knives, steel ball rounds—we only had a few of those—and steel plating all did damage."

"So did running them over," Viv said. "I think. The elf we hit didn't get up right away, but I guess she could have been stunned."

"Or that scary elf killed her, too," I said. "It felt as if he was...disappointed, maybe? Like that other elf let him down or something, and death was the reward for that."

"We can only speculate," Malcolm said. "For now, we need to get our wounded and our dead home."

"We can't leave yet," I said. "Malcolm, the barrier is gone, and elves are free to enter our world. This place is way too close to civilization."

"I have an idea," someone near the portal said. It was Mike, staring up at the empty doorway that occasionally rippled like heat haze. "We can make it look like the barrier is still there."

"Illusions," I said. "But that will only work here. I don't think you can create an illusion that covers all the slips throughout the world."

"It's not a perfect solution, but it will give us some breathing space." Mike rubbed his hands together. "Get Dallas and Smitty—"

"Smitty is dead," Jeremiah said, his voice flat and angry.

Mike swore. "Then it will have to be me and Dallas. I wanted—it doesn't matter. But we should act fast."

"Move the elves' bodies back through the portal," Malcolm said.

"And someone activate the emergency wardstones for transport back to the Gunther Node."

I stood there, feeling useless, while everyone around me leaped into action. Even Viv left my side to help Jeremiah. I watched Mike and Junie Dallas doing things by the portal until it occurred to me I wouldn't be able to see the illusion. So I turned away and found a place near the last undamaged Humvee where I could wait to be returned home.

Now that the crisis was over, or at least over for now, I felt cold and sick over what I'd experienced. But what made me feel even worse was the knowledge that I'd made it possible for elves to enter our world. That it had been the oracle's insight didn't make it better. After what I'd seen the scary elf do, I couldn't see a way that this was anything but a tragedy. Then I remembered Judy lying in a pool of blood and couldn't stop crying.

Malcolm found me when my tears had mostly dried up and I was more or less calm again. "It's time," he said, and then, "What's wrong?"

"What happened to Judy?"

"Alastair saw her in vision, and we sent bone magi to retrieve her. Mike doesn't know yet—he told me years ago never to tell him when personal matters might interfere with a mission. So don't say anything, please." Malcolm put his arms around me and held me close. This time, he seemed to be moving more freely, and that cheered me up a bit. I'd never wanted so badly to be home with my family.

The stone magus who transported me via wardstone brought me, not to the Gunther Node, but to the shed in my backyard where we kept our personal wardstone. I was grateful beyond belief that someone had known what I needed. I thanked the magus in a daze and ran for my back door.

The house was dark and quiet, with only a few lights burning in the great room whose windows faced the backyard. Lucia raised her head when I entered. "Don't slam the door, Davies, she's only just fallen back asleep," she said, and I realized she held Jenny half on her lap and half resting on a couch cushion.

My heart gave a little thump, and I quietly crossed the room to kneel next to Jenny. "She was awake? I don't even know what time it is."

"About two-thirty, and she had a nightmare an hour ago." Lucia sounded grim. "She said she saw elves—she didn't say elves, but she described the vision you told me about. Elves fighting humans."

I closed my eyes. "I hope she didn't see her father fighting them. I don't know if I could convince her that he's safe short of showing her a dead body. Lucia, I can't—"

"She's strong. She'll figure it out," Lucia said. "Did you get the news about Judy Rasmussen?"

My heart constricted. "Did they reach her in time?"

"Alastair's vision sent a team there directly after Campbell's people left following you. She's healed and resting at home." She stood, lifting her sleeping armful gently. "Now, take her to bed."

She handed Jenny to me with some effort—my daughter was getting lanky and too heavy to carry comfortably—and I thanked her and carried Jenny up to her bed. She stirred when I laid her down, but just enough to say, "Mommy," and fall back asleep. I watched her for a moment, then checked on Alastair and Duncan. Duncan was soundly asleep, his arms and legs flung wide as if he meant to conquer his bed territory. Alastair, though, said, "Mom?" when I quietly opened his door.

"I'm sorry, I didn't mean to wake you."

"No, I woke up when Jenny cried and then I couldn't fall back asleep. I was too worried." He sat up and rubbed his eyes. "What happened?"

I couldn't tell him everything was all right, even though by some definitions that was true. "Your visions helped. They saved Aunt Judy's life, for one."

"I was scared at first, but Dad said you would be safe, and I didn't see any visions that showed you getting hurt." Alastair drew his knees up and hugged them. "But a lot of people died, didn't they?"

I suddenly felt so weary I wanted to lie down on Alastair's floor and sleep for a year. "They did. We'll talk about it tomorrow, all right? I'm really tired, and Daddy will be home soon and he's tired too."

"But—"

"Alastair, how about you ask me a question that will reassure you? Enough for you to sleep, anyway."

Alastair bit his lip. "Are there more elves coming?" he finally asked.

I nodded. "I'm afraid so. Not soon, maybe, but...they are coming."

I didn't think that was a reassuring answer, but Alastair looked relieved. "All right. Good night."

"Goodnight, honey."

I closed the door and stood for a moment with my hand on the knob. Then I walked back downstairs to wait for Malcolm. And probably to be interrogated by Lucia. Too bad Lucia couldn't be put off as easily as my son.

CHAPTER 21

As if my body hadn't gotten the message that the situation was serious, I slept like a log for six hours, waking briefly when Jenny crawled into bed beside me just before dawn. Around nine, Malcolm shook my shoulder. He was already fully dressed. "Lucia wants us at the Gunther Node in an hour."

I groaned. "This is because I wouldn't let her interrogate me last night, isn't it? Or—this morning, I guess."

"She said we can't waste time, and we need a strategy now. And I agree with her." Malcolm picked up Jenny, who yawned and blinked. "Mother is coming over to watch the children."

"I didn't realize she was back." Malcolm's mother Madeleine liked traveling and was rarely home longer than a few weeks. Last I'd heard, she was in the south of France.

"She ward-stepped home a few hours ago at my request." Malcolm shifted Jenny into a better position. "I'm afraid there's no time for anything but cereal."

"I don't think I could manage anything more solid, anyway."

I showered quickly, then shoveled Cheerios into my mouth until I felt reasonably full and not queasy. Night-Noon butted against my knee the whole time, giving a good impression of a starving cat who believed cereal was an appropriate cat food. Maybe it was, for elven caracals.

Duncan hovered nearby while I ate, not speaking, just petting Night-Noon's head behind her ears. Finally, feeling unsettled, I said, "Is something wrong?"

"We did all right, right?" Duncan asked.

He sounded so uncertain my heart went out to him. I put my arms around him and cuddled him close, something I hadn't done for a while because Duncan resisted shows of affection he didn't initiate. "Duncan, you and Alastair did *wonderfully* well. You did exactly as I always hoped you would when your gifts were needed. Thank you."

"I don't like it when I see things I didn't ask for," Duncan murmured into my shoulder. "I'm afraid I'll get it wrong."

That response was unexpected. "Duncan," I began, then fell silent, feeling I needed to be careful in what I said next. "I've made you feel that your prophecies are really important, haven't I? Important enough that misunderstanding them could be bad."

Duncan nodded.

"Well, I shouldn't have done that. It's not true, sweetheart. Yes, our prophecies help people, but it's okay if you don't interpret them right, especially if they show things you don't understand. Prophecies are for guidance, not to make everything turn out perfectly. And I'm sorry if I made you feel you had to be perfect. *I'm* not perfect, and I've been doing this much longer than you have." I kissed the top of his head. "Duncan, you should decide for yourself which prophecies you're going to share. It's your oracular gift, not mine."

"It was different when I was helping," Duncan said. "Like I got to choose. And I saw—"

"Saw what?" I prompted when he didn't finish that sentence.

He shrugged, but this time I didn't feel he was concealing anything. "I saw one of the elves. He didn't look like the others, not all skinny. I saw him like he was looking at me, and it felt like he saw me watching him."

Instinctively I felt he was talking about the scary elf who'd wrecked the Humvee, but I reminded myself that there were no doubt millions of elves and probably many of them weren't abnormally thin. "Do you think that was real, or were you imagining it?"

Again, Duncan shrugged. "I couldn't tell. But if he could see me, doesn't that mean it's dangerous to try to have prophecies about elves? Because they might learn things about us."

A chill ran through me, and I hugged Duncan again. "That is incredibly wise, Duncan. I'm glad you told me. We'll have to be careful, huh?" I released him and ruffled his hair, and he ducked away from my hand just like always. "Grand-mère is coming to stay with you, and I'll make sure she knows you're allowed extra video game time. I think you've earned it."

Duncan grinned and ran away. A moment later, I heard the television turn on. Well, extra screen time wouldn't hurt, and it was true, he and Alastair had earned a reward.

Soon after, Malcolm and I were driving north to the Gunther Node. Traffic was lighter than usual, but it felt like we were moving in slow motion, as if every other car on the road was going faster than we were. I guessed the illusion came from my anticipation of this meeting. So far, no one had criticized me for freeing the barrier—and it had felt like giving a creature its freedom—and I'd overcome the despair that had temporarily made me feel guilty over doing what the oracle had revealed. But I was pretty sure very few people, particularly adepts, were going to nod understandingly when I said a prophecy had made me do it.

"You're nervous," Malcolm said. "There's no reason for that."

"How do you know?"

Malcolm tapped his fingers in a rapid rhythm on the steering wheel. "You make that noise when you anticipate something awful. Relax. You did the right thing."

"And now you're a mind reader." I sighed. "Malcolm, I can't stop wondering if there was a better way to do things. If I should have waited to bring down the barrier until the Savants were gone, or something."

"The Savants were beating us by virtue of greater numbers." Malcolm's voice was low and angry. "We might have left to regroup, yes, but that would simply have put them in control of a slip with an open portal, and eventually they would have discovered the need for steel weapons. What you did saved lives."

"I hope others see it your way." I leaned my head against the window. "Ms. Stirlaugson won't."

"Ms. Stirlaugson is a reactionary," Malcolm said, still sounding angry. "She would like things to not only stay as they are, but to return to an impossible past. There is no way this could have ended that would satisfy her, because all the possibilities disrupt the status quo. Don't be afraid of her."

"I won't." It was only a tiny lie. I wasn't so much afraid of Stirlaugson as I was of all the Wardens who agreed with her, some of whom I liked and hoped respected me.

When we reached the Gunther Node airplane hangar, in addition to a couple of the node's small white vans, a maroon Jeep was parked at the base of the rise. Cassie and Gabriel got out as we parked. "I'm glad to see you," Cassie said. "The directions were good, but nobody told us what to do when we got here." She gestured at the open-sided structure. "I'm guessing this isn't the Gunther Node."

"No, just the way in." I led the two adepts to the center of the white circle painted on the concrete floor. It had twists and spurs and looked like a crown of thorns. They watched curiously as Malcolm spoke into the old-fashioned telephone handset attached to the back wall and then joined us in the circle, taking my hand. "It takes—" I said.

The world blinked, and we were in the middle of the three-story-tall concrete cavern that was the Gunther Node's transit hub. "—just a second," I concluded.

"It's enormous," Gabriel said. "Where is this place?"

"I don't know. Lucia won't say, and I think it's because she doesn't know, either. The rumor is it's outside Camas, across the river. All we're sure of is it's underground." I waved at Lucia's assistant Dave Henry, who approached us with his usual ground-eating stride.

"She wants everyone in Yellow 14," Dave said when he was near enough for speech. "Hey there. Cassie and Gabriel, right?"

Gabriel nodded. Cassie said, "Who is everyone?"

"You'll see," Dave said.

We followed the yellow line painted on the floor through the enormous opening with a rim also painted yellow. The line ran straighter than most of the corridors in the Gunther Node, joined now and then by lines of other colors, but by the time we reached the door labeled 14 in big gold vinyl cutouts, only the maroon line remained next to the yellow one.

Dave pressed a spot to the left of the door that looked just like the rest of the wall, and the door retracted into the wall. Impulsively, I said, "How do you know where to press?"

Dave looked at me in surprise. "There's a visual overlay to mark where the sensor is...and I guess that means it's an illusion." He grinned. "You've been walking around this place for more than ten years thinking we're all magicians, is that it?"

I blushed, but it was pretty funny. "I guess I thought it was some special skill."

"Nope. Just good old-fashioned magic." He gestured for me to enter ahead of him. Cassie, Gabriel, and Malcolm followed.

The Gunther Node had so many rooms I didn't think I'd ever be surprised by what it contained, but unexpectedly, Yellow 14 surprised me. Curved benches forming concentric rings broken at intervals so people could pass surrounded a thigh-high octagonal platform whose center glowed with warm yellow light, like a recessed light fixture set in the floor instead of the ceiling. A few people, none of whom I recognized, sat on the benches, not very close together. They looked like people giving strangers plenty of elbow room, though I guessed at least a few of them knew each other.

Someone I did recognize stood by Lucia, next to the platform. I'd met Rick Jeong ten years ago, and we'd become good friends since that time. He was in his thirties, but because of a side effect from his bone aegis that slowed his aging, he looked no more than nineteen. Ever since the death of his friend and colleague, Darius Wallach, Rick had become the Gunther Node's resident mad scientist, fond of pushing the boundaries of the Wardens' knowledge of magic and its possibilities.

Rick didn't look up from the tablet he and Lucia were examining, so I found a seat on a bench about midway from center and waited. If I was wrong, and Lucia intended to yell at me, I wanted to delay that moment as long as possible.

Malcolm sat beside me, with Cassie and Gabriel just beyond him.

Cassie said, "That's extraordinary. What does it show, other than the globe?"

I turned, startled, as Malcolm said, "I don't recognize any of the markers."

"Slips," Gabriel said. "There's the one outside Pocatello, and the one near Camas, and I imagine the red one—"

The penny dropped. "It's another illusion, isn't it," I said, so mournfully Malcolm laughed and took my hand.

"Why is it you can't see illusions?" Gabriel asked.

"Well," I said, "I'm—"

"Davies, get over here," Lucia said. I hopped up and sidled along the curve of the bench to one of the aisles. Rick smiled when I approached, which relieved my mind somewhat. He was too good a friend for me to want to alienate him.

"All right, everyone, listen up," Lucia said. "I'll sum up so everyone's on the same page. At some time before one-thirty this morning or there-abouts—" She glared as if our failure to record the exact time was a moral failing— "our Wardens confronted Michael Castellan's group, called the Savants, at a place where another parasite reality is connected to our own."

"It's not exactly a parasite," I began.

"That depends on the distinction between—" Rick said.

"That's enough, both of you," Lucia said. "The distinction is irrelevant. But, fine. Another reality, maybe a parasite, maybe not, is connected closely to ours at the point where the two groups encountered each other. During that confrontation, Haley—where the hell is she?"

"On her way," one of the strangers said.

Lucia shook her head in mock despair. "It's like none of you care that I can tear off your limbs and beat you to death with them."

"Metaphorically," the same stranger said.

Lucia glared at him in a silence that went on just a little too long for comfort. "Right. Metaphorically," she finally said. "As I was saying, Haley opened a portal between the realities that permitted the Savants to go through into the other reality, which our allies tell us is called Faerie."

Someone made a choked sound that might have been a laugh. "Got a frog in your throat, Cameron?" Lucia said sarcastically. "No? Do you mind if I finish? The portal worked one way because of the barrier put there a thousand years ago to stop the parasite reality's inhabitants from entering ours."

It occurred to me that if any of these people were hearing these facts for the first time, they'd have a lot of questions about what Lucia was leaving out. It must be nice to be so respected and, yes, feared that nobody interrupted your lectures.

"That was when Davies, thanks to an oracular prophecy, found a way to dissolve the barrier," Lucia said.

I was grateful she'd included the part about the prophecy, because all eyes were suddenly fixed on me, and despite my resolve I quailed inside. I made myself stay calm and hoped that translated to my appearance.

"The absence of the barrier allowed elves to enter, and five of them did. Most of them were killed by our people, and the last retreated," Lucia said. I shot a sidelong glance at her, but she didn't look as if she was lying. Technically, none of that was a lie, but I remembered how the scary elf had sauntered back through the portal, how he'd moved like none of us were a threat to him. That hadn't been a retreat.

"Davies, tell us what you know about the barrier," Lucia said.

"Um—what do you mean?" I stammered.

"We're trying to establish the effects of it being gone," Rick said. "It will help if you can tell us what it was made of, how you destroyed it, things like that." He held a stylus over his tablet and looked ready to start taking down my every word, which of course made me even more nervous.

"I, well," I began, "it wasn't destroyed, really. I mean, yes, it's gone, but—" I caught Lucia's eye and straightened my spine. Blathering wouldn't help anyone.

So, instead, I told them everything I could remember. How I'd known what to look for because of my experience with the oracle and closing off the invaders' world. The sensation of being enfolded in something warm and pliable. My vision of the tiny magnetic cubes. And, finally, how I'd showed the barrier how to disperse itself so it was free.

When I finished, no one spoke for several seconds. Then Rick said, "So there's no way to get it back? Reassemble it?"

"No. Wherever it's gone, it's not coming back. I think—" I glanced at Cassie and Gabriel, but they looked no more or less shocked than anyone else. "I think there might have been a human intelligence in there once. Maybe the adepts know more about how the barrier was created—they were responsible, after all."

"I've never heard any suggestion that a human was incorporated into the barrier, but it would make sense," Cassie said. "It would explain a lot about how we've always had trouble impressing our will on it, if there was a person in there. But we really don't know."

"Anyway, it felt like it had an identity," I continued. "Maybe it wasn't a person, maybe that was just because it was over a thousand years old and developed consciousness over time, like Abernathy's did. Whatever it was, it was glad to be free. Like it had been trapped, or something."

"Don't worry," Rick said, though I didn't think I looked in need of reassurance. "Reassembling the barrier was always at the bottom of the list of possibilities."

"Which leaves us with the cold fact that our reality is once more open to invasion," Lucia said. "This time by intelligent opponents whose fighting skills may surpass our own, and who are immune to many, maybe most, of the weapons we're used to wielding."

"Way to look on the bright side, Lucia," someone drawled.

"Don't make me come over there, Hutchison," Lucia shot back. "Conti's illusion should hold them for now, if we assume the elves have had a millennium to learn to fear the barrier and won't try to interact with it to learn the truth. But we also have to assume the illusion won't hold forever. Jeong?"

Rick cleared his throat. "I've come up with a way to alert the Wardens when an incursion happens. But we'll need the help of the adepts." He pointed at what to me was empty air above the lighted platform. "These blue markers represent the thin spots, the slips, we either know about or have detected. The red one is last night's encounter."

"What do you mean, detected?" Gabriel asked.

"The slips have a sort of polarized effect that registers with the

Pattern—that's a magical device we used to use to track invaders, but our glass magi have repurposed it. The trouble is that the polarization effect can be very slight, and while eventually we'll have the Pattern tuned to those, well, frequencies, we can't count on that happening soon enough. So we'd like you adepts' help in identifying the slips you know about." Rick did something on his tablet that made everyone look at the globe I couldn't see. Sometimes my ability was seriously annoying.

"We can do that," Cassie said. "It will take a day or so to contact everyone, but I'm sure they'll want to help." She was looking at me, not at the globe, and her expression was too grim for what was a very positive statement.

"They'll be mad, won't they?" I said. "About the barrier. You said your group was among the few adepts who believe the barrier should come down."

Cassie hesitated, then nodded. "I'm sorry. They won't believe in an oracle, and even if they did, they wouldn't believe in a prophecy that demanded doing the unthinkable."

"It's all right so long as they help," I said, though I didn't feel all that certain.

"And it helps that one of our allies is an elf," Lucia said. "Gabriel Roarke, what can you tell us about the enemy?" She sounded not at all abashed at outing Gabriel, or classing his own people as our enemy.

Gabriel stood. "I am a thousand years removed from the elves we fought early this morning. What Lucia didn't mention is that the barrier had a corrosive, corrupting influence on Faerie and its inhabitants for those thousand years. What I saw of the elves who fought us revealed that they've undergone a physical change—they're thinner and taller than the elves of my time, their skin is paler, their eyes are unnaturally large, and probably there are more changes that weren't immediately visible. I can pass for human. None of them will be able to."

He lifted his chin as if in defiance. "But elves aren't invulnerable," he said. "Cold iron, or steel if you want to be less poetic, will kill an elf where ordinary bullets won't. Cut off an elf's head, or cause enough blood loss, and he'll die as readily as a human under the same circumstances. Elves can be suffocated, and they can be drowned."

"You sound like a race traitor," another Warden commented from behind me.

Gabriel's sharply angled eyebrows arched to his hairline. "I'm sure I do," he said. "But you might consider that I've made myself a traitor by allying with humans. I married a human woman. I don't even speak the same language those elves do. They will not be gentle with me just because we're nominally the same race. And I intend to defend myself and those I love with the same force I suggest you do." He sat and took Cassie's hand in his.

"Enough insulting our guests, Matthews," Lucia said without turning around. "Roarke is right. We can't afford sentimentality. We have to act as if the elves intend the destruction of humanity as much as the monstrous invaders did." She drew in a deep breath and let it out explosively. "So. We're going to monitor the slips for elven incursions. I want a team of stone magi assembled within the hour to plant ward-stones near each slip so we can ward-step immediately to anywhere the elves come through. All the major nodes have stepped up ammunition manufacture, making steel ball rounds to equip every Warden willing to put their life on the line. Anything else?"

Rick raised his hand just as if he was in elementary school. "What about the Savants?"

A murmur ran through the room. Lucia hissed and got silence. "My information says their leader, Michael Castellan, led their retreat, which is bad news as he is certainly a force I don't want to disregard. He's got to regroup, but eventually he'll be back. There's nothing we can do about the Savants except watch out for them. Leighton, how many slips do they control?"

"We're not sure," Cassie said. "I don't think more than fifteen in North America, maybe one or two others around the world. We can show you the ones we know about for that map. Castellan is wealthy and connected, but the Savants have only been around for fifty years, and their founders weren't makers of binding stones—those makers are the ones who know where all the slips are."

"And the Savants don't dare enter the portals yet," Malcolm said. "They were much less prepared to fight elves than we were, and they lost many more people in that battle. Even with Castellan still leading them, they're not a present threat."

"Fine," Lucia said.

I stopped myself raising a hand as Rick had. "What about Ms. Stirlaugson? Does she know about any of this?"

Lucia snorted. "Stirlaugson and I are going to have a conversation this afternoon. Don't worry about it."

"But she's going to—"

"I *said* don't worry about it, Davies. Stirlaugson's reaction isn't important." Lucia glared at me, and I backed down. Besides, what else could I say that wouldn't sound whiny? That I was afraid Stirlaugson would yell at me for letting elves into our world?

"Ms. Stirlaugson has much to answer for, given that she trusted Castellan," Malcolm said.

"Yes, and don't think I won't use that to the hilt," Lucia said. "That's all for now. You stone magi need to organize your teams—Jeong will direct you to the most urgent locations. The rest of you, you have your orders. Now, get."

Everyone rose. I turned to face Lucia, and the room swung wildly with me. "Wait," I said, which was all I had time for before the prophecy overtook me.

The swooping, rushing sensation faded, leaving me atop a high plateau from which I could see miles and miles of untamed land, yellow-tan with blotches of grayish green under an overcast sky. Wind battered at me, but although I could feel it against my body, my ears heard nothing. The silence felt like a toothache, throbbing and occasionally sending a twinge through me.

I turned in place and found myself looking at a mountain so tall I had to tilt my head to see its top, which was dusted with snow in places. And emerging from the mountain was a city. "Emerging" was the only possible word; the city seemed to grow from the rough, irregular cliffsides, its walls stark and angular, its roofs the same color as the mountain and therefore nearly invisible. Gates at the base of the city, where it touched the plateau I stood on, glinted pink-gold in the light of a sun I hadn't seen.

As I peered more closely at the gates, an invisible hand gripped me and swept me across the plateau until I stood at the base of the city, in front of the gates. They were made of copper, not tarnished as I'd seen copper turn when it was exposed to the elements, but shiny and bright as if someone polished them every day. Then the gates swung inward, and I was face to face with an elf.

He didn't look as emaciated as the elves we'd fought, though his skin was as chalky as theirs and his white hair hung in loose hanks around his angular face. He stared at me, and I was surprised to see he looked as startled as I felt. I had absolutely no doubt he saw me.

The elf took a step forward and extended a hand. In a voice that sounded like a question, he said something in an alien language—

—and with that, I was back in Yellow 14 and Lucia was supporting me with a hand under my elbow. "What did you see?" she asked.

I shook my head. "An elf. And he saw me."

Murmurs rose up all around, some people exclaiming over my words, others repeating them for people who hadn't heard me, because I hadn't spoken loudly. Lucia's expression became grim. "He saw you?"

"He did." I shook my head again, more slowly this time. "I think it was a warning. Duncan suspected it, too."

Malcolm came to my side. "Duncan did? Helena, what does it mean?"

"I don't know," I said, "but I feel like our troubles are just beginning."

About the Author

Melissa McShane is the author of many other fantasy novels, including the novels of Tremontane, the first of which is *Servant of the Crown; Burning Bright,* first in The Extraordinaries series; and *The Book of Secrets,* first book in The Last Oracle series.

She lives in the shelter of the mountains out West with her family, including two very needy cats. She wrote reviews and critical essays for many years before turning to fiction, which is much more fun than anyone ought to be allowed to have. You can visit her at her website **www.melissamcshanewrites.com** for more information on other books and upcoming releases.

For news on upcoming releases, bonus material, and other fun stuff, sign up for Melissa's newsletter **here**.

The Book of Harmony
The Book of War
The Book of Destiny

THE NOVELS OF TREMONTANE
Pretender to the Crown
Guardian of the Crown
Champion of the Crown
Ally of the Crown
Stranger to the Crown
Scholar of the Crown
Servant of the Crown
Exile of the Crown
Rider of the Crown
Agent of the Crown
Voyager of the Crown
Tales of the Crown

COMPANY OF STRANGERS
Company of Strangers
Stone of Inheritance
Mortal Rites
Shifting Loyalties
Sands of Memory
Call of Wizardry

THE DRAGONS OF MOTHER STONE
Spark the Fire
Faith in Flames
Ember in Shadow

Printed in Great Britain
by Amazon

24928421R00134